# THE
# TORCHBEARERS

# THE TORCHBEARERS

## A DARKDEEP NOVEL

## ALLY CONDIE
## BRENDAN REICHS

BLOOMSBURY
CHILDREN'S BOOKS
NEW YORK LONDON OXFORD NEW DELHI SYDNEY

BLOOMSBURY CHILDREN'S BOOKS
Bloomsbury Publishing Inc., part of Bloomsbury Publishing Plc
1385 Broadway, New York, NY 10018

BLOOMSBURY, BLOOMSBURY CHILDREN'S BOOKS, and the Diana logo
are trademarks of Bloomsbury Publishing Plc

First published in the United States of America in September 2020
by Bloomsbury Children's Books

Bloomsbury books may be purchased for business or promotional use.
For information on bulk purchases please contact Macmillan Corporate
and Premium Sales Department at specialmarkets@macmillan.com

Library of Congress Cataloging-in-Publication Data
Names: Condie, Allyson Braithwaite, author. | Reichs, Brendan, author.
Title: The Torchbearers / by Ally Condie and Brendan Reichs.
Description: New York : Bloomsbury Children's Books, 2020. | Series: [Darkdeep; 3]
Summary: Middle-schoolers Opal, Nico, Tyler, Emma, and Logan find their friendships tested
as never before when the townspeople panic, something cryptic surfaces from within the
Darkdeep, and a newcomer arrives with an agenda.
Identifiers: LCCN 2020015776 (print) | LCCN 2020015777 (e-book)
ISBN 978-1-5476-0255-1 (hardcover) • ISBN 978-1-5476-0256-8 (e-pub)
Subjects: CYAC: Supernatural—Fiction. | Monsters—Fiction. | Houseboats—Fiction. |
Friendship—Fiction. | Northwest, Pacific—Fiction. | Horror stories.
Classification: LCC PZ7.C7586 Tor 2020 (print) | LCC PZ7.C7586 (e-book) | DDC [Fic]—dc23
LC record available at https://lccn.loc.gov/2020015776
LC e-book record available at https://lccn.loc.gov/2020015777

Book design by Jeanette Levy
Typeset by Westchester Publishing Services
Printed and bound in the U.S.A. by Berryville Graphics Inc., Berryville, Virginia
2 4 6 8 10 9 7 5 3 1

All papers used by Bloomsbury Publishing Plc are natural, recyclable products
made from wood grown in well-managed forests. The manufacturing processes
conform to the environmental regulations of the country of origin.

To find out more about our authors and books visit
www.bloomsbury.com and sign up for our newsletters.

For Soman,
best friend, best hair, best human

# THE
# TORCHBEARERS

# PART ONE

# DOOM

# 1

# NICO

Nico Holland kept his head down.

Someone was following him.

*Or something.*

He shook off the disturbing thought. Nico walked fast, shoulders hunched, his jacket collar swept up to avoid as much notice as possible. A frigid November wind dug under his shirt and twirled his light brown hair. Nico ignored it, making his way from the park area above Otter Creek toward the heart of downtown Timbers.

He was headed for the waterfront. Specifically, the old Custom House, and the secret Torchbearer office he and his friends had discovered hidden beneath it.

*Maybe this time we'll actually get inside.*

Their last attempt had been thwarted by too many prying eyes. After the inexplicable creature attacks over the past two months—including the mass destruction on Halloween—the town was on permanent high alert. Getting anywhere unnoticed was becoming impossible.

As Nico hustled along the empty blacktop, a long shadow stretched across his path ahead. Nico slowed to a stop, nervously eyeing the tree line.

Nothing. Swirling pine needles. Green branches.

And something black and sinuous, scurrying up the trunk of a longleaf pine.

Nico swallowed. *Twice in two days.*

Was it a raccoon? Way too big for a squirrel. Then Nico tensed. He didn't want to run into a black bear cub. Or, more accurately, the cub's mother, which wouldn't be far away, and wouldn't like human company crowding its young.

From the upper boughs, Nico caught a flash of yellow eyes. They pulsed once, then winked out. He shuddered, peering into the murky canopy. But whatever had been there was gone.

*Just an animal. Keep moving. You're being paranoid.*

Nico turned down a two-lane road cutting through the woods surrounding his neighborhood. Minutes later he reached town square, sighing in relief as he spotted Tyler Watson sitting alone on a park bench. His friend was fidgeting nervously beneath a giant papier-mâché turkey hanging from a light post. The gobbler held a sign that read *HAPPY THANKSGIVING!*, but the *H* and both *G*s had blown off in the wind.

Short and slender, with dark skin and bright, inquisitive eyes, Tyler was doing the worst job of acting natural Nico had ever seen. Their eyes met. Tyler nodded stiffly, then rose and did a rigid power-walk over to join Nico on the corner of Main Street.

Tyler glanced left, then right—the caricature of a secret agent. "Anyone see you leave?"

"No, but . . ." Nico shot a glance at his back trail. He shook his head roughly, mainly to convince himself. "I saw something in the trees, but it was probably nothing. This is stupid. I'm getting all in my own head about an overgrown woodchuck."

Tyler frowned as deep as the Pacific Ocean. "Hey, I've seen weird stuff too, lately. There were wet tracks on my driveway this morning. Paw prints. Big ones."

Nico grunted. "That could be a stray dog, though."

"Or a stray figment. It's happened before, dude. Plus, Emma thinks something's been prowling around her yard at night. Heck, even *Logan* is spooked—said he heard a scratching sound outside his kitchen window right before bed. He did *not* investigate."

Nico didn't respond, mostly because he feared the same thing. As the new Torchbearers, he and his friends were tasked with controlling figments that escaped from the Dark-deep, a terrifying black well they'd found in the basement of their houseboat clubhouse. If new imaginings really were emerging again, without warning, it'd be the worst news possible.

Tyler shook his head. "I'm just saying, we've all had prickling feelings lately. And whatever I saw climbing over my back fence yesterday didn't move like a golden retriever."

Nico was about to respond when he noticed an old woman in the park, wearing a long raincoat. She was standing a dozen yards away and not moving, watching Nico and Tyler as they huddled on the street corner. Playing it cool, Nico gave the stranger a friendly nod.

The woman didn't respond. Or blink. She continued staring at Nico with gleaming eyes.

Nico felt a tug on his elbow. "You know that lady?" Tyler whispered.

"Nope. And she's creeping me out. Probably thinks we're vandals. Let's get out of here." He and Tyler started toward the docks, leaving town square behind. Nico cast an anxious glance back over his shoulder. The old woman was gone.

Nico's foot caught on the sidewalk and he stumbled. Tyler steadied him by the elbow. "Watch your step, slick."

Nico ignored the jab, scanning the now-empty plaza.

*Did she run somewhere? Or hide behind a tree? Man, this town has gone bonkers.*

And Nico hadn't told Tyler everything yet.

"There's more bad news," Nico reported sourly as they

headed downhill. "Carson and Parker were loitering a block from my house, pretending to fix a flat. But I saw them both mount up as soon as I rounded the corner."

Tyler squeezed the bridge of his nose. "Carson is convinced you meet with monsters. For lunch dates, I guess."

"I cut through the woods and jumped a creek. I might have lost them, but we should be careful."

Tyler nodded, zipping past a crate of squashes and corn outside the general store. "Any trouble getting out of the house?"

Nico shook his head. "My dad's been at work since seven this morning." Nico's father, Warren Holland, worked for the Park Service, which was headquartered in the very building they intended to infiltrate. *Focus on that problem. We've got enough to worry about.*

Tyler frowned. "So he's at the Custom House right now? That's suboptimal."

Nico shrugged. "He'll be upstairs in his office. We just need to sneak into the basement."

Nico suddenly heard the squeal of bike tires. He grabbed Tyler by the front of his hoodie and yanked him under the awning of Ms. Alikhan's flower shop. Holding his breath, Nico watched as Carson Brandt and Parker Masterson coasted by—Carson wearing a deep scowl, Parker looking bored.

Tyler sighed as the boys disappeared from sight. "They won't leave it alone, will they?"

"Would you? Carson was on the beach during Dark Halloween. He saw the worst of it."

A church bell rang three times, startling them both. The flower-shop door began to creak open behind them and they lurched back onto the sidewalk.

Hazy sunlight burned low and orange over foam-crested waves that stretched to the western horizon. A few locals were out and about on the main thoroughfare. Mr. Taylor was sweeping the front steps of his ice-cream parlor, casting dark looks at anyone he didn't know. Mrs. Campbell was peering through the blinds of her nail salon, notepad in hand, ready to record whatever she deemed suspicious. A choking tension filled the air, one that never quite went away.

Dark Halloween had definitely left its mark.

That's what people called the night when a horrifying army of figments marched from the sea and rampaged through the streets of Timbers. Half the town swore that the beach attack had been a complete hoax, masterminded by the awful YouTube personality Colton Bridger. Those people believed the creatures were fake—either costumed hooligans or fancy special effects to get footage for Colton's megahit online streamer, *Freakshow*.

But the other half—those who'd faced ravenous figments on the dunes, or encountered walking nightmares in their driveways later that evening—knew the monsters had been *very* real. And they were thoroughly freaked out about it. Carson Brandt was definitely in that camp.

Mayor Hayt was as well—she'd been at ground zero when the figments swarmed. As a result, the local government had now adopted a siege mentality. There was a curfew for kids after dark, and the Turkey Trot had been cancelled. Timbers didn't seem to have much luck with public events. Paranoia was infecting the town like a slow poison, but no one had any idea what to do.

Only the five Torchbearers knew what really happened, and Nico and his friends weren't about to reveal their secrets. Not if they could help it.

But *everyone* in town agreed on one thing—they hated the reputation Timbers had acquired, both as a fake-monster haven and as a dangerous, haunted backwater. Outraged citizens were looking for someone to blame. Which made getting around undetected a chore.

Tyler stopped abruptly, squinting in the glare of the dipping sun. "Crap, they're coming back."

"This way!"

Nico ducked into a dark alley behind Piro's Deli, jogged to a pair of rusty dumpsters, and darted behind them. Tyler slid in close beside him, his mouth curdling. "Oh man, these things stink like month-old ham. I'm dying."

Nico slashed a hand for quiet in the gloom. "*Shhh!* I hear something."

A moment later, Carson's voice carried down the narrow, foul-smelling lane. "I'm telling you, they went in there. I *saw* Nico. Who else wears a jean jacket?"

Parker's response echoed off the brick walls. "Who would hang out behind Piro's? That guy hates kids. And do you smell that? Those dumpsters are full of moldy cheddar. I'm never eating a hoagie again."

Carson's voice held the tinge of obsession. "I bet Nico's meeting his creature friends back here. This is the perfect place for it."

Nico heard the rapid tick of walked bicycles. He gritted his teeth. How would he and Tyler explain hiding behind a dumpster? Parker was bigger than both of them put together, and Carson didn't seem all there these days.

Nico began to sweat.

"There's no such thing as monsters, dude." Parker sounded annoyed. "Face the facts—you got duped by *Freakshow*. Stop being a drag and let's go play video games."

"I know what I saw, okay? You weren't there. Whatever jumped me on the beach was *not* a special effect. There were . . . that thing . . . I could see it *drooling*! If Logan and Nico hadn't—"

"Those guys were part of the act," Parker interrupted. "Look at Emma. She was working for the show! The whole thing was a prank to make the town look crazy. What we *should* be thinking about is how to get back at those losers. Everyone at school feels the same."

A door screeched open with a flood of fluorescent light. Nico pulled Tyler between the grimy dumpsters just as Piro

Gekas emerged from his deli, carrying massive bags of trash. He moved past where the boys hid, tossing the garbage bags up and over the top. Then he jerked to a halt and glared down the alley.

"Hey!" Piro snapped. "What are you two doing back here? Rooting in my waste bins?"

"Nossir!" Carson squawked. "We, uh . . . we were looking for my, um . . . my football."

"No footballs here!" Piro growled, jabbing a finger. "Go! *Now.* This is no place to play."

"Yes, Mr. Gekas!" Parker said hastily. "Sorry to bother you!"

Nico heard the boys awkwardly backing their bikes out of the tight space. Piro glowered their direction a moment longer, shaking his head and muttering. Then he stomped back inside.

Nico slid out from between the dumpsters, gasping for fresh air. "Ugh. Gross. Let's bail."

Tyler made a gagging noise. "Oh man, the hot-ham stench got in my mouth. I'm burning this sweatshirt when I get home."

The door closed behind Piro, returning the alley to semidarkness. But in that murk, something moved.

Nico froze, adrenaline pumping into his veins.

A shadow was hugging the wall just beyond Piro's door. The form was vaguely human-shaped. As Nico stared in astonishment, an odor like hot peppers tickled his nose. Nico thought he glimpsed a wrinkled face—the old woman from the park?—but it disappeared in a wispy swirl of dark fur and gleaming yellow eyes.

Nico stumbled backward into Tyler and the dumpster.

"Hey, watch it!" Tyler griped. "You made me touch something wet!"

The shadow flitted down the alley and disappeared. Nico was left blinking in the half-light.

"Something wrong with you, man?" Tyler asked. "I think we can slip out now."

"Did you see that?" Nico whispered.

"See what? The bag of expired mayo? Yes, and I can't unsee it."

Nico squeezed his nose. Was he seeing things? Had his brain gone on temporary vacation?

"Let's get out of here," Nico said. "I need to clear my head."

"Amen to that."

They eased back onto Main Street. There was no sign of Carson and Parker. Or eerie shadows.

Nico sighed, then rubbed his eyes. *Stress is getting to me.* He dug out his phone to see if he'd missed any messages.

He had—a text from Logan Nantes. The message wilted Nico's mood even further.

"You talk to Emma?" Nico asked, putting his phone away.

"She's not coming," Tyler grumbled, scratching his forehead. "A group of *Emma-mazing!* fans are camped out in the woods across from her house. She says they usually get hungry and bug off at lunchtime, but not today. Until they leave, she's a prisoner."

Nico grunted. Emma Fairington had played a starring role on *Freakshow: The Beast* as Colton Bridger's blue-eyed, local-cute-kid helper. The popularity—or notoriety—she'd gained from the show had helped launch a hit YouTube channel of her own. But fame had a price. Emma now found it harder than any of them to fulfill her Torchbearer duties. This was the third time in two weeks she was going to miss a meeting.

"Logan can't make it either," Nico said. "He just texted the group. Said he bailed on his shift at the houseboat yesterday, so he's going there now to make sure everything's okay. And since *my* dad refused to let me out of the house all weekend, that means no one's been to the island in almost four days."

The boat in Still Cove was their clubhouse and secret hideout, and home to a mysterious force the Torchbearers were sworn to protect—the Darkdeep. Hidden in the houseboat's bottommost chamber, the Darkdeep was a swirling black well that, if entered, scanned your mind and brought figments of your imagination into being for a short period of time. Some were delightful. Others, not so much.

These creatures had threatened to overrun Timbers more than once in the weeks since Nico and his friends found the vortex lurking there, unattended. They'd learned that the Darkdeep itself was even more dangerous than the figments it created, but they still didn't know all the answers. Or even most of them.

Which made it doubly important to keep a close eye on it.

A task they'd been failing at miserably.

"Heads-up. There's Opal." Tyler nodded toward the docks. "Oh man, I hope she doesn't run into the Doofus Bros. They might've pedaled that way."

Nico started, his mind still lingering on that unsettling shadow in the alleyway. He glanced up to see Opal Walsh's long black braid swish out of sight as she strode downhill ahead of them. He and Tyler got moving, trailing her, keeping a safe distance. Groups attracted attention these days, and they didn't want to be noticed.

"Think we can sneak in under the stairs?" Tyler asked in a hopeful voice. "I hate that trapdoor, but I like the sewer route even less. I already hugged a dumpster this afternoon."

Getting into the Torchbearer office the easy way—through the Custom House lobby—had been tough since Timbers became a police state. Logan solved the problem a week ago by finding a large drainage pipe accessing the building from below, but it was *not* a pleasant trip. Nico got shivers just thinking about the cold, dank passage.

*Better than getting caught by Dad, though.*

He glanced at his watch. "The lunch rush should be over, but I'm not sure the foyer ever clears out in the middle of a workday. And we can't stand around in there, waiting." He grimaced. "I think we have to go in ugly."

"Parker's not wrong about the kids at school," Tyler said abruptly. "Lots of people gave me the side-eye today. If we were unpopular before, we're outcasts now. Half our classmates think we're in league with legit monsters, and the others think we lied to embarrass everyone. What a mess."

Nico shook his head. "Let's catch up with Opal."

They reached the waterfront and found Opal waiting a block from the Custom House. The building's front entrance hosted steady foot traffic as workers briskly entered and exited Timbers' largest office building. Opal's dour expression confirmed Nico's fears.

"We'll have to go the back way," Opal said. "Are the flashlights still down there?"

"I think so," Nico muttered.

Tyler groaned. "Any chance we could put on fake mustaches and pretend to sell insurance?"

Opal chuckled darkly. "I think it's the uncivilized route for us."

Nico led them back up the block, turning into a narrow lane that ended at a wooden fence. Beyond it, waves crashed against a tumble of heavy rocks below. Nico kept an eye on the street as Opal pried a loose board aside and carefully wriggled through the gap. The boys quickly followed, emerging onto the seawall bordering the harbor.

They walked single file along a ragged, crushed-shell trail atop the barrier, angling toward an abandoned dock, where they scurried beneath its rotting timbers and regrouped. Holding his nose, Nico moved deeper into the recessed space, to where a canvas bag sat alongside a circular concrete hole burrowing below the building. They had reached the sewer gate.

Nico dug into the bag and removed three flashlights, powering them one by one. "Remember to breathe through your mouth."

"That's worse," Tyler huffed. "The funk gets into your taste buds, and I already had a mouthful of dumpster trash."

Opal tilted her head. "Did what now?"

Nico and Tyler spoke in unison. "Don't ask."

Opal rolled her eyes. "Let's get this over with." Not content to wait, she fired ahead. Nico rubbed a hand over his face and followed. Tyler reluctantly crept in last.

"No rats today, please," Tyler whispered in supplication. "I'm begging. Man do I hate rats."

The opening was no more than five feet tall, forcing them to hunch as they shuffled along a narrow concrete shelf that ran above the main drainage channel. The stench hit Nico like a physical blow. Gagging, he scurried as fast as he could, nearly bowling into Opal at the first turn. He didn't look directly at where his flashlight beam fell. He didn't want to see anything.

"I'm going to be sick," Tyler moaned behind him.

"Well, you're in the right place for it," Nico quipped.

Opal made a second turning, into a larger section where they could all stand. Another grime-crusted channel led to an old metal door secured by a padlock. Opal unlooped the chain—they'd severed its rusty links days ago, and only kept it there now for show. Setting the obstacle aside, she turned the door's handle and pushed with her shoulder.

The portal inched backward with a shriek that jangled Nico's nerves, but they were far beneath the Custom House and he knew the racket couldn't be heard from up above. The trio wormed through the narrow opening and slammed the door shut behind them. Nico took his first full breath in minutes.

"We've *got* to find a better option," Tyler spat. "I can't handle that reek every time."

"It's the only entry point that isn't watched," Nico wheezed, fanning his nose. "You think I enjoy it?"

"Can we go, please?" Opal said. "We're already late and I want to get to work."

The lightless chamber was an old-fashioned boiler room, unused since the Custom House was retrofitted with a modern HVAC system decades ago. They crossed to an unremarkable closet and entered it one by one. Shelves stacked with ancient paint cans lined each side. Nico approached the back wall, put his hands against two bumps in the concrete, and pressed at the same time. There was a slight click.

A line of concrete blocks swung inward on silent hinges.

They had arrived.

# 2

## OPAL

A wall clock ticked in the silent chamber.

Opal had got it working again with a pair of AA batteries. When they'd first discovered the office weeks ago, the clock's hands had been frozen at 12:31. Who knows how long the timepiece had hung there, immobile, waiting for a Torchbearer to restore it to working order. The technology was as old and out of date as everything else in the Torchbearer office.

Opal squirmed behind the lone desk, a battered scrap of parchment in her fingers. In front of her, Nico sat with his elbows on the conference table filling the center of the room. Tyler stood beside a row of steel filing cabinets, leafing through an old folder. He'd spearheaded the effort to restore the office to functioning condition, taking a strange joy in wiping away years of dust and grime. Opal was just glad she'd finally stopped sneezing.

They'd found this place by following a series of clues Thing had given to Opal, first through mental nudges, and later through direct telepathic communication. Like the house-boat itself—and the ceremonial vault hidden within the tunnel running under Still Cove—this room was a closely held Torch-bearer secret, guarded for generations. The records placed there covered decades of the Order's secret work.

Opal glanced at a massive bureau against the far wall, flanked by two towering bookshelves. Inside the open top portion was a stack of old nautical flags and a seascape of the Washington coast painted by Yvette Dumont, the original founder of the Torchbearers. Opal got a chill every time she looked at the canvas. That image had led them to the Rift, and all that happened afterward.

Including Thing's maddening note-in-a-bottle, which they'd received through the Darkdeep just when they'd thought the danger might finally have passed.

She read the second-to-last line. *There's something here that doesn't belong.*

Opal glanced up, mumbling the final line out loud for the thousandth time. "Or, I should say, someone."

"It's me," Tyler deadpanned.

Opal rolled her eyes. "Just focus on *your* task, okay?"

Tyler shrugged. "I'm all focus, ma'am. I possess a razor-sharp clarity of thought on the issues at hand. Shall I demonstrate?"

He didn't wait for an answer, crossing his arms and lifting his chin. "When the Darkdeep began spitting out figments on its own—a *serious* problem—we determined the cause: the Rift, a pesky hole in space-time linking our world to Thing's planet by way of an empty Void between dimensions. This portal lurks at the bottom of the ocean, beneath a decommissioned oil platform built by the Torchbearers." He paused. "Am I going too fast for you?"

Nico covered his face and groaned.

Opal's eyes found the ceiling.

Tyler plowed onward, undeterred. "The Rift and the Darkdeep are connected in a manner we don't yet understand. We also don't know how to reseal the gateway, as the chemical formula used by the old Torchbearers is presently unknown. Then a bunch of nasties tried to cross over from Thing's world and wreck shop, but we fought like indomitable battle lions and shut those fools down."

"You mean the Beast did," Opal countered. "You were cowering on the platform with the rest of us."

Tyler studiously ignored her. "*Thus*, the main thrust of our research: to determine the status of the Rift, and whether I will be needed once more to fix everything with my inspiring bravery and gigantic, stupendous brain." He nodded heavily, then smiled wide. "Lecture complete."

Nico snorted, leaning back in his chair. "The only way to *fix* things is to hunt down every scrap of information we can about the Rift. We don't know if the plan we worked out with Thing actually solved the problem."

Opal frowned. "How can we ever be sure? The oil rig is destroyed. It's not like we can scuba five miles out and inspect a hole in reality on the ocean floor."

"I've heard worse ideas," Nico grumbled. He shifted uncomfortably. "We *do* know for certain that we didn't restore the old seal that failed when the Rift was left unattended. So we still have to finish that job, at least. And hope it's enough."

Tyler placed a dog-eared file back into its drawer. "Right now, all *I* want to figure out is what's been creeping through my mom's rosebushes at night." He blew out a deep, shuddering breath. "What about you, Opal? Ready to report any findings to the group?"

Opal thought of the strange thumps she'd heard in her attic the night before. Lately, all the Torchbearers had bizarre stories to relate—of shadows, and sounds, and suspicious tracks. At first she'd been skeptical, but Opal was starting to take these rumors more seriously. That morning at dawn, she could've sworn something was hovering outside her bedroom window. But when she'd ripped open the blinds, there was only dark, billowing mist and a flicker of yellow-gold. The memory sprouted goosebumps along her arms and legs.

"Hello?" she heard Tyler say. "Earth to Opal?"

Nico flinched. "That's not as funny now that we know

other planets exist. Those Takers had an open doorway to attack us. We have to make sure it's permanently closed."

Opal shook her head to clear it. Tyler took that as an answer to his question and turned to a new drawer.

After Dark Halloween, the group had changed how they worked. Rather than play tug-of-war trying to solve riddles collectively, each Torchbearer was now tackling a specific problem on their own. Everyone had a dedicated space where they could compile notes, images, theories, whatever. Opal's was already the most chaotic. The office was starting to resemble some kind of police situation room.

Opal was in charge of the note-in-a-jar Thing had sent back through the Darkdeep weeks ago. She'd been closest to the little green creature before Thing returned to its home world, so Opal had taken on the task of figuring out what the message meant. For background, she was researching Yvette Dumont, the founding Torchbearer. Back when the Rift first formed, Yvette had made the initial contact with Thing and saved its life. Maybe something in her story would help.

Nico was investigating the bizarre phenomena that had plagued Timbers while the Rift was open. Though the algae bloom off Razor Point had dispersed and the lightning storms stopped, Nico worried about lasting effects. Opal didn't think there was much point to his research—they couldn't control nature, after all—but as the son of a park ranger,

Nico took environmental threats seriously. The Rift was practically all he thought about now. He had tide charts spread out across the table, and often complained that the sulfur stench hadn't left Still Cove.

Tyler was focused on what being a Beastmaster truly involved. Ever since coming face-to-face with the Beast on Dark Halloween—and somehow communicating with it using his algae stick—he'd been obsessed with contacting the ancient sea monster again. Yet another thing Opal wasn't sure about—in her mind, steering clear of a giant alien carnivore from another dimension was by far the safest course.

And then there was Emma. She was supposed to be tracking the *Freakshow* disaster online—steering conversations away from thinking Timbers was a monster haven—but she spent most of her time on her YouTube show, *Emma-mazing!* It drove Tyler and Nico nuts. Opal privately agreed with them, though she stood up for Emma whenever the other girl wasn't around. But facts were facts—the Torchbearers needed *less* attention on their hometown, not more. Emma was gathering followers by the thousands, a budding Colton Bridger in their midst. She wasn't even there today, which Opal could tell had Nico's blood boiling.

*Neither is Logan.*

Opal frowned. His excuse was acceptable, but this wasn't *his* first missed meeting, either.

Logan was tasked with discovering everything he could

about Torchbearer history, but he seemed more interested in growing his online souvenir business. Opal knew Logan was making a killing—his new gear mocked *Freakshow* and their incredible flameout on the beach—but she feared he was making enemies. Yet Opal couldn't deny his talent for turning nonsense phrases into cash. Logan was the only thirteen-year-old she knew with a 401K. And the extra money came in handy for Torchbearer expenses.

So many threads, but they were *all* trying to figure out how to permanently seal the Rift. The problem ate at Opal every day. She swallowed a groan. It was a lot.

"A *few* reports will be late, I guess," Tyler grumbled. "Since Emma and Logan didn't bother to show up."

"Emma tried," Opal said. "It's not her fault that Internet weirdos are spying on her house."

Nico's head shot up. "Then whose fault is it?"

Opal winced. Sometimes the underground boardroom felt stifling. She missed the houseboat's high ceiling and drafty showroom, and the cool mists cloaking the island's black pond. But with Timbers on lockdown, getting to Still Cove had become increasingly difficult. She felt a twinge of unease that Logan was out there all alone. Cell service never reached that far. *We really should go in pairs.*

"At least Logan is watching the Darkdeep," Nico added. "Emma's just schmoozing with her fans."

"That's not fair," Opal snapped.

Nico lifted an eyebrow, then looked away.

"She's always doing something for that show." Tyler sounded exasperated. "Like she forgot the Torchbearer oath."

Nico nodded sharply. "We already have a job. And, um— *it's kind of important.*"

"It's not just Emma who's spaced out," Tyler huffed. "I swear, school today felt like a minefield. Some kids are still freaking about another possible monster invasion, which makes them suspicious of everyone else. Those dopes think whoever sits next to them in the cafeteria might be a bogeyman in disguise. And the others think we're pranksters ready to ambush them in the bathroom wearing monster masks. It's insane."

Opal nodded, her forehead scrunching. "In class, I can't tell who's friends with who anymore. People keep switching cliques. Having fights. Yesterday, I saw the reading club huddled under the bleachers, planning an evacuation route."

Nico scoffed bitterly. "Someone wrote 'Monster Lover' on my locker in Sharpie."

Tyler held up an index finger. "Ten bucks says it was Carson."

Opal sighed. She wished Emma and Logan had come today. She wished Thing's note was more clear. She wished she could talk to the little green creature again, just once.

But such thoughts led to dangerous places. Opal wasn't ready to get *that* crazy.

Not yet, anyway.

"Did you find anything else about the first Torchbearer?" Lips pursed, Tyler glanced at the ceiling. Then he snapped his fingers. "Suzette Fremont. There has to be a file on *her*, right?"

"Yvette Dumont," Opal corrected. "And no, nothing yet."

"What about you, Ty?" Nico asked. "Anything new on our scaly friend?"

Tyler picked up a warped book he'd found in the bureau. "Actually, yeah. I'm reading between the lines here, but it seems like the *Beast* actually chooses the Beastmaster. Like, there were former Torchbearers who wanted the job, but the Beast didn't accept them."

Tyler fell silent, fidgeting with his collar.

Opal crossed her arms. "Well, what happened to them?"

"They seem to have been, um . . . chomped."

"Great." Opal rubbed her face. Though they'd never seen the Beast actually *eat* anyone, it was an enormous razor-toothed monster from another world. She didn't love that Tyler—who used to be the most cautious of them all—was clearly enamored with the creature.

"So how *does* the Beast pick a Beastmaster?" Nico's face seemed a shade paler.

Tyler licked his lips. "It brings something from the sea and lays an offering at the person's feet."

"Like a cat with mice." Opal winced. "The Beast either

chews you up or leaves a dead ocean carcass on your door-step. And you *want* this job?"

Tyler looked away. "I don't know. Yeah. I think."

"So you're not a full Beastmaster yet," Nico said, rubbing his chin. "Bummer. I thought maybe it was done when you waved that glowing algae in its face." Tyler had communed with the Beast once before, and the huge leviathan had even battled Takers with them at the Rift. But whatever alliance they'd forged wasn't necessarily permanent.

*Super. One more thing.*

Tyler squared his shoulders. "The Beast *did* respond to me on Dark Halloween, so maybe—"

"Oooh, that reminds me!" Opal dug into her backpack, pulling out the old leather notebook she'd found on the boat, the one with spiky flowers drawn in the corner of each page. She'd been using it to collect notes on Yvette Dumont.

Opal removed a folded piece of paper tucked within its pages and displayed an indigo-colored monster, rendered in childlike strokes. "A kid I babysit drew this the other night. Ingrid was there on the beach. She must've actually witnessed the Beast's arrival."

"Jeez." Nico ran a hand over his mouth. "Poor kid."

"This is pretty good," Tyler muttered, examining the picture. "The scale is off, though."

Opal took the drawing back. Tyler seemed reluctant to let it go. "Ty, you should be careful. The Beast saved us once, but that doesn't mean we understand it. Or can control it." Tyler drew in a sharp breath, but Opal quickly changed the subject. "Nico, what about you? Anything new about the oil rig, or what the Rift might be doing underneath it?"

"No," Nico muttered. He slumped back in his chair and spoke louder. "The news basically missed the whole thing. I found one local article about the platform going down in the storm, but nothing else, and the link only had thirty views. With so much other stuff going on, I guess the story slipped by. No one's figured out that the rig was used by Torchbearers to control the Rift." His expression grew pensive. "I *did* find some other weird news. There's a huge red tide off the coast of Australia, and no one knows its cause. It looks exactly like ours did." He spun his phone around so they could its screen.

Opal peered at the image. It mirrored what they'd seen encircling Razor Point.

"Not great. But these blooms *do* occur naturally, right?"

Nico nodded. "There's more. Crazy things are happening at Yellowstone National Park. Last week their sulfur pools turned different colors, and now a few geysers are spouting sky high and off schedule." Nico made air quotes with his fingers. "It's all 'unexplained.'"

He tapped his screen again and slid the phone across the table.

*JUST ONE OF THE GEYSERS: LITTLE CUB ERUPTS AS HIGH AS OLD FAITHFUL.*

Opal read a few lines before passing the phone to Tyler, who gave the story a cursory scroll. "Cool," he said lightly, handing the phone back to Nico. Nico took it with an injured expression.

Opal frowned. Like Tyler, she thought Nico was getting sidetracked, but she understood the disappointment of feeling like you're onto something and no one else caring. Nico had backed her wild hunches before, even when she was the only one hearing Thing's voice inside her head. "That does seem strange," Opal said, making her tone interested. "Especially the part about the sulfur pools. You think it might connect to the rotten-egg stench in our pond?"

"I dunno, maybe," Nico said seriously. "We know that sulfur bubbled up because the Rift was out of control. Maybe this is something like that?"

Opal formed a thoughtful expression. "Could be."

Nico grinned, gave her a grateful nod. Opal felt better. Nico hadn't been smiling a lot lately. It was good to see one sneak up on him.

He also hadn't gotten a haircut recently, and his brown hair was curling over the edges of his ears. He looked kind of cute. Opal's heart ticked an extra beat. *Why am I still looking at him?*

"Wait," Tyler said sharply. "The name you said earlier was 'Yvette Dumont'?"

"Yes, Tyler. The name of the founding member of the Order hasn't changed."

Tyler spun his book around. "Well, you're welcome then. Because I found *her*."

"Seriously?" Opal rushed over and bumped Tyler aside.

He chuckled, rubbing his shoulder in mock agitation. "That sentence doesn't use a full name, but it says that the first Torchbearer was *also* the first Beastmaster. And look at these initials here—Y. D. I didn't notice before because I forgot French people use the wrong letters in their names. Who doesn't spell *E*-vette with an *E*?"

Opal quickly read the page. Flipped to the next.

"Careful," Tyler warned. "That book's an original."

"What is this?" Opal pointed to the middle of a paragraph.

Tyler shrugged. "I can't tell, because your finger is over it."

Opal grunted in annoyance and read the words aloud. "*The Order's founder also originated the position of Master. Perhaps because both had suffered a great loss at the moment of the Tear, Lotan and Master were bonded for the extent of her life. After Y.D. died, years passed with no accepted Master, until the Lotan itself chose a replacement, an event that was of considerable astonishment to all.*"

"A great loss," Opal repeated, chewing on the end of her braid. "You think that refers to Dumont's shipwreck?"

Before anyone could answer, three phones buzzed at once. Nico glanced down reflexively.

Shook free. I'm outside the Custom House. Need help!

31

"Emma!" Tyler scrambled to his feet. "What's happened now?"

"Only one way to find out," Nico groaned, rising and striding for the door.

With a sinking feeling, Opal was right behind him.

# 3

# NICO

Nico slipped from the alcove beneath the marble staircase.

"The coast is clear," he whispered, scanning the empty lobby of the Custom House.

Behind him, Tyler stood with his back pressed to the wall. Inside the alcove, Opal swung the trapdoor shut, hiding the stepladder Logan had lowered into the underground hallway accessing the Torchbearer office. This was the riskier way in and out, but it was later in the day, and no one wanted to go back through the sewer if they could help it.

"Hurry up," Tyler said. "If Emma was followed here, we might have a serious—"

"Nico Holland!"

The voice rang across the reception area, freezing the startled trio like department store mannequins. Heart in his throat, Nico turned to face the ancient bank of elevators a dozen yards farther down the wall. His father, Warren Holland, was standing there with his arms crossed, having obviously just exited. *What did he see? Did he notice me coming out from under the stairs?*

Nico swallowed. "Oh, hey Dad. What's . . . um, what's up? We were just playing hide an—"

Warren straightened to his full towering height of six-and-a-half feet. "My office. Now."

From the corner of his eye, Nico spotted Tyler skulking toward the exit, trying to remain unnoticed. Opal was still huddled in the recess underneath the stairs. Nico watched as she tripped the secret catch, scrambled onto the ladder, and climbed back down into the hidden passage. Shrugging guiltily, she closed the trapdoor with a soft click. *Coward.*

"Tyler Watson!" Warren Holland called out.

Tyler stopped dead in his tracks, then pivoted slowly. "Oh, hey there, Mr. H. How's the uh . . . the environment today?"

"Get home, Tyler," Nico's father said curtly. "This isn't a place to goof off. You know that."

"Got it, sir. Good, um . . . good day!" Tyler spun and double-timed it toward the front entrance.

"Tell your parents I said hello," Warren called after Tyler's retreating form. Tyler waved a hand in acknowledgment as he pushed through the doors.

*And then there was one.*

*Me.*

*Ugh.*

"Let's go, Nico."

"Yes sir."

Nico joined his father in the elevator, standing stiffly at his side as Warren mashed the button for the third floor. *Didn't he just come down? What was he doing in the lobby?* It occurred to Nico that either he was about to get the scolding of his life, or his father had been looking for him just now. *He didn't even ask why I'm here.*

They reached the level occupied by the National Park Service. Nico's dad spent most of his time working in the field—the *real* job of wildlife protection, as Warren Holland saw it—but everything required paperwork. Warren had a small office at the end of the hall.

Nico stepped inside and sat on a plain chair facing an equally drab desk. The walls were bare except for a large map of the greater Timbers region tacked up with pushpins. A lone window provided a surprisingly good view of the waterfront. But Nico was staring at his hands, worried that his father was about to unleash on him for violating the sanctity of his workplace.

"I have b—" Warren paused, then sighed. "I have news."

He slumped heavily into his chair, which creaked under his burly frame. Warren Holland interlocked his fingers on the top of his desk. Nico felt his father's eyes and looked up to meet that steely gaze. Time seemed to slow.

"I'm being reassigned," Warren said, in somewhat of a rush. "To Portland. It's a promotion, actually. I'll be managing the regional subbranch. Lots of . . . of time"—he waved an ineffectual hand . . ."managing."

Nico's heart stopped. The walls closed in around him. His vision narrowed to a pinprick, with his father's frowning mouth the sole object in focus. "You've been transferred?" Nico asked dumbly. "Like, for real?"

Warren nodded. "The paperwork came through this morning. We're off to a new challenge."

Nico's brain was struggling to catch up. "How? When?"

Warren spoke with care, his voice echoing strangely in Nico's ears. "My start date is the first of next year, which is helpful. We won't have to rush out of town right away. You can finish the current semester here in Timbers without disruption, then start fresh at a new school."

Nico stood so fast the chair beneath him flipped over. Both hands rose to grip his hair. A thousand protests expanded in his throat, then wrestled each other into silence. He felt like he was choking.

"Son, I know this isn't what you wanted, but—"

Nico turned and fled. He needed *away*. Needed this conversation to end. To be a dream. He ran down the hallway and pounded the elevator button. His father's head appeared in his office doorway. Sad, helpless eyes regarded him.

Nico abandoned the elevator and fired into the stairwell,

racing down three steps at a time. Reaching the ground floor, he streaked through the lobby and burst out into the fading afternoon light. There he paused to catch his breath, but found he couldn't. His heart was pumping madly, like a horse galloping out of control. Sweat slicked his palms, his forehead, his whole body.

*No. No no no no no no no no.*

But it was true. It was real.

He would have to leave Timbers.

"Nico?"

His head rose to see Emma Fairington on the sidewalk across the street, her cell phone perched on a selfie stick. Tyler stood beside her, arms crossed, a scowl twisting his features. A second later Opal rounded the Custom House, gasping in fresh air. She'd obviously come out through the sewer pipe.

Nico tried to collect himself. In a snap, he decided not to say anything about the transfer.

He couldn't. Not yet.

"Emma, what's going on?" Nico said, swallowing the lump in his throat.

"I'll tell you what's going on," Tyler bit off, nodding sharply at Emma. "Her *emergency* was needing help with her next YouTube post."

"Don't be such a buzzkill," Emma said lightly. "I need some man-on-the-street stuff to spice up the footage. I want to record you guys doing funny Beast impressions."

All the anger Nico had bottled inside at his father's news exploded at once. "More attention on the Beast? Emma, did you learn nothing from what happened with *Freakshow*? Stop making our job harder!"

Emma's face dropped. She blinked rapidly, as if holding back tears. "I just thought it would be funny," she said in a small voice. "And that you guys could be on TV."

Opal darted forward and snagged Emma's hand, shooting a glare at Nico for good measure. "We know, Emma. It sounds like a cool idea. Maybe we can film it later?"

Nico's face burned, but he held his tongue. Tyler, however, wasn't dissuaded. His eyebrows formed a disapproving V. "Nico is absolutely right. Not only are you risking Torchbearer secrets, you're putting the Beast in danger, too." He actually stomped a foot. "We don't need people even *thinking* about Timbers. Or its legendary sea monster. That's too risky for everyone!"

Nico felt his irritation surge to match Tyler's. "I know you like making your show, Emma, but another Internet sensation drawing eyes here is the exact opposite of helpful. We should be laying low and waiting for some other goofy town to seize the spotlight. But you keep fanning the flames."

Emma's head rose, and she jutted her chin. "Half this town *personally* saw rampaging figments on Halloween night. The story is *out*, Nico. It's not going away. Maybe we should tell the truth about what we know, and not hide everything like the old Torchbearers." She yanked her phone off its stick. "It's not like they were such great people. The Order held Thing prisoner for over two centuries."

"Tell the truth?" Tyler squawked. "Then what do you think happens to the Beast?"

"What happens if a bunch more Takers show up without warning?" Emma fired back. "We don't even know if the Rift is secure. What if we only delayed the problem, or buried it under that oil platform? Did you ever think about that?"

"Do you really trust the adults around here to handle something as dangerous as the Darkdeep?" Nico said. "We were pretty careful, and things still spiraled out of control. You want Mayor Hayt making decisions about a volatile interdimensional vortex? Or some army unit sent up from Seattle?" He caught and held Emma's eye. "And Tyler's right. What do you think they'd do to the Beast, if they knew it was real?"

"They'd hunt it down," Opal said quietly. "They wouldn't try to understand."

Emma's grimaced. The corners of her mouth sank. "I wasn't trying to risk anything," she mumbled. "And I won't do an episode on the Beast."

"But you can do something else," Opal said quickly, squeezing Emma's shoulder. "After all, your subscribers always want more *Emma-mazing!*"

Emma nodded, wiping her nose. "I have an idea about frogs that's pretty solid. Or I could live stream an investigation into whatever freaked out my fans in the woods yesterday."

Nico frowned in frustration, but tried to hide it. He didn't want Emma doing *anything* that attracted notice, but he couldn't ask her to abandon her show completely. Emma loved it too much. And it really *was* successful—Nico had to admit he was impressed at how quickly her channel had gained a huge following.

Tyler sighed. Checked his watch. "I gotta get home. I'm only allowed short stints out by myself. My parents decided I'm not to be trusted, and they aren't playing around."

Opal glanced at Nico. "I'm free for another few hours. We could check on Logan. Anyone up for a ride out to Still Cove?"

Nico was about to agree, but then his father's terrible words came back to him. Suddenly, he just wanted to be alone. He couldn't keep up this front for long.

"My dad sent me home," he lied. "Maybe I can catch up with you later."

"I'll go," Emma piped, already regaining her good spirits. "I need landscape shots for an episode I'm composing. I'm going to edit in my stuffed tiger, and make it look like . . ."

She trailed off at the pained expressions on the boys' faces.

"I'm out," Tyler huffed. "So long."

"Gotta run," Nico said. "Later, guys."

Fighting a wave of swirling emotions, he turned and hurried up the block.

# 4

## OPAL

Opal clawed an old spiderweb from her face.

*Blech. Uck. Tunnels are so freaking disgusting.*

"I'd *never* put the Beast in harm's way," Emma muttered sullenly, oblivious to Opal's distress as they tromped along the midnight-dark passage running under Still Cove. "How could Ty say that?"

"He's upset." Opal put a hand against the stone wall to steady herself. She didn't love this deep-plunging path out to the island and their houseboat, but it wouldn't help if she tripped and cracked her skull. And it was less gross in there than the sewer she'd slunk through an hour ago. "Your show is super clever, Emma. I'm sure you have a ton of other great ideas."

"I do, actually." Emma snagged Opal's hand in the gloom, nearly triggering a squawk of alarm. "Like, *so* many. For example, what if I acted out classic horror movies using radishes? I could carve little faces on them! Make miniature sets!"

"Sew tiny outfits?" Opal joked, but she was actually kind of into it. She secretly loved playing with dollhouses, even though she was too old. *All that itty-bitty furniture, the teeny plates and cups* . . .

They reached the round chamber at the tunnel's deepest point. Emma's voice echoed over a hand-and-flame symbol carved into the flagstones outside the Torchbearer's hidden vault, which was locked behind a stone wall only a special key could open. "Guess who my newest subscriber is. Just *guess*. You won't believe it."

"Harry Styles," Opal cracked. "No, it's Thor. You're being followed by a Hemsworth brother. Or Natalie Portman."

"Nope. Better."

"Is that even possible?"

"Keep guessing."

"I give," Opal huffed, quickening her steps. They were in the middle of the passageway now, directly under the bay and as far from both exits as possible. She couldn't suppress a shudder. *So much ocean overhead*. The dank smell of salt water permeated the air. "Zendaya?"

"No!" Emma couldn't contain herself any longer. "It's Happy Pig. You know—the guinea pig with the most followers ever on YouTube!"

Opal stopped in her tracks. "But . . . that's not a person."

"Who cares?" Emma clapped her hands in delight, the sound echoing eerily ahead of them. "He has a channel, too."

Opal started moving again. "What does a guinea pig post videos about?"

"Usually dancing animal stuff. Ferrets. Monkeys. One time a bulldog was playing the harmonica."

Opal was silent for several moments. "I really don't understand the Internet."

Minutes later they reached the switchbacks at the opposite end of the tunnel and began the long climb back up to the surface, emerging in a cave on the island's northern side. Opal took a cleansing breath and stepped outside. Tendrils of mist slithered across moss-covered boulders and dark, loamy earth. The foliage had turned November shades of green, gray, and brown.

She and Emma climbed from the gully to the top of a steep ridge. Opal looked down at the dark pond nestled within the island's sharp edges. At its center, a deeper shadow was just visible inside the blanket of encircling fog.

Opal's skin prickled at the sight of the houseboat's weather-beaten exterior. She'd never get used to its haunting presence. The promise of danger and surprise it always sparked within her.

They descended to a short field bordering the pond and the stepping stones leading out to the boat's front porch. Examining the inky surface, Opal realized Nico was right.

There was still a hint of the sulfur stink that had assaulted them weeks before. The streaks of yellow were gone, but where the liquid had once been jet-black, it now retained a smattering of ugly brown splotches.

"What's that sound?" Emma asked from the stone behind Opal, as they worked along the hopscotch path over the pond. A discordant pounding noise was reverberating across the water, slow and methodical. Opal realized it was coming from inside the houseboat.

"Logan must be fixing something again."

Opal bounced up the rickety steps, opened the door, and entered the foyer. She led Emma through a green velvet curtain and into the houseboat's central showroom. A hammering racket echoed from behind a trick wall panel that hid spiral stairs down to where the Darkdeep lurked. Logan's jacket was thrown over a display case.

Opal stuck her head into the secret stairwell. "Logan? What's going on?"

"I bet he can't hear you." Emma slipped past her, hopping down the winding cast-iron steps.

Logan glanced up as they reached the bottom. "Oh! Hey guys."

He wore a short-sleeved button-up shirt with his name embroidered over the pocket, like one of his father's lumberjacks, and a backward Mariners baseball cap to corral his thick black hair. An open toolbox sat beside two long planks of wood on the floorboards next to him. Then Opal realized they *were* floorboards, recently pried up, creating a hole in the false bottom of the boat. Logan was standing inside that gap, looking pleased with himself.

"Need help?" Emma picked up a hammer and attempted to twirl it, but lost her grip and dropped the tool with a loud clang. Everyone winced.

"Um, thanks, but I'm almost done." Logan nodded at the floorboard to his left. "I'm checking for water damage, from when the Darkdeep flooded. The last thing we need is a leak in the hull below this deck."

He slid the warped board aside and grabbed a brand-new one from a stack of planks he must've appropriated from his dad's supply. Opal avoided looking at the opening in the floor. She'd never understood how the Darkdeep—a literal hole in the bottom of the vessel—didn't just sink the houseboat. *We have to be below the waterline down here.*

Opal shivered. Some things you didn't question, because the answers might be too scary to contemplate.

"What's this?" Emma had flipped the old board over and was inspecting its underside.

Beside them, the Darkdeep rippled suddenly. The barest hint of movement. A swirl where none had existed before.

"Um . . . guys?" Opal said hesitantly.

She glanced at Logan. He'd climbed out of the hole and was shining his phone on the plank in Emma's hands.

Something shimmered in the weak illumination.

Emma's eyes sparkled. "Tell me we found buried treasure. Or a hidden stash of adamantium."

Opal bit her bottom lip, squinting at the pitted slat. "Is that like a trademark of some kind? Branded into the wood?"

Logan leaped back. The phone dropped from his shaking fingers.

"Whoa," Emma breathed, eyes rounding. She whipped out her own phone and shoved its light close.

Opal gaped at the dilapidated floorboard, then at Logan, the Darkdeep's twitch temporarily forgotten. She recognized the symbol stamped onto the plank—a pine tree with three stiff, stark branches angled out on each side. Her eyes flicked to Logan's toolbox, and the image etched on its lid. The emblem on the floorboard was clunkier, but the similarity was undeniable. They were definitely looking at an early logo of the Nantes Timber Company.

"It's our mark," Logan said, swallowing oddly. "This old plank came from the Nantes mill."

"Ohmygosh." Emma clapped a hand to her mouth. "Logan, did someone in your family build this houseboat?" She pointed to a floorboard beside the ones Logan had pried up. "These all look the same. What type of wood is that? Did your company sell materials like this in the past?"

"Who knows?" Logan shook his head irritably as Emma began snapping pics. "It's probably just a weird coincidence.

My family's sold basically all the lumber used in this region, for, like, *forever*. You really can't build anything around here without using our wood. I shouldn't be surprised, actually."

"There are no coincidences!" Emma hissed. "Can you check?"

"I might be able to find a sales history or something," Logan said testily. "But keep in mind what we're talking about, okay? Tracking a bunch of random planks from who-knows-how-long ago? I don't know if people even kept records of . . . of"—he swung his hand in a wide arc—"wood transactions back then. I doubt it."

"It *does* confirm that the houseboat was constructed close by," Opal pointed out, chewing on her thumb in thought. "I was never sure." Part of her had secretly wondered whether the Torchbearer's floating museum had been assembled in this dimension at all. That riddle, at least, was now answered. *But who built the place, and when?*

Opal glanced back at the Darkdeep. Its surface had settled again, but a faint glow remained. She edged a step closer to her friends.

"Send me those pics later," Opal said to Emma. "You want them too, Logan?"

Logan had slipped back into the gap and was crouching, feeling around near his feet. "Shoot. Where is my stupid phone? My dad said if I lose this one I have to buy a replacement myself."

"What are you standing on, anyway?" Emma asked.

"The outer hull. The boards I was checking create a deck above it. I'm standing on the last line of—"

Logan froze. Then he ducked down out of sight. Seconds later his hand emerged, dumping his cell phone beside the opening. But Logan didn't rise, continuing to root around below the flooring. His muffled voice carried from below. "What in the world . . ."

Emma glanced at Opal, who shrugged back.

"There's stuff down here!" Logan called out excitedly. A beat later a grimy metal lockbox slid up through the hole, clanking down next to Logan's phone. It was largish and square, about the size of a breadbox, and covered in hard-crusted grime. Opal's nose wrinkled at its moldy scent, but she felt a thrill at the same time. Maybe they really *had* discovered buried treasure.

Logan's head reappeared, covered in dust. He stood and awkwardly wriggled out of the hole, holding a worn baseball in his left hand.

Logan slumped back on his heels, staring at the ball. He looked like he couldn't breathe.

"What is it?" Opal asked, eyes darting from Logan's sheet-white face to the object clutched in his fingers.

"This . . . this baseball belonged to my . . . m-my grandfather," Logan managed, his face a mask of shock. "I've seen it before—in pictures at our hunting cabin, and around the house. He carried this thing around so much it became like a local legend. He'd hold the ball when giving speeches, or addressing everyone at the company Christmas party. Grandpa would pick it up and start tossing it to himself almost every time he left his office."

Logan spun the ball in his fingers and thrust it toward Opal. "Look—see that long scuff down the side, between the stitching? Grandpa's story was that Babe Ruth hit this clear out of Yankee Stadium on his only trip to the East Coast. According to him, it bounced right into his hand as he was walking down the street." Logan gazed down at the ball, his expression a mix of wonder and horror. "When I was little, I'd search for this baseball in any picture of him I came across. And it was always there, like a lucky charm. I wondered where it went after he died." His head whipped to Opal, eyes wide. "How can this be *here*?"

Opal opened her mouth, but no sound came out. She had no idea.

Logan pivoted abruptly and set the ball aside. He grabbed the metal box and yanked roughly on its blackened latch, but the lid wouldn't budge.

"Logan, hold on." Emma eased the container from his white-knuckled grip and wiped a layer of grime from its face. An old-fashioned combination lock appeared, the kind with dials you have to align into the proper numerical sequence. "This is like a portable safe. Pretty heavy, too. I bet it's made of steel. We might have to cut through the lock with a butane torch to get inside. I think my parents sell them at the shop, though!"

Opal felt a strange anticipation building in her gut. "What would the Torchbearers have felt like they needed to hide *on their own houseboat*?"

"What do you mean, Torchbearers?" Logan snapped. His cheek was twitching spastically.

"Well . . ." Opal looked somewhat surprised. "Who else would have put those things down here?"

Logan shook his head once, hard. Then he snatched one of the loose floorboards, put it back in place, and started pounding nails into their former holes, his mouth set in a rigid line. Opal wasn't sure if he'd completed his inspection, but finding that baseball had clearly rocked Logan's world. He seemed completely shaken to find something so familiar in such an otherworldly location.

*I would be, too.*

"Logan," Opal said quietly.

He didn't respond, finishing with the first board and moving to the second.

Opal reached out, resting a hand on his shoulder. Logan tensed, his eyes squeezing shut. The hammering abruptly ceased.

"We have to find out how the ball got down there. You know that, right?"

He pulled away. Logan rose stiffly, lifting the box and holding it tightly to his chest, ignoring the dirty streaks it left on his work shirt. He took a deep breath. "I . . . I'll look into it, okay?" A beat passed, then, "Just don't say anything to Nico or Tyler yet. Not until I . . . until I know more."

"Sure, Logan." Emma shot a worried glance at Opal, who made a calming-hands gesture back at her friend. Emma nodded doubtfully.

There was a splash behind them. All three kids spun.

A thin stream of black liquid was arcing up from the center of the Darkdeep. The flow remained steady for a moment, filling the room with a deep, earthy scent, before it faded to nothing and the well stilled. Then a huge expulsion of sour air bubbled up through the water, roiling its surface before fading with a hiss.

Silence filled the room. Opal found she couldn't break it. The eruption had reminded her of . . . what? A geyser? She didn't know a lot about geology, but that's what it looked like.

A memory of the Rift explosions knifed into her thoughts. Opal felt a twinge of panic.

"Oh, man." Logan ran a hand over his eyes. "That can't be good."

"That's an understatement," Emma whispered. "Why is the Darkdeep *burping*?"

# 5

# NICO

$A$ textbook struck the locker next to Nico's.

He jumped backward in surprise as the book thunked heavily to the floor, pages scattering from a broken spine. A shriek of outrage reverberated down the hall, along with the dull thud of a knee connecting with . . . something.

Nico turned to see Carson, face green, keeling over at Megan Cook's feet. He made a weird moaning gurgle that turned Nico's stomach. Parker was hastily backing away from Megan, holding her backpack out in front of him in what looked like surrender. Megan snatched it from his fingers and stormed down the hall. Stares and whispers dogged her every step. Despite the clear "a-fight-just-happened" sounds, no teachers emerged from their classrooms.

Timbers Middle School was teetering on the brink.

Emma appeared beside Nico, kicking the broken textbook aside as he closed and spun his lock. "Do I even wanna know what that's about?" he asked with a weary sigh.

"Carson and Parker are attempting to search people's bookbags," Emma explained matter-of-factly. "They're checking for 'monster-attracting devices,' apparently. In the courtyard this morning, Carson said he's going to flush out any demon-kids who might've summoned the attack on Dark Halloween."

Nico shook his head. "And Megan?"

"Had no interest in having her things examined."

"She made that pretty clear."

"Indeed. Carson threw her math book as a warning, but he misread the situation."

Nico squeezed his nose. "Carson ran into me and Logan on the beach during the figment attack. He witnessed us battling that sphinx monster, right before the Beast showed up. So why are he and Parker wasting time messing with Megan?"

Emma laughed dryly. "I guess they're leaving no stone unturned. Hopefully all stones will be as difficult as she was."

Nico nodded in a distracted manner. Emma didn't miss it.

"What's wrong?" she asked, her big blue eyes clouding with concern. "You were quiet all through Biology."

Nico slumped back against his locker. "I might as well tell you. My dad's transfer is officially official. We're moving to Portland in January."

Emma gasped. "Nico, no!"

He nodded, a wave of heat rushing to his face. "It's true."

Emma was about to say more when a wadded paper ball

struck her in the forehead. Someone in the hallway shouted, "Down with traitors!"

Nico whirled, anger hot and ready, but the anonymous missile-chucker had already slipped away. Students moved in tight-knit groups down the corridor, eyes roving for threats. The book club guys—Ryker Harrison, Phoenix Payson, and Carter Bradshaw—zoomed by with their heads down and shoulders hunched. Dallen Brynner and Kayden Hepworth were huddled in a corner, recording everyone with their phones.

Paranoia infused the air. Nico thought Timbers Middle might be the epicenter of freaking out for the entire town. The place was ready to explode.

Emma grabbed his arm. "Let it go, Nico. I'm fine. It's just paper."

"What is going *on* these days?" Nico growled, still searching for the culprit.

Emma shrugged, then dropped her voice. "People are scared. Remember, some of these kids actually *saw* the Beast. They weren't prepared for it like we were. The fact that they're panicking makes perfect sense."

"What's that about the Beast?" Tyler asked, sidling up to them as the crush of students in the hall began to thin. He eyed Emma with suspicion.

Emma gave him a level look. "We were discussing how kids in this school are on the verge of melting down, and that it's a pretty reasonable reaction given what happened. Where have you been, anyway?"

"I had to miss first period." Tyler frowned sheepishly, rubbing his mouth. "My mom has me talking to this doctor-lady twice a month. It's fine—she's nice. But I'm pretty sure if I tell her the whole truth, it won't turn out well. Like, I'll-live-in-my-pajamas-at-a-hospital not well."

"When did you start therapy?" Emma asked curiously. "There's zero wrong with that, by the way. Talking is good."

"I've been going since the day *Freakshow* aired their last episode." He flashed a wry grin at Emma. "You and I have been best friends forever. When my parents saw that you were *starring* in the series, they decided *I* must've had something to do with it, too. They were . . . concerned. I'll use that word."

Emma winced. "Sorry. If it's any consolation, I'm not allowed inside Mr. Harvey's A/V shop anymore. He chases me away every time I pass his store window. He called me a 'carpetbagging opportunist,' which I had to look up. It's not a compliment."

Tyler snorted. "Not sure why that should make me feel better. And don't act like it's all been bad. You've been getting free ice cream from Mr. Taylor any time you ask."

Emma smiled wickedly. "He wants me to film a scene inside his shop. Free advertising."

They were interrupted by Opal joining them. "The bell's in two. Something up I should know about?"

Emma's face fell. She shot a troubled glance at Nico, who looked away.

"Um, Nico has som—"

"Guys! Guys!"

Logan was streaking down the hallway, waving madly. He reached them in a wild rush, jostling into Tyler and Opal. Nico tensed. One of his fists slammed down by his side, striking the locker behind him.

Emma shot Nico a confused look, then her eyes widened. She edged between the two boys.

"You're not going to believe this!" Logan was trying to catch his breath. Opal watched him with rapt attention, which somehow made Nico even more angry.

"Opal and Emma already know," Logan wheezed, "but on the houseboat yesterday, we found an old combination safe and a baseball that used to belong to my grandfather."

"Wait, *what*?" Tyler squawked.

The hall had totally cleared. The bell could ring at any moment, but no one moved.

"I was pulling up warped boards in the Darkdeep chamber—to check for water damage—and we saw a plank with our logo on it. Nantes Timber, I mean. The stuff was *underneath* it, in the crawl space between the floor and the hull." Logan was talking rapidly, his words tumbling on top of one another. "I was pretty freaked out, so I took everything home and checked the ball against some old family photos. It's the same one. There's no question."

"What about the lockbox?" Opal asked.

"Wouldn't open," Logan replied. "But I'm sure I can figure it out eventually."

Scowling, Nico opened his mouth to say something scathing, but Emma grasped his forearm. His glare swung to her. "Just wait," she whispered. "This might be important."

Nico tensed, but he held his tongue. The others seemed to miss the exchange.

"Once I was sure," Logan carried on, "I started thinking about that particular logo. Like, when did the company start using it? Could I narrow down the year? So I went to my dad's office and started rooting around. And found this!" Logan flourished a folded piece of paper that had been stuffed in his pocket.

Opal eyed the crumpled document. "And that is . . ."

"A purchase order," Logan said proudly. "For lumber sufficient to construct one custom-designed houseboat, delivery to be made locally. The details were only recorded in the company president's private business ledger. In this case, by my great-grandfather."

Everyone was stunned to silence, including Nico.

Finally, Emma spoke. "Who took delivery, Logan?"

Logan beamed with delight. "A man named Spartan Hale."

Tyler slapped both hands to his head. "His last name was Hale? No chance he's not related to Roman!"

"Has to be!" Logan crowed in triumph. "And since Roman

Hale was the houseboat's final caretaker—and the last member of the Order before us—it means I found a clear link to the Torchbearers!"

Logan's bragging smile was more than Nico could stand. "Boy, you Nantes jerks think you're *so* freaking great!" he shouted, startling everyone. He shouldered past Emma to stand eye-to-eye with Logan.

Overhead, the bell rang. No one reacted.

"Huh?" Logan blinked at Nico. He actually looked hurt. "Nico, my great-grandfather helped *build* the houseboat, and my granddad must've actually gone aboard at some point, even down the hidden staircase. He could've seen the Darkdeep! I think that's pretty important."

Nico's lips curled into a snarl. "You think your stupid family matters more than anything else. It's all you care about."

Logan stared. "Dude, what are you talking about?"

"Nico's dad got transferred," Emma blurted, snaking around Nico and dodging his incensed look. "To Portland. They leave next semester."

Nico felt Tyler's hand grip his shoulder. Opal was gaping at him, mouth rounded in shock.

His eyelids began to burn.

Logan's face crumpled. "Oh no. Nico, man, I'm so sorry. I didn't want that to happen. If there's any—"

"Didn't want it to happen?!" Nico exploded. "Your *father* is the whole reason we're getting kicked out of town."

"I already apologized for that," Logan shot back, heat rising in his voice. "I told him to stop, but we both know their feud has a life of its own."

"Awesome," Nico said bitterly. "Well now *I* get a life of my own in Portland. And it's your family's fault."

Logan's face turned bright red. "If *your* dad hadn't made an enemy of the whole town with those stupid owls, none of this would've happened! You've never once admitted that your father dug his own hole by making everyone in Timbers furious. It wasn't just my dad that wanted him gone, you know!"

"He led the pack," Nico replied coldly. "And used dirty tricks to rig the system."

Logan bumped chest-to-chest into Nico. "Who are you calling dirty?" he asked softly, a dangerous glint entering his eyes.

"In your family, who isn't?" Nico spat back, his hands balling into fists.

Opal shoved between them. "That's enough, both of you! Everyone needs to calm down and take a breath. We can settle this, if you'd just—"

She was cut off by a deep growl that fluttered Nico's stomach. Startled, he glanced down the hallway, then nearly shouted in astonishment.

A large black dog was standing at the opposite end of the corridor. As Nico watched, it padded closer, exposing ice-white canines and hard yellow eyes. The animal approached slowly, a deep rumble echoing from its jaws. A whiff of something spicy—almost peppery—filled the air. The lights in the hallway seemed to dim.

Nico felt goosebumps erupt all over his body. *That smell* . . .

Tyler, frozen in place, spoke out of the side of his mouth. "Why . . . why is Cujo inside our school?"

"He doesn't look friendly," Emma whispered back. A thin sheen of sweat had appeared on her forehead.

The animal advanced another few steps, golden eyes gleaming. The group reflexively backed up.

"Okay, so . . ." Logan was dry-washing his hands. "A mongrel got in somehow. We just have to scare it away. Or alert someone. Before it chews on us."

"That's pretty big for a dog," Opal breathed. "*Too* big, guys."

"It's a wolf," Nico hissed. "Must be down from the hills outside of town. They never enter occupied buildings like this unless . . . unless something's not right with them."

"What, like *rabies*?" Emma whimpered.

The wolf stalked closer, then stopped, no more than twenty feet away.

Nico stayed very still, avoiding the animal's gaze. He didn't want to set it off. But there was nowhere to run. The corridor was empty, with all doors shut. No one had the slightest idea what was happening in the hallway. If this wolf attacked, they wouldn't be able to get away in time.

The wolf sat back on its haunches. Glared with unblinking yellow eyes. Its lips peeled back, and Nico was struck by an impossible thought—that the animal was *smirking* at them.

The lights seemed to dim another notch. Shadows drifted toward the wolf, making it harder to see. The yellow eyes flared like a strobe light. The piquant scent increased.

Nico blinked as the wolf's body flickered somehow, almost shifting in phase. Then it stepped forward, breaking the spell.

Flashes blazed inside Nico's head. He rubbed his forehead in shock.

"What just happened?" Tyler whimpered, tears leaking from the corners of his eyes. "It's like I just stared into the sun."

Beside him, Emma gasped. "Did . . . You guys? I think that thing got *bigger*."

"Not a wolf," Opal whispered. "It might be a figment."

Logan grimaced. "But whose then?" Opal shook her head.

The creature bayed suddenly, shattering the stillness. Everyone jumped.

Nico was done waiting to be chomped. "Run!"

As one, the group spun and tore down the hallway in the opposite direction.

Nico heard a sharp growl, then the click of long claws raking the linoleum. Rounding a corner, he spotted the cafeteria straight ahead. He pointed without breaking stride. "In there!"

Another earsplitting yowl. Nico glanced back, saw that the creature was stalking them at a trot, letting them flee before it. *But not get away.* The strange grin was still plastered on its lips. The wolf's yellow eyes pulsed with a mysterious inner radiance. The reek of spices swept over Nico and he gagged.

*Those eyes. That smell. Where . . .*

Logan reached the doors first. He slung one open and waved everyone inside. "Hurry!"

Everyone scrambled into the lunchroom in a mass of frightened limbs. Logan slammed the door shut. Opal spotted a janitor's cart, yanked out a mop, and shoved it through the door handles in a makeshift barricade. Then she and Logan backed away to where the rest of the group was huddled a few steps beyond the threshold.

Something heavy pressed against the doors. The mop held.

A beat passed, then a terrible screeching sound filled the air as something tore at the metal.

Abruptly, the noise ceased.

Nico swallowed, unsure. "I think . . . maybe that thing is . . ."

A fist pounded against the door, causing everyone to jump. An angry female voice boomed from outside the cafeteria. "Who's in there? You'd better come out *right now*, or you'll be living in detention every day from now on!"

Nico paled. "Oh no. It's Principal Kisner."

Tyler put a palm over his eyes. "Better let her in. I'm guessing Dr. Wolfenstein isn't still out there with her, begging for treats."

"Great," Emma mumbled, shoving her hands in her pockets. "This is all we need right now."

Opal removed the mop and opened the door. Principal Kisner was standing in the hallway with her arms crossed, practically shaking with fury. "I want to know who did this . . . this . . . *disgraceful* vandalism!"

As Nico exited, he saw deep gouges scoring the metal doors. Twin swipes, like claw marks.

*But claws can't carve through solid metal.*

*Can they?*

"We didn't do it!" Logan protested. "There was a giant wolf! It was chasing us! Honest!"

Principal Kisner glared at him. She spoke through gritted teeth. "My office. *Immediately.*"

They had no choice but to comply.

Nico moved to follow his friends, but paused, shooting a glance back at the doors. Those scratches were incredibly deep, even for a rogue figment. And what kept bothering him about the creature's eyes?

"Nico Holland!"

Nico winced, then hurried after the others, mind swirling with unsettling thoughts.

*What in the heck were they dealing with now?*

# 6

## OPAL

*The Torchbearers stood me up.*

Every single one of them. Opal couldn't believe it.

She'd texted the group during last period:

Houseboat meeting at 4 p.m. No excuses.

*Looks like they found some excuses.*

Appearing shaken, Principal Kisner had marched them all to her office and interrogated the group about the gouges on the cafeteria doors. Meanwhile, word spread around school that some kind of creature was stalking the halls. If tensions had been bad before, they were a disaster now. Kids were so spooked they refused to change classes.

It didn't help that Opal and her friends were the only witnesses. No one else caught sight of the wolf, but that didn't stop Carson from working the rumor mill, talking about how the Torch necklace weirdos had summoned a pet monster to play with and lost control. Opal thought even a few teachers had regarded them warily as the day dragged on.

All in all, things couldn't have gone worse.

Which was why she'd called the meeting. Plus, Opal desperately wanted to sort things out between Nico and Logan. That wound would fester if they didn't confront it head-on, but neither boy so much as glanced at each other after leaving the principal's office. Another catastrophe they didn't need.

So here she was. Alone.

*Maybe they're all just late?*

Yet that wasn't even what bothered Opal the most. She began reviewing her notes on Yvette Dumont to avoid thinking about what Emma had told them in the hallway.

*Nico.* Moving. To Portland. In less than two months!

Opal squeezed her eyes shut. A hole in her stomach threatened to consume her.

Somehow, *that* problem felt too big. Bigger than the Rift, or the Darkdeep, or strange wolves that seemed to twist and change right in front of your eyes. Opal knew she was being ridiculous—those issues were way more important than a friend moving away—but she couldn't seem to face the idea of Nico's leaving town. *If he goes, everything will change.*

Opal flipped through the closest book she could grab, examining the same few snippets she'd found weeks ago. It wasn't much, and none of it groundbreaking.

Yvette Dumont had been shipwrecked off the coast of Oregon in 1741. She became the first Torchbearer. She'd placed Thing in its jar to save the little green alien, but then kept Thing there against its will, believing the creature's presence on Earth created a balance between worlds that kept the Rift sealed. And that's where the trail went dead.

Or had, until yesterday. Opal opened the worn leather notebook she'd found on the houseboat and now used every day. She recorded two new facts Tyler had discovered in the Torchbearer office: *Yvette Dumont was also the first Beastmaster. She suffered a great loss at the time of the Tear.*

Opal gnawed on her braid, idly coloring in the hand-drawn flower at the bottom of the page with a purple marker. She'd drawn opal stones in the opposite corners to match the aster blossoms, perhaps as a way to make the notebook feel more like her own. But pretty sketches didn't help solve either of the mysteries plaguing her.

What happened to Yvette Dumont, and why had Thing sent that cryptic note?

With a snort of frustration, Opal glanced at her latest notation.

The Tear.

That's what old Torchbearers called the moment the Rift first opened.

But *why* had a giant rip in space-time occurred at all?

Minutes ticked by as she stared at nothing, working the

question over in her head. Getting nowhere yet again, she glanced at the clock. Opal told herself the others were just having a hard time getting away—everyone's parents were on edge, and paying closer attention to vague excuses and long absences. A trip to the principal's office definitely hadn't helped, although no one was actually suggesting *they* made those scratch marks.

But Opal had picked this time of day strategically. Most adults weren't home from work yet.

And really. *No one* could make it?

She sat back with a loud sigh. There was so much to do.

The houseboat was a mess. People had been rummaging through display cases and chests—looking for items that might help with their research—but not putting things back. No one had updated the inventory in weeks, or made notes about Dark Halloween in the Order's official logbook. And they all kept missing their Darkdeep-watching shifts.

Meanwhile, who knew if the Rift was still boiling with Takers at the bottom of the ocean?

Opal had missed a watch herself last week—Kathryn Walsh had stopped her daughter in the driveway and demanded they watch a self-defense video together. Like Tae-Bo would help them fight off figments.

She rose dejectedly and trudged toward the trick wall panel, passing the empty pedestal. Opal ran a hand across its smooth surface, her fingers tracing the circle where Thing's jar had rested for so many years. In the end, the tiny alien had helped them survive. It had proven to be an ally and friend.

But did Thing really expect her to act on nothing but a scribbled warning?

*Probably.* That was how the confounding little creature operated. Opal smiled ruefully as she tripped the catch to the hidden staircase. *Might as well do a quick check on the Darkdeep.* She had one foot on the top riser when the houseboat's front door slammed. Opal heard someone bound through the foyer, the entry curtain swishing aside as Emma burst into the showroom.

"Sorrysorrysorry!" she called out, tossing down her bookbag. "I'm super late, I know."

"Too many selfies?" Opal snapped, then immediately regretted her tone. At least Emma was here, which was more than could be said for the boys.

"No," Emma replied crisply, eyes flashing. Pond mist had wilted her curly blond hair, and her cheeks were bright red from the cold. "My mom needed help at the store. Dad's not feeling great. Plus, I had to go over *everything* about the animal attack at school. I have the distinct impression that my mother does not believe me."

"I'm sorry," Opal said, and meant it. "My mother hounded me, too. Is everything okay?"

"Ha! *Hounded.* Good one. And yeah, things are fine—my dad just has the flu, I think. Wait, are we the only ones here?"

"Yes. And it's probably time for me to head home anyway."

Emma bit her bottom lip. "Sorry again for being late. What did you want to meet about? The wolf? Did you notice how it, like, *changed* when you looked at it?" Opal watched a shudder wrack her friend's body.

"It wasn't a normal wolf, for sure." Opal took a deep breath. "I just felt like we needed to talk. There's a lot going on, and we have to fix this thing between Nico and Logan."

Emma nodded sadly. "That fight was horrible. It could have been any of us."

"Um, not really." Opal gave Emma an odd look. "Logan's dad actually pushed for the transfer."

"That's not what I meant." Frowning, Emma began fiddling with her hoodie's zipper. "We're all way overstressed. Even you and I are sniping at each other these days." Her expression turned sheepish. "That's part of the reason why I film *Emma-mazing!* sometimes, even when I know I should be handling Torchbearer stuff. It's a break from the pressure. And with my show, I'm the only one in charge, which is nice for a change."

Opal understood. There were times when she wanted to throw her hands up and quit this whole mess.

Emma dropped to a knee and opened her backpack, digging around inside. "I almost forgot—I found something interesting. About the Nantes family."

"Really?" Opal crouched next to her. She knew Logan wanted to investigate his family's Torchbearer connections alone, but she couldn't help being curious.

Emma nodded without looking up. "I was running searches on Reddit, scanning for any Beast-related threads that might cause us trouble—nothing came up, by the way—when I found a link to an old property management archive for Timbers. Turns out, there are records that go all the way back to the town's founding, but the earliest ones are only in hard copy at the library." She rocked back on her heels and held out a sheaf of legal-sized papers with grid-like drawings on them. "So I went in for a look. You can't check any of this stuff out, but I got Old Lady Johnson to let me make copies of the oldest documents. She even let me do it myself, which I couldn't believe."

Opal frowned at the sketches. "I'm not sure what I'm looking at."

"Plats."

Opal raised an eyebrow.

Emma winked. "Parcels of land. When they first mapped out Timbers, back in the 1700s, they wrote down who got which lots, mostly along Otter Creek. That's what Mrs. Johnson said, anyway. But look!" She tapped a square of faded handwriting. *"Edward Nantes, craftsman, .78 acres. The Row."* Her gaze rose to meet Opal's. "That must be the original Overlook Row!"

"Cool," Opal said, as supportively as she could. "But we knew Logan's family has been here since the beginning. There's a statue of Edward Nantes in town square, and they still live on Overlook Row *now*. If not in their original house, then one just like it."

Emma held up a finger in riposte. "Proof of something is never pointless," she said primly.

Opal nodded, her eyes drifting to another lot farther down the street. Its label jumped out at her. An electric shock arced along her spine.

*Y. Dumont, chemist, .63 acres. The Row.*

"Whoa." Opal stabbed the listing with her finger.

"Holy crap." Emma shifted for a better look. "How did I miss that?"

"That has to be our girl, right?" Opal asked gleefully. *Finally! More about Yvette Dumont!*

Emma's face glowed. "Makes sense. She was a founder, and had to live *somewhere*."

Opal recorded the land info in her notebook, then drew a rough copy of the plat on a second page. She could barely contain her excitement. They'd suspected Yvette had lived in Timbers, of course—where else? There were no other towns nearby in that time period. But this confirmed it. And now they knew her occupation. *Maybe this is the break we needed . . .*

"That isn't *your* new house, is it?" Emma nodded at

Opal's sketch. The Walshes had recently moved to Overlook Row, a fact Opal's mother liked to tell anyone who'd listen.

"Sadly, no." Opal smiled wryly. *That* would've been cool. For a moment, she fantasized about finding a trapdoor in her bedroom, one that led to a Torchbearer treasure vault. "Our house was built in 1824. My mom talks about it nonstop, so I know the exact date. Plus, we're on the other end of the street." She leaned closer to the plat, scanning the tidy, antiquated writing. "It's neat that they wrote professions on here. Is that common with these kinds of records?"

Emma shrugged. "No idea."

"I wonder what a chemist did back then," Opal mused. "Was it someone who actually did stuff with chemicals? Or was it, like, an old-school pharmacist?" She felt like she'd heard the term used that way before.

"Either way, this is a *very interesting* discovery." Emma lifted her chin imperiously.

Opal chuckled. "Yes, it definitely is. Great find, Em."

Emma's eyes positively sparked.

Opal looked back at the schematics. "Do you—would it be okay if I—"

"Take them," Emma said with a snort. But something in her tone caught up to Opal midway through gathering the papers. "Hold on. What's the catch?"

"No catch." Emma popped to her feet and rezipped her bookbag.

Opal watched her friend through narrowed eyes as she placed the photocopies in her own backpack. "Let's check on the Darkdeep before we go. See if it's still farting."

They moved to the stairs. When Emma cleared her throat halfway down, Opal hid a smile.

*Here it comes.*

"Just, you know," Emma mumbled, as they reached the lower chamber, "I've been thinking. We should get the boys to take Thing's message more seriously. It might be really important, but who knows what it means? I think we have to find out. We may even need to . . . to go in again."

Across the room, the Darkdeep belched. Black water shot into the air, kissing the rafters.

Both girls jumped backward in alarm, but the ripples faded quickly. The dark liquid stilled as if the expulsion had never occurred.

Opal glanced nervously at her friend. Emma stared at the now-silent pool, eyes serious.

Turning back to the well, Opal tried not to shiver.

They'd entered the Darkdeep before, even knowing it was dangerous.

To flee a figment horde. To battle a Taker. To access the Rift.

When necessary, they did what was necessary.

But there was always a risk. Nightmares that emerged afterward.

Thing's words rang in Opal's head.

*There's something here that doesn't belong.*

*Or, I should say, someone.*

Opal suddenly had to know who it might be.

# 7

# NICO

Tyler's scarlet vestments rippled in the steady breeze.

*Bathrobe*, Nico thought. *He's wearing his dad's terry-cloth bathrobe.*

His friend was standing on the island's small beach, legs planted wide, an old book wedged in the crook of one elbow as the other hand waved an algae-covered stick high over-head. Tyler faced Still Cove as if confronting it. His eyes were shut and he was humming to himself.

Nico shook his head. His patience was already gone and they'd only been there ten minutes.

"Why the bathrobe, man?" Nico blurted finally.

Tyler shushed him with an annoyed glare. "It's the color, ignoramus. I'm attempting to attract a vicious predator. I figured red might get its attention. Like a bullfighter."

Nico snorted. "Bulls *charge* when attracted, you know."

Tyler flinched, but then his brow furrowed. "Will you please let me do this?"

"By all means, continue. It's going great so far."

Tyler clicked his tongue. "This book isn't exactly a how-to manual, Nico. It just says that former Masters were able to summon the Beast by"—he glanced at an ancient page—" '*forging a spiritual connection with the Lotan so as to commune with its primordial essence.*' " Tyler looked away. "So, like . . . that's what I'm doing."

Nico shrugged. "Tell me why we want to summon the Beast again?"

"So we can learn how to make it go away."

Nico blinked rapidly a few times. "Makes sense," he managed finally. "Lure a killer alien sea monster here, so we can . . . ask it to leave."

Tyler rolled his eyes. "Look, we need to know if I can command the Beast or not. Or at least control it. I *was* able to communicate with it that once, during the beach attack. I think." He shot another reproachful glance at Nico. "And that *sea monster* saved our butts against the Takers at the Rift battle. Don't act like it didn't."

Nico nodded reluctantly. "It did. No question. I just worry that the Beast had its own reasons for fighting Takers, and now we might just be a tasty afternoon snack."

By the shiver that ran through Tyler, Nico knew he wasn't the only one concerned. But Tyler had declared himself the next Beastmaster, and he was determined to revive the old connection between Beast and Torchbearers. Which was why they were both freezing their butts off on this lonely, windswept beach, instead of investigating whatever the heck that wolf thing had been. *At least he has that bathrobe to wear. Looks pretty warm.*

Tyler turned back to the slate-gray sea. Still Cove was as smooth as glass, with barely a wave despite the whipping gusts assailing both boys as they stood near the waterline. It didn't seem possible that sky and water could act so independently, but little about Still Cove made sense. *It's why no one ever comes here but us.*

Tyler lifted his algae stick once more. Eyes closed, he seemed to be chanting something, but his words flittered away on the swirling wind. Nico held his tongue for as long as he could, but the air was bitingly cold, and he was starting to lose feeling in his toes. He was about to whine again when Tyler dropped his arms in frustration.

"I don't feel anything," Tyler snapped. "No connection, no vibe. Nothing. Maybe I need more algae."

Nico kept his tone as neutral as possible. "Let's go to the houseboat and regroup. Opal wanted us there an hour ago anyway. I'm sure the others are all still spooked about what happened this morning."

"You mean the crazy-eyed super-wolf that clawed through a metal door?" Tyler tugged his robe closed. "Um, *yeah*, I imagine they are. So am I. That *had* to be a figment, right? But how?" With an exasperated grunt, Tyler chucked his algae stick into the cove and shuffled over to stand with Nico. "Hey, you know Logan might be at the boat, right? Opal's text went to everyone."

Nico felt his pulse accelerate. "I hope he is."

"No no *no*." Tyler scolded, crossing his arms. "Enough of that nonsense. Logan may have been a jerk about your dad's transfer at first, but he had nothing to do with how it actually went down. That was his dad. And we *both* know he doesn't want it now."

Nico scowled. "He didn't seem too broken up about it at school."

"Then you weren't looking hard enough. Logan feels terrible. Like he's partially responsible."

Nico's glower deepened. "Because he *is*. You were there when he taunted me in the cafeteria last month. Logan's the one who told me about it! He was *gloating*. Right to my face."

Tyler frowned, ran a hand over his scalp. "We've been working with Logan for a while now. Through a lot of hard, bad stuff. You know he's been solid. I thought we put this feud to bed a long time ago."

"I'm about to have a bed in Portland, Ty. So I guess we closed the matter too soon."

Tyler's head dropped. "I'm just sick about this. Is there anything your dad can do?"

Nico's tone was acid. "Probably, but he won't. His pride always gets in the way." He made a deep voice that mimicked his father's. *"I go where they tell me, son. It's not my place to question the decisions of my superiors. You'd do well to act accordingly."*

"Maybe we could sabotage it somehow?" Tyler stroked his chin thoughtfully. "You said the move is kind of like a promotion? What if we screwed up something your dad is responsible for, so that he doesn't get the new job and has to stay."

Nico rubbed the back of his neck. "Believe me, I've actually considered it. But what if that got him fired instead? Then I'd still be moving, only my dad would be out of work. Plus, what do we know about espionage? We'd just get caught, and then I'd spend my teenage years in Portland under house arrest."

Tyler sighed. A beat later he looked sharply at Nico. "Hey, did you read that thing about Old Faithful going haywire?"

The subject change caught Nico off guard. "Huh? No, what?"

"I saw my mom's Facebook this morning. Somebody had posted an article about that famous geyser. The one in Yellowstone? Last night it erupted in bright yellow."

Nico gave his friend a squinty look. "Old Faithful went to the bathroom?"

Tyler spread his hands. "I'm just telling you what it said. The geyser used to shoot out regular water, but now the flow is coming up like neon highlighter fluid. Apparently stinks like a sewer, too. The park rangers are bugging out. The article ended with a whole list of weird events that happened there over the last week."

"Stank yellow liquid?" A chill course through Nico's veins. "Sounds like what happened here when the Darkdeep went nuts."

Tyler nodded, eyes worried. "Could be a coincidence. But also, maybe not."

Nico dragged a hand through his hair, silently berating himself. *He* was supposed to be keeping an eye out for any freaky environmental stuff, but Tyler had found the most troubling signs yet. This definitely sounded like a Rift problem. But all the way in Wyoming? How did that make sense?

What was going on at the Rift anyway? Nico knew they needed to check on it, but that was now basically impossible. The oil rig had collapsed, and the Rift was below that wreckage, socked away at the bottom of the ocean. It might as well have been on Mars. *Sooooo frustrating.*

"Let's get to the houseboat," Nico repeated, with as much authority as he could muster. "We need to figure out some way to recon a sunken platform." He hesitated for a sec, then added, "But maybe don't tell Emma about Old Faithful right now."

Tyler halted midstep. "Don't tell Emma? Why not?"

Nico's shoulders rolled in a guilty shrug. "I don't know.

I just don't want this to become a YouTube story. We don't need anyone out there connecting dots, or thinking about Timbers at all. Emma's lost sight of that."

A bit of heat crept into Tyler's voice. "Are you saying you don't trust *Emma* now? Just how many Torchbearers are on your *unreliable* list at the moment? Me?"

"Don't be ridiculous." Nico was suddenly angry, too. "I'm out here with frostbite on my ears trying to have your back." Then he gave Tyler a look. "But you're honestly telling me that the exciting adventures of *Emma-mazing!* don't make *you* nervous? After all, the Beast is our biggest secret after the Darkdeep."

Tyler looked away. Nico knew his words had hit home, but he didn't celebrate. It felt terrible losing trust in Emma.

Logan, however, was another matter. *We never should've let him through the door.*

"Come on," Nico said, gripping his friend's bony shoulder. "The showroom has to be warmer than this beach. I'm sure we can tell Emma everything. I wasn't being fair."

"She wouldn't sell us out," Tyler insisted. But was there a slight hitch in his voice?

"Opal's gonna kill us both for blowing off her text," Nico said. "I hope she understands about the bathrobe."

Tyler's face grew sickly. "Maybe you should go on ahead. To, like, smooth the way."

Nico snickered. "No chance. We'll face her together. And

next time I'll bring a bathrobe, too. My mom has this fluffy peach-colored one. That'll attract ol' Beastie for sure."

Tyler laughed. They turned and started up toward the tree line.

Behind them, a tremendous splash sounded.

Both boys spun, then danced back as a ragged wave crashed onto the beach and rolled up the sand. Out in the bay, a thick line of wake was sliding away from the island, arcing toward the mist-choked mouth of Still Cove and the wide Skagit Sound beyond.

Nico's mouth had gone dry. "Um, Ty?"

"No idea." His friend had paled several shades. "Maybe I'm . . . I'm not so far off after all."

Beyond them, the water smoothed, then went as still and silent as glass.

# 8

# OPAL

Opal knocked on Logan's front door.

*How old is this house, anyway? Was it here when Yvette Dumont lived down the block? Did she ever climb these steps?*

Two months ago Opal had been standing in the same spot, tasked with checking on Logan after he'd tracked them to the houseboat and come face-to-face with the Darkdeep. Nico and the others had hidden behind garbage cans while she'd done the dirty work of finding out if Logan was going to tattle.

This time Opal was alone, but her purpose was the same. She wanted to know what Logan was up to.

He answered the door himself. "Hey. What's going on?"

"We need to talk," Opal said, then she cursed under her breath as Logan's little sister bounced onto the porch.

"Ooh!" Lily Nantes grinned wide. She wore an apron and

was holding a giant bag of apples. "Do you want to talk to Logan *alone*?"

Opal cut to the chase. "Yes, I do." Her gaze flicked to Logan. "Like, right now."

"*Or*," Lily said, drawing out the word, "you could forget my doofus brother and come bake pies with Mom and me. We're making all the family favorites. Mom's is apple crumb. Dad likes coconut cream. *I* prefer chocolate chip cookies."

"That's not a pie," Opal pointed out.

"Is so," Lily said. "Chocolate cookie pie. I invented it."

"Maybe later."

"Fine, *whatever*." Lily started skipping down the hall, but then she spun at the last second. "What's your favorite pie, Opal?"

Opal blinked. "Lemon meringue."

Lily nodded her acceptance before turning away once more.

Logan kept a hand on the doorframe. "Look, I know you said for us to meet at four, but those two grabbed me right after school and it's been *The Great British Baking Show* ever since. I can't get away."

Lame excuse. Though he did have flour in his hair.

Opal made no move to leave.

Finally, he stepped aside. *Reluctantly?* "Do you want to come in?"

Opal entered the foyer and followed Logan to his father's

study. A welded conglomeration of metal gears and blunted mill tools hung behind the enormous desk, which looked as solid and heavy as a tugboat. A puffy white cat uncurled from an armchair next to the unlit fireplace, stalking past them as if they'd purposely ruined its nap. Framed pictures and old books lined the shelves.

Logan slid the doors closed once the cat had made its leisurely exit. "Yeah?"

Before Opal could answer, the doors popped back open, causing her to jump.

Logan's father entered the room. "You're needed in the kitchen, son." Sylvain nodded at Opal. "You two can speak tomorrow at school."

Opal's mouth formed a tight line. She felt a sudden rush of anger. *This man is responsible for Nico having to leave Timbers. I bet he's been gloating about his victory all week long.* Mr. Nantes didn't appear exultant at the moment, but who knew what went on behind those piercing blue eyes.

*Although . . .*

Looking closer, something seemed a bit wrong with Logan's father. He wore his usual jeans, plaid flannel, and work boots, but his face appeared haggard. Sylvain Nantes typically gave off an indomitable vibe. His nickname around town was "Paul Bunyan"—used by some with respect, by others in a kind of fearful awe.

But at the moment he seemed kinda . . . beaten down. Used up.

Opal succumbed to a wild impulse. "Nico's dad got transferred," she blurted.

"I heard, Opal." Mr. Nantes shot a warning glance at his son before meeting her eye. "I know you're friends with Nico, and I'm sorry he's moving, but that's life in the Park Service. Transfers are part of the job."

"But *you* requested Mr. Holland's transfer."

*Holly moly, what am I doing? Taking on Paul Bunyan himself? In his own office?*

Sylvain's cheek twitched, though the rest of his face remained impassive. He cleared his throat. "I can assure you that I don't run the Park Service. Where'd you hear a rumor like that?"

"From me." Logan's voice shook, but only a little. "You were bragging about it. I told the whole school weeks ago."

Mr. Nantes passed a hand over his face. Opal was struck by how tired he looked.

Sylvain sighed. "That was just me blowing off steam. Now look what I've done." He placed a calloused hand on his son's shoulder. "Let me be clear: I could no more get Warren Holland transferred out of town than I could stop him from prioritizing a few dozen owls over honest people's labor."

His gaze drifted to the study's bay window, which had a stunning view of the Pacific, even better than the one from Opal's house down the street. He seemed to go far away for a few heartbeats, looking out at the dark water. Something in his posture wilted, like he was barely able to muster the will to explain himself.

Opal didn't care. She felt a wave of indignation surge over her. *I'm being lied to.* "You're the most powerful person in town," she pressed, astonished by her own temerity. "The Nantes family always calls the shots in Timbers. Since the very beginning."

To her surprise, Sylvain began to laugh. Low and bitter, it rumbled through the room.

Logan stared at his father in shock.

"It's true," Opal shot back, her ears growing hot. Was he laughing at her? "You, and your dad befo—"

"Actually," Logan cut in, "why don't we talk about Grandpa for a second." His voice was rough. Logan's face paled, even as dots of red bloomed on his cheeks. He dug into his hoodie and pulled out the baseball he'd found on the houseboat. "This was his, right? The Babe Ruth ball with a scuff on it?"

When Sylvain saw the baseball, his jaw dropped open. He took a halting step toward his son. "Where did you get that?"

"I think you know." Logan thrust the ball toward his father, trying to get him to take it.

Sylvain Nantes recoiled as if snakebitten, dropping both hands to his sides. He strode quickly to the front door and opened it. "Opal, it's late. You should—"

"I'll *tell* you where I found it!" Logan insisted doggedly, stalking his father into the foyer.

Sylvain spun, eyes tight, every muscle in his body rigid.

"Whoa, whoa, whoa!" Opal hissed, waving at Logan. "Take it easy! Don't say anyth—"

"When was your last visit to Still Cove, Dad?" Logan's voice cut like a razorblade. "It took me a while to put it all together, but I finally did. Grandpa didn't stuff his baseball under the floorboards. *You* did. When was the last time you checked out the houseboat?"

"Logan!" Opal cried. *"Stop talking right now!"*

But his father only covered his eyes. His shoulders drooped, and a long sigh escaped his lips.

Sylvain Nantes slowly closed the door. And locked it.

---

Opal couldn't believe what was happening.

She was sitting across from Sylvain Nantes in his study. Logan had just told him about the houseboat. And his father clearly hadn't been surprised.

"Our family has *always* been Torchbearers?" Logan repeated, as if unable to process what he was hearing.

Staring at the ceiling, Sylvain nodded unhappily.

Logan pressed both fists to his temples, gaping at his father. "You're saying that *Grandpa* was a Torchbearer?"

Another reluctant nod.

Logan's twinkling eyes shot to Opal's. "This is so cool!" he whispered, but then his attention snapped back to his dad.

"So why aren't either of your names recorded in the Order's ledger? And why didn't you tell *me* any of this, if it's some kind of family tradition?"

"Because I am *not* a Torchbearer." The iron had returned to Sylvain's voice.

Opal felt a spasm of unease. They'd lost control of their secret. An *adult* knew, and not just anyone. Logan's father had the power to change everything if he wanted to.

Mr. Nantes sat forward in his chair, his expression stony. "I want nothing to do with it."

"But—" Logan began.

Sylvain cut his son off with a raised hand. He glanced at Opal, and this time, she realized he wasn't just exhausted. He was . . . heartbroken. Sylvain leaned heavily on the desktop, dropping his gaze to its scarred surface.

"When I was old enough, my father took me out to Still Cove. Just like your great-grandfather had done with him. He showed me the boat and Torchbearer vault, and introduced me to Mr. Hale, who at that time was still a young man. Then my father . . . led me downstairs to witness the Deepness." Sylvain shuddered once, uncontrollably. His glare rose from the desktop and pierced them both. "I learned about the Rift, the Traveler in the jar, the Torchbearer code, all of it."

"Even the Beast?" Logan asked.

Sylvain stiffened. "You kids have been busy."

"So *you* were supposed to be a Torchbearer." Opal's tone was delicate. "But you . . . you didn't do it?"

Mr. Nantes slumped back in his seat, deflated. "I knew immediately that I didn't want any part of that mess."

Part of Opal understood. "It's a lot to take in," she agreed. "Keeping watch, making sure the gateway stays closed." Her eyes popped. "Do you know how to seal the Rift for good?!"

Sylvain shook his head sharply. "No one does. That's why the tradition is passed down."

Logan gave his father a hard look. "So you just didn't want to do the work? It was too much trouble to watch out for rogue figments, and keep our town safe?"

"That's not what it was," Sylvain snapped. "Don't presume to understand my motivations."

Logan was unrelenting. "You were here on Dark Halloween! You *knew* what was happening. And said nothing!"

Sylvain tensed. His voice was barely a whisper. "I *thought* I knew."

Opal watched Sylvain's expression roil, as if he struggled with some terrible burden. Then his cheeks went slack. He sighed again, a long, hopeless exhalation, his gaze drifting to the window once more. After another endless moment, he resumed speaking. "It's the part you probably don't know yet. The . . . the worst of it. The one thing the Torchbearer Order never wrote down." He set his jaw. "When those monsters marched from the sea, I . . . I assumed the day had finally come. I don't think I ever forgave my father for telling me about it."

Goosebumps erupted up and down Opal's limbs.

Logan leaned forward, his whole body quivering. "What did he tell you, Dad? What don't we know about?"

Sylvain turned to look at them, eyes sorrowful and resigned. "That the end of the world is coming, son. It could already be on its way. And there's absolutely nothing you, I, or anyone else can do about it."

# PART TWO

# THE MESSAGE

# 9

# NICO

Nico's heartbeat pounded in his ears.

"The end of the world? Logan's dad really said that?" His shocked expression morphed into a glower. "What a bunch of garbage. Why am I not surprised the Nantes family thinks they're the center of the universe?"

Opal shook her head firmly, eyes tight as she paced the showroom. Her chin trembled. Nico realized she looked shaky, like she was trapped in a car rolling downhill with its brakes out and a cliff looming ahead.

"Nico, his dad *knew* stuff." Opal absently wiped moisture from her upper lip. "Torchbearer secrets! And some things aren't up for debate. Logan found his grandfather's baseball under a floorboard right beside the Darkdeep, and his dad *admitted* putting it there. His father also knew the combination to open the lockbox we found, too. Those aren't tricks—Sylvain Nantes has 100 percent been aboard this houseboat!"

Nico glanced at a row of glass cases gleaming in the early morning sunlight. Under Tyler's ruthless direction, layers of dust had been obliterated, but the showroom still had an abandoned vibe. An aura of age and neglect. *How long since anyone but us walked these aisles?*

He felt a rush of panic. Opal's revelations were terrible. Coming so soon on the back of his dad's transfer news, Nico wasn't sure he could handle the strain. *I'm about to lose my house, my friends, my hometown. Now even the secrets I swore to protect are exposed.*

*Oh, and maybe the world is going to end.*

"Explain it all again," he said quietly, hoping the crack in his voice had gone unnoticed.

Opal nodded. "I went to see Logan, one thing led to another, *blah blah blah*, and suddenly we're in this crazy confrontation with his father about the baseball. Sylvain said flat-out that the Nantes family has been Torchbearers since the founding of Timbers. But get this—they never logged their names on the Order's roster."

Nico shook his head in bafflement. "Why?" He jabbed a finger at the ancient, slug-stained record book they'd found inside the tunnel vault, which Tyler had placed inside its own display out of respect for its importance. "We have the entire list of Torchbearers right there. If Logan's ancestors were so important, and took the oath, why didn't they sign where it matters? The last name is Roman Hale—who we already know about. There's not a single Nantes on the ledger."

"Sylvain mentioned Hale by name," Opal countered. Was there frustration in her voice? *At who? Me?* "He said their family never went on record in case the Order was exposed. But they financed, supplied, and disguised the operation, dating back to the days of Edward Nantes and Yvette Dumont. The idea was that if anyone ever discovered the Darkdeep, *they* wouldn't be connected, and could handle the problem without suspicion."

Nico abruptly paced away, crossing his arms. Finally, he turned back. "It makes sense," he admitted grudgingly. "You'd want part of the group fire-walled in case the worst happened." Nico squeezed his forehead, then ran a hand over his face. "Still. You're telling me that a long line of Nantes jerks served as head Torchbearers, but never took credit for it? Doesn't sound like the people I know." He paused. "Maybe they just wanted a way to weasel out of trouble if things went bad."

"They kept their own records." Opal spun and dug something from her bag, a battered gray booklet about the size of an iPhone. "This was inside the lockbox, along with an album of grainy old photographs. Logan's going through those now—he thinks his dad boxed up all the family Torchbearers stuff to get rid of it—but he asked me to bring this ledger here for safekeeping. It's a private listing of every Nantes who joined the

Order. The ones picked as Torchbearers didn't even tell their spouses or kids if they weren't also chosen—no more than three people knew the secret at any given time."

Nico stared at the logbook like it was wrapped in a dirty diaper. "How'd Logan convince his dad to give up the combo? And why store their secret family history on the boat?"

"Logan asked for it point-blank, and Sylvain just told him. Right in front of me, like he was in a daze." Opal grimaced. "His dad isn't in good shape. Logan doesn't trust him to keep any of this stuff protected. He tried to bury it once already, after all."

Nico blinked. "Because of the end-of-the-world thing?"

"Sylvain *believes* it, Nico. You should have seen his face. He's convinced we're all doomed, but he wouldn't tell us why."

Nico grunted derisively. "No specifics, just 'everyone's gonna die'? I'm not buying it. Maybe Logan's dad has a screw loose." He glanced at the entry curtain. "Why isn't Logan here, anyway? We should *all* examine those pictures, if they really do involve Torchbearer stuff. I know Emma and Tyler are stuck at home, but Logan should be able to do whatever he wants right now. Since his dad knows all about us."

Nico scuffed a shoe on the carpet. He hated that their secret was out.

"He's pretty shaken up, Nico." Opal's gaze carried a touch of reproach. "Logan just learned that his family bankrolled the Torchbearer Order for centuries, and that his dad decided *not* to keep the tradition alive. Or tell *him* about it. I'm not sure which stung worse."

Nico sighed. "Why'd his dad bail on the Darkdeep? It was such a reckless thing to do."

Opal threaded her braid between her fingers. "He didn't answer straight out. Thomas Nantes, Logan's grand-dad, brought Sylvain to Still Cove when he turned thirteen. Thomas showed him everything—the island, the vault, the houseboat, even the Darkdeep itself. Sylvain was supposed to be next in line. But Thomas *also* told Sylvain something else. And it terrified him."

"What?"

Opal shook her head. "He wouldn't say. Then like twenty years passed, Sylvain got married, and Logan was born. At the time, Thomas Nantes and Roman Hale did all the Torch-bearer work, and they were still trying to involve Sylvain. He played along until his father died. But when Thomas passed away, Sylvain came here and buried the lockbox and his father's baseball under the floorboards. Rejecting that part of his family's past, I guess—the whole Torchbearer legacy. Sylvain stopped talking to Roman Hale outside of work at the mill, and hasn't been back to the houseboat since."

Nico's eyes grew hard. "And when Hale went missing?"

Opal shrugged. "I guess Sylvain assumed Hale had run off and quit, like he did."

A thought occurred to Nico. "When the Rift went beserk, and figments attacked the beach, Logan's dad must've known what was happening. But he never came to check on the Darkdeep. Or went out to the Rift, as far as we know. Not once!"

Opal gave a grim nod. "He said we wouldn't understand. I'm telling you, the man has totally given up. He assumed the end of the world was here, and just accepted it."

Nico stared at Opal, his mouth falling open. "That's . . . that's horrible!"

"Logan felt the same. He was furious. But it didn't faze Sylvain. He seems convinced that whatever the danger is, it's irreversible, and maybe already underway."

Nico chewed the inside of his cheek. "What *precisely* did he say about the end of the world?"

Opal took a deep breath. She appeared to be running the conversation back in her mind. "He said that the Rift was just the beginning, and that nothing could protect our world from what lies beyond. That the Darkdeep was only part of it. Then he turned and went upstairs." She paused, her voice turning sad. "He didn't even hug Logan. It's like his dad couldn't show any emotion at all."

*I know what that's like sometimes.* But Nico forced away the unexpected twinge of sympathy for Logan. "So that's all? Nothing else?"

Opal thought a moment. "Wait. He said time was running

out. I remember because it didn't make sense when we were talking. Sylvain blurted out that no one could contain a Rift, on either side." Her eyes widened. "He also said that *he* wasn't the only one who thought so."

Nico's ears perked. "Not the only one? What does that mean?"

Opal snorted nervously. "Who knows? Maybe Sylvain is pals with other Torchbearers."

The hairs on Nico's neck stood up. "You mean like Roman Hale?"

Opal's face had paled. "Maybe. But now that I think about it . . . that's not how it felt at the time. And I think he used the present tense."

Nico sat down hard on a bench. Pressed his fists into his eye sockets. "Oh man, I can't handle much more of this."

He felt a soft touch on his back. Nico tensed. Opal was standing beside him, one hand resting between his shoulder blades. Her fingertips radiated heat like sudden fire.

Nico didn't move. Didn't want to break the contact. A rush of emotions coursed through him.

"I'm so sorry you're moving, Nico."

Opal's voice was gentle. Fragile. Nico didn't look up.

"It's not your fault," he said, fighting to keep his voice even. "I'm just gonna miss . . . I hate that . . ."

"Same."

She lightly brushed his neck. Nico nearly shot ten feet

into the air. But he didn't pull away. They weren't looking at each other. Nico couldn't. He'd gone tomato red and was terrified Opal might see. *What in the world is happening to me?*

"Maybe you could come visit some time?" Nico said softly, uncertain what words would come out until after he spoke. "A ferry runs to Coupeville on weekends. From there I'm sure there's a bus down to Portland, or, or . . . whatever."

He heard a swift intake of breath. "Yeah. Sure, Nico. That'd be fun."

They stayed frozen like that for an endless moment. Opal's hand on the back of his head, Nico unmoving, eyes closed as if resting. He thought these might be the scariest heartbeats of his life. *Say something, doofus.*

He opened his eyes. Eased back until they could see each other. Opal was facing away, a scarlet flush infusing her cheeks. *What's bothering her?*

"Opal, I . . ."

She turned back, but they didn't meet eyes.

"Yeah?"

"I . . . I just want to say tha—"

An echoing boom thundered up through the floorboards.

Opal and Nico leaped apart as if electroshocked.

Nico's gaze whipped to the wall panel hiding the Dark-deep. "What was that?"

Opal was smoothing her jeans and hair. "Nothing good. Let's go see what gave the Darkdeep indigestion this time."

"Right." Nico stumbled after her as she arrowed for the secret staircase. "Right, yeah."

At the bottom of the steps, they found the well slowly bubbling. A weird odor permeated the room, like sour milk. Or a dog that ate cheese that didn't sit well. Opal moved straight to the edge and peered down. "Nico, look!"

She pointed into the Darkdeep.

An object was bobbing in the inky liquid.

Nico knelt and fished it out, being careful not to touch the water. He stepped back, holding a canvas-wrapped parcel no larger than his palm. Nico powered his phone light and examined the mysterious item.

"Another message?" Opal whispered.

Nico swallowed. "Only one way to find out."

He unwound a small metal tie, loosening the cloth. Something dropped into his other palm.

Nico held it up. A beat passed, then he grunted.

"Huh?"

He was holding a small, roughly carved figurine. The material felt like wood, but not a kind Nico had ever seen before. The grain was fine, the figure shaped in strong, simple cuts with an angular lower half that appeared to be a dress. The top was a woman's face wearing a tiny crown on its head.

Beside him, Opal snapped her fingers. "The queen!"

He squinted. "What? Like, a doll?"

"No, no!" Her eyes shone with excitement. "A game piece. This looks a bit like one of the queens from our chess set. The one Thing gave us to get back through the Rift! Remember?"

Nico saw it now. "You're right!"

Opal chewed her lip thoughtfully. "But our set isn't missing either queen. And *those* pieces are made of stone."

"True." Nico's brow furrowed. His gaze dropped to the now-silent Darkdeep. The surface had smoothed, revealing no further clues.

"Why would this show up now?" Opal whispered, almost to herself. "Who sent it?"

Nico felt a lump build in his throat. He choked it back as adrenaline filled his veins.

"I don't know. But we'd better find out. Fast."

# 10

## OPAL

Is it weird having a museum named after you?"

Opal eyed the old-fashioned lettering above the entrance to the Nantes Timber Exhibition Hall.

Logan snorted, pushing through a pair of heavy glass doors. "It's easy if you own the place." He still seemed annoyed she'd dragged him from his house despite everything that had happened. Logan's father had practically gone into hiding, locking himself in his study early that morning and ignoring anyone who knocked.

An elderly woman in a green smock slipped from her stool and beelined for them, clearly delighted to have visitors. The word *VOLUNTEER* was stitched in gold over her right pocket. Her eyes gleamed with the passion of someone who knew a lot of obscure trivia, and couldn't wait to share it.

Opal recognized her—Mrs. Cartwright, who'd owned the grocery store until her daughter took over a few years ago. "Your family does Timbers a great service here," she intoned reproachfully, having heard Logan's snide remark. "Think of everything the town would lose if this collection wasn't preserved."

"Right," Logan said. "We need old saws."

Mrs. Cartwright squinted at Logan, as if unsure whether she was being mocked. "Shall I give you a tour?" she asked hopefully.

Opal felt a stab of angst. It'd be impossible to snoop for Torchbearer stuff with a pushy guide around.

"We're fine on our own," Logan said, and the woman's face fell. "I actually, um, know a lot about this building already."

"Of course you do," Mrs. Cartwright said, making a valiant effort to hide her disappointment. "Thomas Nantes would undoubtably have made certain his grandchildren were well versed in their family history."

"Not all of it, apparently," Logan muttered. Mrs. Cartwright blinked at him.

Opal smiled gamely at their underutilized host. "If I have any questions, we'll definitely come find you."

Mrs. Cartwright's gaze turned a few degrees cooler. "It goes without saying that you will respect the sanctity of this landmark, young lady." She broadened her frosty regard to include Logan as well. "Both of you. This is not a place for silly dates."

Opal felt her cheeks burn. A *date*? Was this woman serious?

"Not a problem," Logan mumbled, suddenly eyeing his shoes. "Come on, Opal." He darted deeper into the building, forcing Opal to scurry after him. Mrs. Cartwright climbed back onto her stool, folding her hands in her lap.

They entered the main chamber of the old mill itself, and Opal's breath caught. She hadn't visited this place in years, not since the fourth-grade field trip. She'd forgotten how high the ceiling was, and the way the old stone walls and wooden rafters made the building feel almost like a cathedral. The heart-pine floor was polished to a glossy sheen, though scars and divots from its years as an active lumber factory were still visible.

Logan barely seemed to notice. He was staring up at a black-and-white family photo that had been blown up into a wall mural. "It's pretty ironic. Whole galleries dedicated to the glorious Nantes clan, but my dad couldn't care less about our *real* history."

Opal nodded at a display memorializing the illegal crackdown of a workers' strike in 1935. "Don't be so harsh. If your father didn't care about the past, he wouldn't have this exhibit here, for example. That history isn't flattering for the company, but he didn't brush it under the carpet. He made sure future generations knew that what happened back then was wrong."

"My *grandfather* assembled most of this stuff. Dad hardly

ever visits. He just pays the bills." Logan crossed his arms. "What exactly do you expect to find here? I'll bet my dad scrubbed the building of anything Torchbearer related."

"We need to explore every possible avenue," Opal said stubbornly, knowing that she sounded like a Scooby-Doo kid. "Your dad rejected the Order before learning all of its secrets. Maybe he missed something important, or didn't know what to look for."

"And we do?"

Opal ignored the jab, wandering into the hall. She began examining displays for any trace of a Torchbearer symbol, or maybe a name they recognized. Opal thought back to the field trip here as kids. Logan was a grade ahead of her, so he hadn't been there. Where had Nico been that day?

She and Nico had stopped being friends before fourth grade, but Opal realized she'd usually stayed aware of him, either at school or around town. Not constantly or anything, just in sort of a *oh, there he is* kind of way. A holdover from the days when they'd been inseparable.

Opal definitely noticed when he wasn't around now. She . . . missed him. Sometimes more than made sense. What was *that* about?

"Look at this garbage." Logan was glaring into a display case packed with eighteenth-century lumberjack mementos. "There's nothing important here, just a bunch of old junk people used to carry around." He pointed to a timeline on the wall that circled the whole room. "All those dates, and none of them matter. Zero to do with the Rift, or the Dark-deep, or *any* of it."

Opal knew it wasn't the museum that was driving Logan nuts. It was his father's rejection of their family history. "Your dad did what he thought was best."

Logan spun, eyes angry. "He cut me out of my legacy!" He flung a hand at a row of exhibits lining the center aisle. "Table-saws. Joists. How to fell an oak. Who cares about that stuff? I never learned anything that *mattered*." Logan sniffed suddenly, color rising in his cheeks. "And it's not just my father. I thought I knew Grandpa. He used to take me fun places all the time. Why didn't *he* tell me our secret? Or show me the houseboat?"

"We were still little kids when he passed," Opal said quietly. "He couldn't put that on you. Plus, Roman Hale was alive back then. Your grandfather probably thought there'd be time to tell you everything later. Or maybe he was hoping your dad would come around."

"That's a lot of maybes." Logan scuffed his shoe against the hardwood, making a basketball-court squeak. "My dad's never been a wimp," he grumbled sullenly. "What could scare him so badly that he didn't even try? And now look at him. He's a basket case."

Opal tilted her head. "He was fine until recently though, right? I wonder what changed."

Logan gritted his teeth. "Dark Halloween. He's been on eggshells ever since that night. I figured it was just monster hysteria like everyone else. But now . . ."

Logan pushed away from the display case, taking a deep breath. Opal gave him some space. Her eye caught on a battered metal lunch box inside the enclosure. It was nearly identical to the one she'd found on the houseboat, right before the Rift crisis. *The one Thing led me to.*

Logan was still fuming. He reached into his jacket pocket, removing the small album of old photographs from inside the lockbox. Logan absently flipped to one of the photos, staring down at his grandfather's smiling face. His other hand fiddled with the Torch necklace he wore every day. "Grandpa is the one who told my dad the end of the world was coming. I finally got it out of him last night. Worse, Grandpa said it would happen *during my father's lifetime*. That's what my dad didn't tell us yesterday—the thing that scared him so badly. He . . . he never got over it."

Opal felt a pit open in her stomach. "*Wow.* He said that to his own son?"

Logan nodded curtly, frowning down at the picture in his hands. It was a nature scene—Thomas Nantes was standing between two towering trees with crisscrossing branches, smiling as he held something round and metal in his fingers. Behind him, a giant spout of frothing water was bursting up into the air.

"Did he say, like . . . when?" Opal found that her arms were trembling.

Logan shook his head. "My dad said the Torchbearers never had a *date* or anything. At first he doubted any of it was real, but then something happened that changed his mind. He still won't say what *that* was."

"The Rift exploded halfway to Jupiter three weeks ago," Opal quipped, attempting a joke. "That might've done it."

"There's more, I'm sure of it." Logan slapped the album down on top of the display case. "But he won't explain! I think something in the news also spooked him. He canceled our newspaper subscription, and some websites are blocked on our computer—Lily found out when she was trying to do homework last night." Logan growled in frustration. "But he won't say, or even come out of his study. He's like an ostrich with his head in the sand!"

A chime sounded. Someone else had entered the exhibit hall. Opal heard Mrs. Cartwright's delighted greeting. This was probably the busiest she'd been in years.

"Oh great," Logan mumbled. "More of the Timbers Historical Society."

Opal glanced back at the battered lunch box inside the glass. An etching caught her eye. She knelt and stuck her nose close. Scratched into its side was the name TOM NANTES. The lid was flipped open, with a folded-up red handkerchief nestled inside. Scattered on the fabric were a handful of old coins.

She moved closer. The coins were the souvenir kind, like you got at tacky stores or in theme-park booths. One was slightly larger than the others. Opal squinted, trying to make out a semicircle of letters running in an arc across its face.

YELLOWSTONE NATIONAL PARK.

The park name was stamped above an etching of a geyser. "PUMP GEYSER" was printed at the bottom. Two giant trees loomed at both edges of the coin, flanking the central image.

Opal stooped closer to examine the engraving. Something about the coin was gnawing at her mind. The geyser's eruption was hauntingly familiar. Like what the Rift had done right before it blew apart. *What the Darkdeep keeps threatening to do.*

Footsteps sounded. A familiar voice echoed across the room. "Hey guys."

Opal straightened. Nico was standing with Mrs. Cartwright a few steps behind Logan. "One of your friends is here?" she announced uncertainly. The look on Nico's face was considerably less than friendly.

"What are you two doing?" he asked, fixing Opal with an unreadable gaze.

"Learning," Opal replied. Then she winced inwardly at how cheesy that sounded. "I think I found something," she added under her breath, trying to attract Nico's attention without tipping off the overeager curator.

"Docs anyone need anything explained?" Mrs. Cartwright asked loudly.

"No, ma'am." Three voices at once. The elderly woman huffed once and retreated to the lobby.

Nico waited until her clomping heels had receded, then tapped an impatient finger on the display case. "You mean that lunch box?" he snapped, sounding skeptical as he swept up one of Logan's pictures and looked it over. "They don't seem unique. Every logger in Timbers probably had one."

Logan stood a little apart from them, saying nothing. He was staring at Nico, who began paging through the other Nantes family photographs while pretending Logan didn't exist.

"I *understand* that, Nico," Opal replied, trying to keep her voice calm. Tension crackled like lightning between the two boys. And, weirdly, between Nico and herself. *Is he mad at me? Why?* Shaking her head, Opal soldiered on to make her point. "But check out the coins inside."

Logan moved to stand on Opal's opposite side, putting her between him and Nico. He peered through the glass, but a moment later he grunted dismissively. "Worthless tourist stuff. I never understood why Grandpa thought these coins were worth displaying." He paused, scratching his chin. "It's probably sentimental. Yellowstone was his favorite place in the world. He went there all the time, even called it his second home."

Logan began to step away, but froze instead, eyes narrowing. "No. *No.*" He put a finger to his lips. "Actually, he called Yellowstone his second *office*. Grandpa said it was a place to be protected at all costs. I always thought he just meant, like, because it was a famous national park, but . . ."

Opal's gaze shot to Nico. "That Yellowstone article you showed us earlier. What was it about again?"

Nico bit off clipped words. "Geysers. They've gone haywire, or something. I'd have to pull it back up."

Something clicked in Opal's head. She snatched the album from Nico, turning to the picture Logan had been staring at earlier. Suddenly it was clear. Thomas Nantes was standing near Pump Geyser, basically recreating the image stamped onto the coin.

Feeling a wave of adrenaline, she slipped the photograph from the album and waved it in the air. "You mean *this* geyser?"

Logan frowned. "Okay. So what? My grandfather wanted to capture the same shot from the coin he bought. Not sure why it matters."

"No, Logan! Look. You too, Nico." She held the photo up so both boys could see it clearly. "He's actually on the opposite side. Those big trees are *behind* him, see? He's in the woods somewhere."

Nico made an annoyed sound. "The man really liked Yellowstone. Logan already said that."

Opal didn't answer him. She was staring in astonishment at the back of the photo, which was mere inches from her nose. "Guys," she whispered. "There's *writing* on here!"

Opal heard two pairs of sneaker squeaks as the boys wedged close.

"Whoa," Logan breathed. "How did I miss that?!"

"It's very faint," Opal whispered back. "In pencil. I barely noticed it."

"What's it say?" Nico urged from over her other shoulder. Three sets of eyes strained to make out the words. Opal tilted the photo, catching the light well enough to read the words.

T. Nantes outside the Y.R. All is well underground.
R.H. - June 1977

Opal nearly squealed. "Roman Hale must've taken this picture! He and your grandfather were on a trip there together. Which could mean Torchbearer business!"

"The Y.R.?" Logan muttered in a puzzled voice. "What could that be?"

"And what's underground?" Nico mused. "Sounds like they were checking on something." Then he realized how close he and Logan were standing and stepped back quickly, glaring at the older boy. For his part, Logan was carefully removing other lockbox pictures, searching for any other inscriptions.

Opal licked her lips, a terrible suspicion brewing in her mind. She reached out and gripped Logan's arm. "*Y.* probably stands for Yellowstone. That just leaves the *R.*"

Logan glanced at her with widening eyes. "Wait. You don't think—"

"What I *think*," Nico interrupted, "is that I'll let you two have your playtime together. Sorry to intrude."

Opal blinked in surprise, then felt her temper slip a notch. "Nico, what the heck? We're trying to solve this!"

"Well, keep trying without me." Nico turned and stormed toward the exit, calling back acidly over his shoulder. "I don't want to *interrupt*."

Opal heard the door slam shut behind him.

# 11

## NICO

Emma was waiting on Nico's front steps.

He spotted her before she noticed him, wrapped up tight in a pink scarf, hat, and gloves. Emma's tongue was wedged between her teeth as she tapped on her phone. A light snowfall was blanketing the ground with fat white flakes that covered the sidewalk.

Nico reached the third riser before she even looked up.

"Oh, hey!" Emma shoved her phone into the pocket of her parka.

"Please tell me you weren't posting another video," Nico grumbled. A terrible mood had dogged him all the way back from the museum. He was still red-hot at seeing Opal and Logan alone together, conspiring without him. Nico actually remembered more about the Yellowstone news stories than he'd said, but he'd wanted out of there immediately.

*I never know what's going on. Never feel the slightest bit of control.*

Emma stuck her tongue out at him. "I was just editing a picture I took of the mountains. I can't believe how fast this storm came on. Looks like we're in for a white Thanksgiving tomorrow."

Nico slumped down beside her and blew into his hands. "It's freaking cold, too. I hate when the weather gets all weird."

"What have you been up to? Opal texted me and Tyler last night, about the big news that the world is doomed. I've been trying to reach you, but your phone is off." She sat back with a look of disbelief. "I cannot *believe* the Torchbearer Order was originally a Nantes family production."

"Don't call it that," Nico snapped, but he softened his tone at the frown on Emma's face. "I'm still getting used to the idea myself. And sorry about my phone." He hadn't felt like talking or texting with anyone, and had shut it off to wallow in the unfairness of the universe. "But get what else we just learned."

Nico hesitated. Why did he say *we*? Opal and Logan had found the clues. *If they* are *clues.*

Emma made a *do-go-on* gesture with one hand.

He sighed. "I just came from the Nantes Timber Exhibition Hall."

Emma snorted. "Exploring the axe-throwing history of our fair town?"

118

"Ha ha." Nico kicked a stray pebble off the porch with his sneaker. "Opal had mentioned wanting to snoop around in there, so I went by her house earlier to see if she was up for it. Her mom said she'd already gone, and that she'd stopped by Logan's on the way. They went together without telling anyone."

Emma put a hand on his shoulder. "It makes sense, Nico. He'd know the most about the museum, right?"

"I guess." Nico scowled. "Whatever. The point is, there's another lunch box in there like the one from the houseboat, only this one's inside a glass case as part of an official display. It's filled with cheap souvenir coins from Yellowstone National Park, and one in particular shows something called Pump Geyser. Then Logan remembered his grandad was way into Yellowstone, and he has this tiny album of photos from the lockbox. One of the pictures showed Tom Nantes at the exact same place as what's stamped on the coin, and the shot was taken by Roman Hale. The inscription says they were checking on something called the Y.R. that's underground."

Emma's foot began tapping excitedly. "Tyler told me about the geysers going crazy! With sulfur, maybe. Do you think there's a connection? And what the heck does Y.R. mean?"

"The inscription didn't say." Nico gave an exaggerated shrug. "But maybe there are more Torchbearer secrets hidden there."

Emma's eyes got big. "Whoa."

Nico stood abruptly and hunched his shoulders. "Not that we'll ever know. This is what I hate most—having all these stupid pieces, but no way to put them together. It's maddening."

"Why can't we know?" Emma asked, her tone one of honest curiosity.

Nico snorted. "Emma, Yellowstone National Park is like two thousand miles away. You wanna hike it later tonight?"

Emma popped up beside him, a devilish gleam in her eyes. "No. We should take a plane."

---

Nico's father was sitting in their kitchen, reading about the mating habits of whales. *Classic.*

Nico strolled into the room, trying for casual and failing horribly at it. "Hey Dad? Remember how, when you first took this job, you said we could visit other national parks?"

Warren Holland looked up with a frown. "Yeah. You and your brother showed zero interest."

"What if I *was* interested. Say, like . . . now."

Warren Holland put his book aside and crossed his arms. "Out with it."

On cue, Emma bounced into the room, beaming a megawatt smile. "Hi, Mr. Holland! Is it true? Can you really get us there for free?"

Warren's gaze flicked between the two of them. "Hello, Emma. Good to see you. Can I get you where?"

Emma's eyes widened in excitement. "To Yellowstone! Nico said that with your job, you can book free seats on a government shuttle the Park Service runs, and we could hitch a ride for Thanksgiving. My parents already said yes! I can't *imagine* how cool it'll be to see Old Faithful. I bet we can even find a restaurant that serves turkey!"

"Yellowstone?" His eyebrows arched in surprise. "I mean, yes, it's possible. There just so happens to be a flight from Skagit Regional to Jackson Hole every Wednesday." Nico's father drilled him with a baleful stare. "I see you've been looking through my private work papers, son."

Nico tried to keep his face straight. "So we can go?"

"Just hold on." Warren's mouth curled like he smelled something foul. "Why do you want to go to Yellowstone all of a sudden? We don't have a place to stay, and Thanksgiving is tomorrow."

"Rob already said he's not coming home from Gonzaga," Nico countered, using his older brother's absence as a convenient wedge. "If he's skipping the whole break to stay at college, why shouldn't we take a vacation? What did you plan to cook, anyway?"

Warren's expression became defensive. "I thought we'd go to Timbers Cafe, like always."

Nico gave his dad a look. "They have cafes in Wyoming,

too. And you said before we could stay at an empty ranger cabin if one wasn't being manned. I bet some are open over the holiday."

Warren swiveled to look at Emma, who maintained her overwide smile. She hadn't actually asked for permission yet, but Emma swore she could convince her parents to let her go if the trip was already in place. If not, Nico would just go by himself.

He really, really hoped Emma could join him. Two days in a cabin with his surprised, surly dad was not what Nico was aiming for.

Warren gave Emma a penetrating glare. "Emma, are you *sure* you want to miss having dinner with your family?"

Emma nodded so hard her head threatened to wobble off. "I don't like stuffing, and they all just sit around watching football anyway. When they're not gobbling up chili or asleep on the couch. I want to see geysers!"

Warren still had his arms crossed. He went silent, seemed to be going over the idea in his mind.

"It'd be nice to have one last trip with Nico before you guys move," Emma said quietly. Was that a real quaver in her voice?

Something loosened in Warren Holland's countenance. He glanced at his son with tired eyes.

"Let me make some calls."

---

"Pumped!" Emma crowed, snapping her seat belt into place. "I am pumpity-*pumped*, pumped *up*. Let's do this!"

"Take it easy!" Nico chuckled, as he strapped himself in beside her. Then he shook his head in honest wonderment, leaning his head against the airplane window. "I can't believe this is happening. How'd you make it work?"

Emma cracked her knuckles in front of her. "Confidence, my friend. See the goal, be the goal, *achieve* the goal." She made a 'shoots, scores' motion with her hands, holding the follow-through for him to see.

Nico covered his eyes and mock-groaned. "Lame. So, so lame." Then he dropped his hands. "But I can't argue with results. We just conjured a visit to Yellowstone out of thin air. Merry Thanksgiving, every one."

Emma's grin soured briefly. "I wish Tyler and Opal could've come."

Nico got busy fiddling with his air vent. "They wanted to. But not many parents are up for something like this—last-minute air travel, on a freaking holiday. I still don't know how *you* pulled it off."

"I worked my parents' soft spots." Emma giggled wickedly. "I own those suckers."

"Tyler said they'd keep digging while we're gone. He's got a new Beastmaster theory he wants to try out, and Opal is obsessed with learning more about Yvette Dumont." Nico sat back in his seat. "Honestly, I'm not sure how all the Nantes and Dumont history is supposed to help us control the Rift, but . . ."

"Knowledge is power," Emma countered, shoving her overstuffed backpack under the seat, then kicking it deeper for good measure. "And be fair—the clue Opal found on that photo is all we really have to go on. We stand on the shoulders of greatness."

Nico snorted. "You're like an inspirational quote generator right now."

Emma grinned ear to ear. "Why, Nico, that's the nicest thing you've ever said to me. Make sure your reach always exceeds your grasp. No fear. Carpe *all* the diem."

Nico laughed out loud, drawing a few glances from the assorted government personnel also taking the mostly empty flight. They'd gone to a special gate at the airport and boarded directly on the tarmac. His father was sitting a few rows back from them, with the other adults. The entire group was listening to Warren as he explained something about seagull migration patterns. It occurred to Nico that, if their rapt attention was any indication, his father was kind of a big deal. *Who knew?*

A voice rattled over the PA system. "All passengers, please take your seats and stow your carry-on luggage."

There was a slight commotion at the front of the plane—someone hustling up the mobile stairs at the last instant. A flight attendant with pursed lips shepherded the latecomer down the aisle. "Take anything open, hon, and buckle up."

As the flyer shuffled into view, Nico felt his jaw drop open. He could not believe who he was staring at.

"Logan?!" Emma screeched in delight. "What are you doing here?"

Dragging a huge duffel bag, Logan was nearly out of breath. He plopped into the aisle seat next to Emma. "*Oof.* Barely made it. I've wanted to visit Yellowstone my whole life."

"But . . . but . . ." Nico's mouth worked like a fish. "How did you know?!"

"Opal told me," Logan answered with a wheeze. "She and Tyler don't know I decided to tag along, but this could be important. I can't get that photo inscription out of my head. And there was no time to get in touch with you guys. So, here I am!" He took a deep breath. "That was close."

Nico watched in horror as the flight attendant sealed the outer door and pronounced the plane ready for takeoff.

"Just *hold on.*" Nico made a chopping motion with both hands. "This isn't even a commercial flight!"

"Not true," Logan replied. "I spoke to a nice woman named Gail about it on the phone. The airline holds a block of seats open for your dad's department, but anyone can buy the leftovers, if you know the right people. As it happens, I do," he said smugly.

"So your mom took care of it," Emma snarked.

Logan's good humor was unshakable. "Like I said—the right people."

Nico sat back and jerked his jacket smooth. "Well, don't think you're staying with us. You might've wormed onto this flight, but you're not weaseling into our cabin. Enjoy sleeping in the snow drifts."

Logan grunted. Then he unbuckled and stood up, peering toward the back of the plane.

Nico stiffened. "Hey, what are y—"

"Mr. Holland?" Logan called out.

Warren stopped speaking and looked down the aisle in surprise. "Logan?"

"Yessir. My parents said I could come along. Okay if I stay with you guys, too?"

"Um, sure, son. No problem. It's a decent-sized cabin." Warren fired a glare over the empty rows at Nico, who had twisted around in horror. "A little warning would've been nice, but it's no big deal. Happy to have you along."

Nico slumped back down in his seat. His father was being nicer than his usual gruff self, probably to assure Logan that he didn't harbor any ill feelings toward him. *But now he's annoyed with* me. *I swear, this Nantes kid!*

"Well," Emma said slowly. "Looks like we're all here."

"Ready for a grand adventure!" Logan boomed, his voice cheery as he resnapped his seat belt. "I wonder if they'll have an in-flight movie?"

Nico's head dropped into his hands.

# 12

## OPAL

**Come to the marina ASAP!**

Opal felt the urgency of Tyler's text as she watched a group of dockworkers drag a battered shipwreck from the sea. Terrence Watson—Tyler's father and the official harbormaster of Timbers—was shouting instructions at the half-drenched men as they used heavy ropes to haul the broken vessel up a boat ramp. A small crowd had gathered, zipped up in heavy coats as they observed the salvage effort.

Opal slipped past them and headed over to the foot of the long pedestrian pier, which was empty. No surprise, since a frigid gale was cutting across the waterfront like a butcher knife as sleet fell in fitful bursts.

**Where are u,** she was about to text back, but a second later Tyler appeared, leaning into the wind with his hood up and parka zipped to the chin. "Happy Turkey Day. Crazy weather, right?" He waved at the snow and ice swirling down around them. They rarely had blizzards in Timbers during November.

"At least it's not glowing orange or something," Opal joked. "What's going on?" She pointed to the drowned boat, which was now listing sideways on the pavement of the marina parking lot. The boards beneath Opal's feet were slick with ice, and she kept one hand on the railing. "Is that what your text was about?"

At that moment Tyler's dad called out something to his crew. The workers began to disperse, some murmuring ominously to each another as they cast unhappy looks at what they'd reclaimed from the ocean.

Tyler's lips pursed inside his parka cocoon. "That's Mr. Reamer's fishing trawler. And he's got quite a story to tell."

Opal glanced back at the wreck. "What happened to it?"

"You'll see, come on." Tyler began angling over toward the damaged boat, being careful where he placed his slippery feet.

Nonplussed, Opal hurried to follow.

"My dad got the call this morning," Tyler said when she drew even with him again. "Reamer was hysterical, howling about how his boat was sinking. Everyone knows he sleeps out there half the time, anchored in the harbor, so my dad high-tailed it down with his crew and they managed to get lines on it before the ship went completely under." Tyler shivered, glancing up at the slate-gray clouds dumping snow onto the boardwalk. "Reamer is a lucky man. It's not a good day for a swim. You think Nico's flight took off okay?"

"I hope so," Opal said. "The weather might be better inland."

They neared the wreck, which had been partially covered by a ragged blue tarp. Tyler's dad waved. He was the only one left in the lot—everyone else was trudging uphill, the back-breaking work done, no doubt heading straight for their mashed potatoes and gravy.

Opal spotted a jagged hole in the bottom of the vessel. She stopped. "Wait. Tyler, you don't think this was a Beast attack, do you?"

"I don't know, but we'd better check it out." Tyler cinched his hood tighter, so that only his eyes and nose could be seen. His voice became muffled. "Let's hope Thing just came back for a visit, and he and Reamer got into a fight."

"Not a chance," Opal replied instantly. "Thing's too busy sending impossible messages." She put a hand into her pocket, running her fingers over the rough-carved edges of the queen from the Darkdeep. She'd taken to carrying it around everywhere, though she couldn't say why. Then Opal realized Tyler was eyeing her strangely.

"Um, *yeah*, Opal. I was kidding. I doubt Thing would sink boats in the harbor."

Opal forced a smile. "I was joking, too."

Tyler gave her an odd look, then shrugged. "Anyway, I want a closer look at the damage. Just in case we *do* have a Beast situation on our hands."

Opal stiffened. "I think your dad's coming over here."

"Don't worry, I got this." Tyler cocked his head and called out. "Hey Dad! What a mess. Can we have a look?"

Terrence Watson nodded, wiping sweat from his forehead. "But don't touch. The insurance people won't like it." He nodded to the waterlogged boat. "I think old *Lemon Capers* is finally done in. Alec Reamer is up in my office right now, talking to the money men. I hope he's telling them a different story than he told me, or they might decide he's crazy and not pay out his claim."

Opal felt a chill run through her. "What's he saying, Mr. Watson?"

Terrence shook his head. "I can hardly stand to repeat it. Alec says he woke up to find a *bobcat* prowling his foredeck. Scared him half to death. When we fished him out of the drink, he was babbling on about glowing yellow eyes. Said the cat went over the side when he yelled at it, then a dark shadow slammed into *Lemon Capers* and she started to list. I'd chalk the whole thing up to bad tacos and a weird dream, but *something* broke that hull."

Opal's breath caught. *Yellow eyes.* She thought of the wolf attack at school, but no one would confuse that shaggy mongrel with a bobcat, not even a groggy Alec Reamer. *And neither animal looks remotely like the Beast*, she realized. Still, something about the story worried her in a way she couldn't quite name.

Tyler was squinting at his father. "So Mr. Reamer thinks . . . a large . . . *cat* . . . sank his fishing boat? Fifty yards out in the harbor?"

Terrence couldn't help but chuckle. "I told you. He'd have better luck blaming it on the Beast. Or the Loch Ness Monster. My guess is, Alec set his anchor wrong or its line snapped, and he drifted onto the breakwater in this heavy breeze. Wouldn't be the first time, but it'll probably be the last."

Mention of the Beast seemed to stir Tyler into action. "I've *got* to see this. We'll be quick, I promise."

"Hurry up, then. Sneak a peek. I feel terrible for old Alec, but you and I got cranberry sauce waiting for us at home. I'll see if the folks inside need anything else from me. Meet me by the car in ten."

"Thanks, Dad. We won't touch anything, promise."

Tyler waited until his father had entered the harbor office. Then he hurried over to the vessel, lifting a corner of the tarp. Opal eyed a gaping hole in the side of the ship. She was about to suggest they take pictures for their records, just in case, when Tyler ducked through the hull.

"Tyler!"

Opal went in after him. The fracture punched straight

through to the hold, and she discovered they could stand upright. Light seeped in weakly around the edges of the plastic covering. "You promised not to touch anything?"

"I'm not," Tyler said primly, putting his hands in his pockets. "But I never said I wouldn't go inside."

Opal was about to argue the honesty of that interpretation when a blast of wind rattled the boat. A spicy, peppery scent filled her nose, causing it to crinkle. Then her eyes popped. "Tyler, do you smell that?"

Tyler nodded slowly. "Just like at school. In the hallway when the wolf attacked. Weird."

"More than weird," Opal said quietly. "Suspicious. The same smell at two different animal confrontations?"

Tyler snorted. "What, you think the wolf and bobcat are working together? Is this the Cartoon Network?"

Opal gave him a flat look. "I'm just saying, it's strange. Maybe something in the woods is causing wildlife to act aggressively. Like an invasive plant, or bad water. Or maybe . . . maybe . . ." Opal ran out of words. She gave up. "Okay, I don't know. But don't forget Reamer mentioned glowing yellow eyes."

Tyler rubbed his neck nervously. "I was *trying* to forget that part."

Opal was about to say more when Tyler swung his backpack around and unzipped the main pocket. "While we have a second, look at this. I was going to show it to Logan first—you'll get why in a minute—but he texted back that he's on his way out of town."

"What?" Opal said, startled. "To where?"

Tyler grinned. "He said Yellowstone. Bought a seat right next to Nico and Emma."

"Oh *no*."

"Oh yes."

Opal imagined Nico's face as Logan strode onto that flight. She shook her head. "Emma should be able to keep the peace, I guess. She's good at that. But I can't believe Logan's dad let him go." Opal dropped her voice. "You know, given . . . everything he said."

Tyler spread his hands. "Maybe Mr. Nantes figures nothing matters anymore. Or maybe Logan pitched a sad story. Like, *let me see the world before it ends!*" He batted his eyelashes.

"Be serious." Opal reached for the zip-locked bag Tyler was holding out. Inside was a sheet of ancient paper, its corners practically crumbling. "What's this?"

"Something I found wedged inside my Beast book," Tyler said. "This document was jammed up into the spine near the back."

Opal removed her phone and played its light over the weathered paper. "I wonder wh—"

Then she saw it. Halfway down, written in a firm, elegant script: *Yvette Dumont, governess.*

"It's a ship's manifest." Tyler was on his tiptoes, peering over her shoulder. "Basically, just a passenger list. My dad dreams about finding a sunken treasure someday, so he likes to collect original records about shipwrecks. Logbooks. Insurance claims. Newspaper clippings, whatever. We're both pretty into it. So I've seen one of these before."

"Plus, it says *MANIFEST* right across the top."

Tyler grinned. "Note the year of the voyage. 1741. And I like the name. The *Dauphin*."

Opal pointed to where the page ended in a jagged tear. "Some names are missing."

"Like every stupid thing we ever find. Incomplete. But it's another set of facts for the fire."

Opal began reading the list. "It looks like these passengers signed the manifest themselves."

"History-book people had great handwriting," Tyler said. "And better names. Lieutenant Commodore Caraway? That's *fire*."

"Tyler." Opal glanced up, eyes bright. "This is *great* work! We have the roster of Yvette's ship. The one that sunk back when it all started."

"It's definitely not nothing. Also, check out that stamp on the back. Guess who preserved this document for the Timbers archive? He must've found it washed up on shore or something."

Opal flipped the page over. "Edward Nantes. Of course. Man, that guy was *everywhere*."

Tyler chuckled. "That's why he's got a statue in town square, I guess. And why I was looking for Logan first. But you can keep that with your Dumont files if you want. I don't have any use for non-Beast-related relics."

"Thanks." Opal carefully placed the document in her backpack. Outside, the wind moaned, and *Lemon Capers* tilted slightly.

"Time to go," Opal squeaked.

"Right behind you."

They slithered back out through the hole and replaced the flap. Opal glanced around quickly, but the marina was empty. She was about to head across the parking lot when Tyler snapped his fingers.

"One more thing!" He reached back into his bag and removed a rectangle of dyed canvas—aquamarine in color, with some kind of blackish blob in the middle. "Remember all those flags in the Torchbearer vault? Well, I found *this* bad boy in the Torchbearer office. In the bottom of that bureau."

Opal bit her bottom lip. "Um. Cool?"

"Hold up. I've got it upside down. Now do you see it?"

For a second, Opal felt like she was failing a Rorschach test. But then . . . "Oh."

The central blob now looked an awful lot like the Beast, only sitting back on its hind paws. Opal realized the background color of the flag matched the glowing algae Tyler had used once to communicate with it.

Tyler's voice grew excited as he eyed the fabric. "Maybe

Torchbearers used *this* to signal the Beast. I mean, they couldn't always have had fresh algae lying around. You think they might've run it up on the houseboat? Or flew it on the platform over the Rift?"

Opal frowned. "Do you think it was to summon the Beast, or keep it away?"

Tyler blinked.

"I'm sure you'll figure it out, Beastmaster." Opal giggled. "Come on, we should be waiting at the car when your dad comes out. I'm *definitely* hitching a ride home."

As she turned, something flitted at the edge of her vision.

Opal glanced back at the wreck.

Under the tarp, two golden orbs glowed.

Opal gasped.

The circles vanished.

Something rattled inside the wreck, then a splash sounded.

Opal was left gaping at the rippling seawater, trying not to panic.

# 13

# NICO

"Okay Dad, we're going!"

Nico had one hand on the doorknob. Emma slipped into her backpack straps, trying to act like this getaway attempt was totally normal. Logan was already outside, having stayed out of Nico's way as much as possible in the tight quarters of the ranger cabin. They'd barely exchanged five words all last night. Emma had been left to fill in the conversation gap. Even her relentless cheeriness had faltered by the end of the evening.

*Now we have to bail.* They didn't want Warren Holland tagging along.

Nico's father looked up from his breakfast of steak and eggs. The three young Torchbearers had quietly bulldozed through bowls of cereal, anxious to get down to business. *What* business, exactly, Nico didn't really know, but their return flight was first thing the following morning, so they didn't have time to waste.

"Wait," Warren said gruffly, wiping his mouth. "Nico, it's only seven o'clock. Where do you think you're headed?"

"Old Faithful!" Emma said cheerily. "I want to see it go off, and the next eruption is in thirty minutes or so."

Nico's dad had managed to secure a two-room cottage on the north bank of the Firehole River. The sturdy log cabin was tucked into a glade of lofty mountain hemlocks, only a ten-minute walk to Upper Geyser Basin and Old Faithful itself.

Warren scratched his beard. "Well . . . I was planning to stop by the field office and visit the education center. While I'm here I can compare Wyoming climate stats to what we have in the Washington database. Plus, they've been logging owl territorial patterns for years, and that kind of data could be relevant to—"

"Great," Nico blurted. "We can do our thing while you do yours, then meet up for lunch." He held his breath, hoping the lucky break held. His father would never be described as an overly protective parent—Nico had prepared more meals for himself than he could count—but Nico hadn't been sure they could get away clean. He and Emma wanted to poke around for more than just peculiar eruptions.

*And Logan. Don't forget that jerk is here for the entire trip.*

Nico was still furious about it.

Warren sat quietly for a moment, frowning. Then he nodded slowly. "Follow the dirt trail out back until it links up with the geyser basin walkway. That leads all the way down to Old Faithful. There might be a crowd by the main attractions, even during the holiday, so stick together. Under no circumstances are you to leave the marked footpaths. People have *died* in this park. This whole area is a geothermal minefield. Understood?"

Nico nodded swiftly, then shot out the door before his father could say more.

"Come on," he hissed at Emma as she hurried to keep up. "Don't let him reconsider!"

Nico zoomed past Logan, into a beaten grass field surrounding the cabin. He didn't slow until he reached the densely packed forest beyond. A crunchy layer of snow coated the ground, leaving clear footprints as they hustled through the trees, down a natural trail, and onto a wide pathway leading to the geyser viewing area. From this side of the river, the park buildings nearest to Old Faithful were still out of sight.

"Slow down," Logan grumbled.

"Keep up," Nico clapped back. "Or don't. I couldn't care less."

"What a *beautiful* morning!" Emma said brightly. She began to whistle.

The path weaved through a cluster of low, wide pools north of the main attraction site. Emma stopped to snap pics.

"That one's called Aurum Geyser," Nico said, reading from a handout he'd downloaded to his phone. A small vent to the side began to bubble.

"Oh, we're in luck!" Emma crowed. "Kaboom coming!"

Moments later the geyser erupted, shooting a fountain of water twenty-five feet skyward.

Nico stopped fuming about Logan for a second to take in nature's majesty. His jaw dropped as the water kept rising, driving twice as high into the air. The stream turned black, then yellow, before clearing again just before the geyser ceased its roar.

Nico's gaze shot to Emma, then dropped to his phone.

"What was that?" Logan said.

"Maybe what we came for," Emma whispered.

"That's 100 percent *not* normal." Nico was scrolling furiously. "Aurum Geyser isn't known for spewing different colors, and I think it went longer than usual."

"Come on, I wanna see the big fella." Emma tugged on Nico's arm until he continued down the walkway.

Logan laughed delightedly as he trailed them. "They get *bigger*?"

Nico shot a glare over his shoulder. "Dude, did you do *any* research?"

"I figured you'd be all over this dirt-water stuff. I had other things to do."

Nico whipped his head back around. *Tune out the idiot.*

They hurried down the trail toward Old Faithful, reaching a wide section that overlooked a frothing, roiling pool. The liquid swirled brown and yellow, and a horrid rotten-egg stench was wafting from its surface. Nico felt his pulse begin to race. *Just like the pond on our island.*

"I know that smell," Emma moaned. "Is this one supposed to reek like a fart?"

Nico shook his head, glancing at his screen. "This is Doublet Pool. It's usually clear, or tinged blue. Something weird is definitely happening underground."

An explosive sound thundered from somewhere around the next bend. Nico jogged ahead to a viewing area that encircled a shallow, rust-colored pool. Towers of boiling water were firing in rapid succession, creating loud, echoing coughs. As Logan and Emma drew even with Nico, the jets turned yellow, slimy green, then a putrid brownish purple. Nico was trying to pull up his phone's camera when the eruptions ceased abruptly, like they'd been turned off by a wall switch.

Emma gave Nico an anxious look. "Okay, was *that* normal?"

Nico shook his head grimly. "Nope. And guess where we are."

Logan swallowed. "I'll bite: this is Pump Geyser, isn't it?"

Nico nodded curtly, then read from his phone. "*'Pump Geyser is a cone feature located in Yellowstone National Park—'* Hold on a sec. Okay, here we go. '*A small boil builds to a heavy doming of water, which triggers eruptions up to fifteen feet high.*'" Nico skipped ahead. "Says here that the geyser got its name because it sounds like an old mechanical pump. It's supposed to cycle up again after a few seconds."

Yet they watched for nearly a full minute, and nothing happened. The geyser had gone silent. Frustrated, Emma made a hurry-up gesture with her hand. "Were the colors at least right?"

Nico looked up. "Not even close. Too many, and too much."

Logan crossed his arms. "Fine. But what does it mean to us?"

Nico ignored him. Mostly because he didn't have a good answer to give.

Emma chewed her lip as the geyser began thumping again. "How big *is* this problem?"

Nico ground his teeth at being forced to agree with Logan about anything. He spun on the older boy. "Your photo made it seem like there was a Torchbearer connection here, and these eruptions match what we saw in Still Cove before Halloween. But . . . I mean . . ." Nico threw up his hands. "Great. Super. Wonderful. Now what?"

"I didn't promise anything," Logan fired back. "You read the inscription, too."

Nico forced a bitter laugh, prodding Emma with an elbow. "You're not going to believe this, but Logan isn't taking responsibility. Stunning, right?"

But Emma wasn't listening. She was staring. Not at the geyser in front of them, but beyond it, at a line of trees bordering the walkway complex. Her fists were clenched, and she wasn't blinking.

"Emma? What's so—"

"Nico, *look*."

The intensity in her voice got his attention. He turned and tried to match Emma's gaze, even lining up his shoulders with hers. A low whistle escaped Nico's lips.

Facing the geyser head-on, Nico noticed a pair of giant evergreens in the tree line behind it that rose to either side of the boiling vent, like primordial bookends. When the geyser finally erupted again, its massive jet of black liquid rose directly between the forest sentinels.

The similarity was unmistakable.

They were staring at the scene stamped onto Thomas Nantes' coin.

"There it is," Nico breathed.

"Wow," Logan said.

"Let's go!" Emma shouted.

Nico's gaze rocketed to her. "Huh?"

Emma grabbed him by the sleeve. "Nico, the trees are a perfect match, but Roman Hale took his picture from the opposite angle. Meaning he and Thomas Nantes were standing on the *other side* of those trees. Trust me on this, it's what I do! I think there's something back there!"

"But, my . . . my dad." Nico couldn't think clearly. "He said not to . . ."

Emma tilted her head. "We've been playing him all along, Nico."

"What's the matter, Holland?" Logan's dark eyes glittered. "Afraid?"

Nico bit back a mouthful of bile. "Come on, Emma. Let's find a way across these rocks."

Looking left, then right, they crept off the footpath, picking a careful route across uneven stony ground. After several heart-stopping minutes—Nico was sure someone would sound the alarm at any moment—they reached tree line and stood directly between the towering twin pines. A threadbare game trail ran between them, cutting sharply left before plunging downhill.

"There's a natural path," Nico stated.

"So let's follow it," Logan snapped. "Duh."

Jaw clenched, Nico took the lead again, scrambling down the muddy decline until it leveled into a boulder field. The trail reached a narrow clearing no wider than twenty feet across. Then it disappeared.

Nico paused, examining the rocks surrounding them. He let out an exasperated growl.

"Dead end?" Logan asked.

"Maybe we missed something," Emma suggested.

Nico punched his thigh. "How is that possible? This is the only route possible behind those trees." But then a set of boulders to his right caught his eye. A gap two feet high and three across lurked at the base of the rocks.

On the left-hand stone, something twinkled in the sunlight.

Nico moved closer, realized something was etched into the granite.

A torch.

*Jackpot.*

"In there!" Nico squealed, pointing at the pitch-black hole in the ground.

The opening was dark and thoroughly uninviting. Cold air flowed from its lightless mouth, whiffs of sulfur souring the stale current. Nico would've bet his life savings that Torchbearer secrets were hidden inside that fissure. He was also certain of another thing—that he really, really didn't want to go in there.

Emma shivered from head to foot. "Um, you guys first."

Logan didn't move.

Nico sniffed. Rubbed his nose. Then he dropped to his knees and crawled inside.

The gap was claustrophobically tight for roughly ten feet, then plummeted steeply, widening into a natural chute that dropped into the all-encompassing gloom. Nico powered his phone light and slip-slid down into the dark maw. *Please don't be a geyser at the bottom.* When his sneakers touched level stone again, Nico felt more than saw that he'd entered a much larger chamber. His hip jostled a stack of wood and he aimed the light.

Torches.

Emma and Logan crashed down behind him as Nico grabbed a pair of weathered brands. He pulled a lighter from Emma's bag, sparked the wheel, and ignited the torches, handing one to her.

"Thanks, I'll get my own," Logan said sarcastically.

Nico hid a nasty smile.

The cave was huge, like an underground amphitheater. Their thin circles of light didn't reach the far wall. Nico's heart thudded. He swung his torch slowly, scanning the cavernous space. He spied a blacker smear of darkness ahead and cautiously moved forward.

The floor sloped downward slightly, like a shallow bowl. A dark hole gaped in the center of the room, breathing up cold air from unknown depths.

Emma crept to its edge and peered down. The drop appeared bottomless. Nothing reflected from the gap's smooth sides.

"Emma," Nico warned. "Not too close. That's a one-way ticket straight to oblivion."

"It's just an empty well." She turned to him, eyes shining in the torchlight. "But maybe it was something else once. Like another Darkdeep?"

Nico tried to calm his nerves. "Could just be a mineshaft. We haven't confirmed that this is a Torchbearer place."

Logan scoffed. "Dude, there was a torch carved on the boulder outside. What else do you need?"

"More," Nico said curtly. "Lots of people use torches."

Emma's gaze slid over Nico's shoulder. She pointed a shaky finger. "How about that, Nico?"

He spun. And his heart nearly stopped.

Another passage had been cut through the chamber's far wall. Two words were carved into the archway directly above it.

*ACCIPERE VICTUS.*

Accept to Overcome. The Torchbearer motto.

Logan giggled a little hysterically. "I'd call that pretty good evidence, huh?"

"Yeah," Nico said in a strangled voice. "I guess so."

Emma put a hand on Nico's shoulder and squeezed. "Do you know what this means? There were *other* Torchbearers! People that had nothing to do with Timbers, or Still Cove. We're not alone!"

"Maybe. Or maybe Logan's grandfather came here and carved that himself for some reason." Nico swallowed. "But Emma, if you're right, you know what else it means?"

She blinked at him. "What?"

"Why have more Torchbearers unless there are other Rifts?"

Even in the torchlight, Nico saw Emma pale. For once Logan remained silent.

Nico snorted. "Exactly."

Logan scuffed his shoe on the stone floor, kicking up a cloud of dust. He turned and aimed his torch behind him, revealing their three lines of footprints across the cavern. "This place hasn't been visited in years. If there's another group of Torchbearers around, where did they go? Why haven't they ever contacted us?"

Nico ground his teeth in frustration. "Decent questions. Let's look for answers."

Emma burst into a tiny laugh. "We're freaking amazing at investigating things though, huh? We found *another* secret Torchbearer place. Opal and Tyler are going to flip out!"

Logan cleared his throat. "We need to see what's down the next tunnel."

"That we do." Emma's voice betrayed her nerves.

*No choice.*

"Okay, then," Nico said. "Come on."

The second passageway was wide and short, leading to a spherical chamber no bigger than a garage. Its walls were smooth and mostly blank, except for a smattering of niches bored into the stone at an equal depth of about six inches. They appeared at varying heights and were unevenly spaced around the room. The trio spread out, examining the holes. Nico couldn't make heads or tails of them.

Logan's voice broke the silence. "There's another tunnel!"

He was completely out of view. Nico realized Logan had stepped behind a lip of rock at the other end of the chamber. He and Emma moved around the outcropping, into a narrow, rough-hewn passage that might have been a natural fissure.

"One more stroll?" Emma said to Nico, her voice thrumming with excitement.

"Okay. But if this cave network goes any deeper, we're turning back. I do *not* want to get lost down here."

Logan shuddered, his torch wobbling in his hand. "We agree on that much, Holland. These'll burn out eventually, and phone batteries don't last forever."

Nico nodded pointlessly in the gloom, fighting to keep his arms from trembling. The thought of blundering around aimlessly that deep underground felt like spiders crawling down his spine. *Get going, then get out.* He pushed ahead once more.

The ragged tunnel made three sharp turns as it steadily dropped. Slowly, a sound was building—a churning, splashing racket Nico found strangely familiar.

The passage exited onto a broad shelf overlooking a dark, flickering cavern.

Something sizzled below.

Nico didn't want to look down, afraid of what he might see.

But he did.

Yellow-green liquid seethed in a huge pool at the base of the craggy chamber.

All the blood in Nico's body drained through his toes.

He was staring into the crackling maw of another Rift.

# 14
## OPAL

Opal knew she'd taken a risk.

But it was getting really hard to visit the houseboat. And on Thanksgiving? No chance.

*Sometimes you have to bring something home.* She glanced at the antique chess set resting on her bed. *No one's using it, and it's not like old chess pieces scream Darkdeep or anything. In fact, the game is probably* safer *here.*

Opal ran a finger across the board—mahogany, inlaid with alternating black and white stone squares in a traditional checkered pattern. Its hand-carved onyx and marble pieces were scattered on her comforter. She stood the queens side by side, then placed the wooden one that had arrived through the Darkdeep in between them. The new version was a poor replica of the pristine stone pieces, but the resemblance was unmissable. This third queen was clearly meant to mimic the original two from the chess set. But why? And who sent it?

Opal nearly screamed at the maddening impossibleness of it all.

She was still ticked at Nico and Emma for not making more of an effort to include her in their crazy plan—she'd found out about the trip in a stupid *text*. Opal's parents never would've allowed her to actually go with them, but being left out stung. After all, *she* was the one who'd discovered the stinking clue!

At least Tyler was around, as trapped in Timbers for the holiday as she was. After getting dropped off by his father, Opal had spent the afternoon eating slightly overcooked turkey and enduring endless family gossip, before finally escaping to her room.

The chess pieces had a pull on her. They felt important. Like a *key*.

Or she was imagining things?

Opal exhaled, glancing at the pile of undone homework on her desk, textbooks buried under a stack of printed articles about Yellowstone. Her eye snagged on the old leather notebook, the one with asters and opals on each page. Opal felt a twinge of guilt. *I guess I've taken a few things home.*

Murmurs carried from the hallway. Her mother was giving a house tour to visiting relatives, and they'd reached the second floor.

Her door swept open without a knock. Opal barely stifled a growl.

"Chess, dear?" Kathryn Walsh lilted, stepping inside. Before Opal could answer, her mother turned to a trio standing in the hall behind her. "Opal's bedroom has hand-crafted crown molding and a sculpted ceiling medallion. All original to the house, of course."

Aunt Grace and Uncle Kelvin made polite "impressed" noises. Opal silently wagered her college fund that they'd been forced into this tour. Renovations were finally complete, and this was the first time her mom had been able to show the fully restored property to anyone. Kathryn pretended not to notice Uncle Kelvin hiding a yawn.

Grandma Heming, however, clasped her hands together in delight. *She's been excited about every tiny thing all day long.* How could anyone enjoy discussing the quality of hand-sewn armchair fabrics? *How'd Dad get out of this?* He and Uncle Eric were downstairs watching a football game.

Mercifully, Kathryn gave her daughter a distracted wave and stepped back out of the room, droning on about light fixtures as she continued down the hall. Of course she left the door wide open.

With a huff, Opal got up to close it, but her father's voice boomed up the stairs. "Opie? You have a friend here! I'm sending her up!"

"Her?" Opal said to herself, edging into the corridor.

Lily Nantes appeared at the top of the stairs, carrying a plate covered in aluminum foil. Catching sight of Opal, she hurried over. "Hi, Opal! I brought you some lemon meringue pie. You said it was your favorite."

Opal smothered a groan of irritation. "Thanks, Lily. That's very nice of you." She stood in the doorway and took the proffered dish, hoping the younger girl would bounce back down the steps.

"No problem." Lily seemed very pleased with herself. "My mom would've finished it off, but I made sure you got some."

"Great." Opal shifted awkwardly, not inviting Lily in. "Um, what's Logan up to?" Like she didn't know.

"He went on some trip with Nico," Lily said casually. "Logan didn't tell my dad, so he's in big trouble. Even though he used his own money, and Mom said it was okay, which I don't get. Still, I bet he's grounded until Christmas."

*If the world lasts that long.*

Opal shoved the disturbing thought away.

"Oh," she managed instead. "That seems . . . strange."

"Dad's been super bummed lately." Lily's forehead scrunched in confusion. "I think maybe he's mad about sports, or something. He's been hiding in his office room all day. Mom says he's avoiding the dishes, but it's still weird. It's *soooo* boring at my house. What are *you* doing?" She peered around Opal into her bedroom. "Oooh, is that chess! Can we play? I learned at school! We had a tournament!"

Opal squeezed her eyes shut. Why hadn't she closed the

dumb door? But then it occurred to her that Lily might know some things about Nantes family history. *I could ask questions.*

"Come check it out." Opal stepped aside. Lily bounded into the room like a happy puppy. In a swift move that Lily didn't notice, Opal scooped up the wooden queen and tucked it under her pillow. She didn't want anyone else to see it.

"Can I be white?" Lilly asked, eyes glued to the ancient board.

"Sure. But I warn you, I'm pretty bad."

"No problem! I've only played a few times."

The game began. Lily moved confidently each time it was her turn, a sly smile tilting her lips. Opal had to think hard before every move. *A fourth grader is smoking me.* But she hadn't agreed to this match for the sport of it.

"So . . . do you have a lot of family in for a visit?"

"Not this year," Lily said, sliding a pawn forward.

Opal brought out her knight, then grimaced as she lost it one move later. "Why is that?"

Lily shrugged. "My aunt and uncle and their family usually come down from Vancouver, but Dad didn't invite anyone this year, so they all went to Hawaii instead." Her voice grew indignant. "Dad said we couldn't go. He *insisted* we stay home, even though nothing important is going on and I never get to see my cousins. Mom didn't speak to him for a whole weekend."

"That stinks." Opal felt a tingle creep across her scalp. *Why couldn't they leave town?*

Lily placed her bishop dangerously close to Opal's back line. "Check."

Opal moved her king. Above their heads, floorboards creaked. Lily's gaze shot skyward.

"Just my family touring the third floor," Opal said distractedly. "Don't worry, no ghosts."

"Oh." Lily looked relieved, and then tried to hide it. "I know that."

"Does your house make weird noises, too? Someone should put up warning signs in places this old."

Lily nodded sourly. "I swear there's been a ton more of them lately. Weird scratching sounds, and once I heard something hiss under the deck. Just the laundry vent, Mom said." She carefully advanced her queen, leaving it open to attack. "Check again."

Opal went still. "Did you see anything? Maybe a wild animal or something?"

"Nope. Like I said, it was just our house being stupid."

*Or a rabid wolf was prowling your yard. Along with a boat-sinking bobcat?* Opal frowned. Now she really was jumping at shadows. *Don't get paranoid. Even Lily didn't think much of it.*

"It's your turn." Lily batted her eyes innocently. "Are you still thinking?"

155

Opal chewed on her fist. If she moved her rook *there*, she'd take Lily's best piece. So why did she feel like a mouse eyeing the cheese in a trap? She glanced at the grim number of her players already lying off the board. An aster was carved into its base of each figure. *What is it with these flowers?*

"Any*time* now," Lily said in a singsong voice.

Opal's suspicion deepened. "Hold your horses."

But she didn't have a plan. How was Lily so good at this?

Kathryn Walsh's voice flitted down the hall. "I know that some people think yellow is simply yellow, but I had *such* a time finding the appropriate shade for the exterior."

Tour at an end, Kathryn had again halted her captives just outside Opal's door.

"This one is called Buttercake. I had it shipped in from England, which was an ordeal, let me tell you . . ."

"Fascinating," Uncle Kelvin muttered.

Kathryn missed the sarcasm. "I shouldn't complain. When you buy a property on Overlook Row, neighborhood covenants require that you maintain the original color, as depicted in an 1857 painting currently on display in the Nantes' home. Some of these buildings predate even that."

"Well, you've done a wonderful job," Aunt Grace said gamely.

"Such history." Opal's mother purred contentedly. "One early resident of this street—whose house, sadly, no longer exists—painted her home purple in tribute to a ward who died tragically."

Opal's head snapped toward the door, the chess game forgotten.

"Purple?" scoffed Grandma Heming, pursing her lips in disbelief. "I'm sure her neighbors were aghast! Where would one even get purple paint back in Civil War times?"

"The 1740s, actually," Opal's mother corrected. "This was an original landowner. Apparently she had some personal knowledge of chemicals and mixed the color herself."

Cheers rolled up from the group watching football downstairs. Uncle Kelvin began edging toward the steps.

"Earth to Opal!" Lily huffed. "You can't stall forever."

"What? Oh, right." Opal slid her rook and took Lily's queen. Her hands were trembling. Her mother *had* to be talking about Yvette Dumont. *My own mom! And she has no idea.*

"*Mistake.*" Lily's hand shot forward and advanced a pawn. Then she tipped over Opal's king. "Checkmate. Sorry. Never take the bait."

"Oops." Opal was barely listening. "Shoot. Good job, Lily."

Kathryn's voice dropped an octave, as if sharing a secret. "This particular landowner was the lone survivor of a shipwreck. She'd been governess to a young girl who, tragically, drowned with all the others. Her body was never recovered."

"Oh *dear*," said Grandma Walsh.

"Why purple?" Uncle Kelvin asked, seemingly in spite of himself. "Was it the girl's favorite?"

"Her ward was named after a flower," Kathryn Walsh's voice faded as the adults headed for the stairs. "I forget which one. The paint color was to match its blossom."

Opal's heart was pounding. *I know a purple flower.*

She glanced at the aster carved on the bottom of her now-toppled king.

"Guess I'll go now." Lily was pouting, perhaps annoyed Opal wasn't heaping praise on her chess skills. "Thanks for playing with me."

"Bye, Lily." Opal barely registered the little girl's exit. Her mind was on tilt.

Then her dad's voice bellowed up once more. "Opal? Dessert is ready! Come down now or I'm eating it all myself."

"Coming!"

Opal's entire body felt electrified.

She knew the girl's name.

*Aster.*

That flower was carved everywhere Torchbearer secrets were hidden.

It represented someone.

A girl whose body was never recovered.

A girl who died?

Or.

A girl trapped where she doesn't belong?

# 15

# NICO

Nico burst into the houseboat's foyer.

Emma was right behind him as he fired through the curtain and into the showroom.

Opal and Tyler were already waiting, huddled beside Thing's former pedestal. They seemed to be arguing—Opal had both hands on her hips, while Tyler was frowning, arms crossed tightly over his chest.

"We found another Rift!" Nico blurted. "It wasn't exploding with Takers or anything, *but we found another Rift.*"

Tyler squeezed his eyelids shut. "So your text said. I'm still hoping you don't know what a mini-volcano looks like."

Emma shook her head rapidly. "Oh, it's a Rift all right. Inside a Torchbearer cave with our motto chiseled in stone and weird holes in the walls. I took pics of everything on our way out so you could see." She waved her phone at them. "Guys, this means there are other Torchbearers!"

Nico held up a hand. "We *think*. We didn't meet one, or anything." He rubbed his face. "But even if Yellowstone really did have its own chapter of the Order, they're gone, too. That cavern was as abandoned as the houseboat when we found it. No one is watching the Yellowstone Rift."

"Y.R. on the photo inscription." Opal smiled a little smugly. "I knew it."

"How are we supposed to deal with a *second* tear in reality?" Tyler moaned. "We can't even take care of our own!"

"Hold on!" Opal glanced at the curtain. "Where's Logan? I have some news to share, too."

"Who cares about Logan?" Nico spat. "We can handle this without him."

"*Handle this?*" Tyler's hands shot into the air. "How are we gonna *handle* this, exactly?"

The front door slammed. A moment later Logan jogged in, red-faced and puffing. "Sorry I'm late! My dad is *livid* I went to Yellowstone. There's currently a Logan-shaped pillow man hiding beneath my bedspread." He giggled nervously. "I'm so dead if he finds out."

Nico pointedly put his back to Logan. "We need to come up with a plan to . . . I don't know . . . find these other Torch-bearers. If they exist."

Tyler blinked at him. "Nico, how in the world are we going to do that?"

A loud thump echoed across the room, causing everyone to jump. All eyes slid to Opal. *Did she just stamp her foot?*

"I. Have. News." Her intensity cowed everyone to silence. "Now that Logan is here, I want you all to listen to me." She paused for a long beat, then continued in a rush. "I've decoded Thing's message."

Nico licked his lips. "For real?"

Opal nodded seriously. "My mom, of all people, said something that helped me finally put it together. And if I'm right about this, well . . ." She shifted uncomfortably. "We have a decision to make."

"A decision about what?" Emma whispered.

Opal waved off the question. "Let me start at the start. I . . . I think I know who Thing is referring to in his letter." She took a deep breath, then walked them through her most recent discoveries. Flowers sketched in the old notebook. A shipwreck named the *Dauphin*. Purple house paint on Overlook Row. "Yvette Dumont was a governess before settling in Timbers, and her charge drowned at sea. But *we* know that storm was actually caused by the Rift."

Nico nodded automatically, but he didn't understand putting this history ahead of what they'd discovered at Yellowstone. "That's great work, Opal. For real. But I don't see how it applies right now."

"Then pay attention!" Opal snapped, tension rising in her voice. "Thing sent us a message-in-a-bottle that said *someone* was there—on *its* world—who didn't belong. Then a game piece appeared in the Darkdeep—a wooden queen that matches the chess set we got from Thing, which is the *only* item from Earth ever to cross the Void both ways. A chess set *with an aster carved onto each piece* and was probably commissioned for a young girl."

Logan scratched his cheek. "So . . . the girl who died in the wreck. Her name was Aster."

"And this Dumont lady painted her house purple as a tribute." Tyler shook his head. "Man, that's sad."

"Or is it?"

Everyone stared at Opal.

She made hand-wiping gestures in the air. "What I mean is—do we really know that Aster died?"

Shocked silence.

Opal dug into her pocket. Held up the wooden queen. "I checked this again, just to be safe. Take a look."

She flipped the figurine over in her hand to reveal its base. Everyone crowded close. Nico squinted, but saw nothing. Then Opal shifted the piece and the light struck it at a different angle. He spotted the faint outline of a flower etched into the strange wood. "Wow. Pretty faded, but it's there. Good job, Opal."

"Thanks." Opal blew out her lips. "Missing it the first time wasn't stupendous, but whatever. I saw the aster eventually."

"Okay," Tyler said slowly. "So this confirms that the

queen from the Darkdeep is supposed to match our chess set. Which means it probably came from Thing, since that's where we got the game in the first place. But what does *that* tell us? Why would Thing bother to carve a fake queen and send it through the Rift?"

Nico's eyes popped. His heart began to pound. His eyes met Opal's.

"You . . . you think Aster is *with* Thing. On its planet, or whatever?"

Opal nodded firmly. "It all fits. She's the 'someone' Thing is referring to. The flower on the wooden queen seals it. The chess set must've belonged to her originally, and Thing sent us a *new* piece with *her* symbol on it. The meaning is obvious. Aster is alive and with Thing!"

Tyler's forehead scrunched in disbelief. "Why wouldn't Thing just *say* that to us? Why all the subterfuge?"

Opal shrugged in honest bafflement. "I don't know, Ty. Thing obviously didn't want to write her name down. Maybe Thing doesn't even know it, or maybe it *needed* us to figure out the answer for some reason. Which we did!"

Nico exhaled slowly. "Okay. So Aster goes down with the *Dauphin*, except somehow she doesn't drown. Instead she gets . . . I don't know, sucked through the Rift and . . . and ends up on another world." His gaze met Opal's again. "But that was two hundred and fifty years ago. Even if Aster survived all that, she'd still have died before the American Revolution."

"We don't know that."

163

Logan gave Opal a look. "Hah?"

She threw her arms out wide. "Thing's world is in *another dimension*. We have no idea how time works there! And think about it—why would Thing send us clues about a missing girl just to later tell us she passed away centuries ago? That doesn't make sense."

"AND THIS DOES?" Tyler thundered.

"Wait a second." Emma squinted at Opal. "Earlier you said that, if you were right, 'we'd have to make a decision.' What did you mean?"

Opal made as if to speak, but paused instead. Her eyes did a circuit of the others.

Tyler's mouth dropped open. "Oh no."

Opal looked down at the floor.

"No no *no*!" Tyler growled, pounding a fist into his open palm to punctuate the words. "We are *not* doing that. Not again!"

Emma's eyes widened. Then she got a speculative look. Nico felt his stomach lurch.

Logan was glancing from face to face. "Not doing what, guys?"

Tyler spun on him. "Don't you see what she's driving at? Opal wants to test her theory. *In person*. She wants to go back into the Void!"

Emma rubbed her chin. "Another Darkdeep dive."

"*Come and see what I have for you,*" Nico breathed. He covered his eyes.

Logan stared at Opal like she'd glitched. "What? *Why?* None of this helps us deal with the new Rift we found at Yellowstone. Or the one five miles from here! *That* should be our focus. If this poor Aster girl got sucked onto another planet, I feel bad for her, but we have our own world to worry about. *Earth.* Right here."

"Is that how you really feel?" Opal asked quietly. "All of you?" Her penetrating gaze traveled the group. Nico found he couldn't meet her eye. "Would you leave *me* there? Or another kid you knew was in trouble?"

No one spoke. Nico felt a ton of bricks land on his chest.

"You wouldn't." Opal crossed her arms. "So why should Aster be any different? We're the only people who can help her."

Nico cleared his throat. "Help her how, Opal?"

There was a slight trill to her response. "We go get her. Bring her home."

No one spoke. Opal's statement had cast a spell over the showroom.

Outside the bay window, the sun moved behind a cloud, and the room darkened. Nico saw his shadow stretch toward the wall panel hiding the Darkdeep. *Into the well. That's the way we'd have to go.*

"I'll do it," Nico said softly.

Emma nearly spoke on top of him. "Me too!"

"Come *on*, guys." Tyler was so upset he was shaking. "What if going back into the Darkdeep wakes it up again?

We just stabilized the Rift in Timbers. Now we know there's another one. We can't risk ruining the balance all over again!"

Opal marched to where her bag sat on a trunk. "We'll bring a balance object. Something to counteract Aster's removal from Thing's world. And . . . we just so happen to have one that we already know works."

Logan frowned. "We do?"

Opal spun, holding the chess set. "Yep."

Tyler looked set to explode again, but he froze, then pursed his lips instead. "Huh."

Nico nodded slowly. "It might work. And while we're in the Void, we can question Thing about the end of the world, and the Yellowstone Rift. Whether there are other Torchbearers or not. That little green blob *has* to know stuff it didn't tell us."

The more Nico considered it, the more Opal's wild idea seemed like the only plan that made sense. How else were they going to learn what they needed to know, with Logan's dad in hiding and all other Torchbearers missing in action, or maybe even long gone?

"Thing might know about Beastmastering, too," Tyler mused. "Crap. We're really going to do this, aren't we?"

Logan put a hand to the bridge of his nose and squeezed. "If we jump into the well, you know it will kick out some figments that we'll have to deal with, right? And we haven't even figured out that yellow-eyed wolf-thing!"

"Hey, I've missed our imaginary friends," Emma joked,

flapping a hand. "Plus, if recent events are any example, we could use the practice."

All eyes shifted to Tyler. He groaned, nodded.

Opal beamed from ear to ear. "Let's get to work."

———————————

Nico inspected the other Torchbearers forming a circle around the Darkdeep. They were all wearing wetsuits. Their last journey had taught them a few things, and everyone wanted to be prepared. They kept diving gear on the houseboat at all times now, in case of emergency.

*And here it is. We're really going back.*

All the way to the Rift, and beyond.

"Supply check," he called out. "Daggers?"

Logan slapped a waterproof bag clipped around his shoulders. "Packed and ready."

"Balance item?"

Opal held a bundle zipped into a dry bag. "Got it."

Nico tried to keep the strain from his voice. "Emma, you have the panic bag?"

Emma wore an airtight scuba backpack. "Snorkels. Fins. Food, water, iodine. Yada yada yada. Let's go."

"Clock?"

Tyler tapped his sports watch. "I'll start the timer as the first person splashes in. Which *isn't* going to be me, by the way."

Nico took a deep breath. Shook out his arms and legs.

"I'll go first. Remember the procedure. Think of the Darkdeep and give in to its pull. When we hit the end of that conduit, swim straight for the Rift under the oil platform. That leads to the Void. We'll regroup there and . . . and . . . see what we see."

"We're ready." Opal's eyes shone in the half-light. "Thank you, guys. I mean it."

Emma squeezed her hand. Nico glanced down at the well, embarrassed.

Below his feet, the Darkdeep waited, as black and motionless as infinity itself.

*Stop stalling. It never gets easier.*

"Here we go," Nico said in an overloud voice. "Stay with the group at all times. If possible."

Words of assent flew around the room.

Nico cracked his knuckles. Bent his knees.

*Three.*

*Two.*

*One.*

He dove in.

# 16

## OPAL

Light disappeared.

So did sound. Touch. Taste. And smell.

Opal hurtled through the Darkdeep, though not a hair on her head stirred.

Black everywhere. Then a sensation of falling.

A blue-green blur appeared and suddenly Opal burst through it. Suddenly she was underwater, grappling with the strong Pacific currents.

She kicked outward, then down, peering into the gray-green depths, looking for the telltale glow of the Rift.

*There.*

Opal dove for the pulsing rip in space-time. At her side, the others did the same.

In moments, the Rift's pull enveloped her, and she was sucked into its shimmering vortex.

An electric shock. A blast of heat.

Then, nothing once more. Only *this* nothing was different. The Torchbearers had entered the Void.

*Took you long enough.*

A lime-green blob with spindly arms and a wide grin was hovering beside a second gash in reality, below the one Opal and her friends had just exited. *Thing.* The alien spoke in the mind-bending way communication worked inside the Void—sending thoughts directly into her head.

Opal shivered. She'd never get used to it.

The group drifted in the strange, prismatic-colored vacuum that existed between worlds. It took Opal a moment to get the hang of moving around again. She closed her eyes, concentrating, and zipped in the direction she wanted to go. That was the trick in the Void—your body did what your thoughts commanded.

*Help!* Logan was floundering in an ungainly circle, exactly as Opal had the first time she'd entered this in-between space. Logan had never been through the Rift before—during the Taker battle, he'd been in charge of stealing a boat and plucking them from the collapsing oil rig.

Opal understood his panic. You couldn't swim or kick like in the ocean. There was no ground to stand on, nothing tangible to grab with your hands.

*Logan.*

His fevered gaze shot to her, a look of distress on his face.

*It's okay*, she told him. *Think about where you want to go. Then it happens.*

He nodded. Gritting his teeth, he let his eyes go unfocused. After a few seconds, he stopped whirling and sank down to where the others had clustered.

Logan flashed a lopsided grin. *Wow.*

Opal gave him a reassuring smile.

Tyler peered longingly up at the shimmering slash they'd come through—the passage back to their world. *I don't like being so far away from it.*

*You're not far*, Thing chided. *Distance has no meaning here.*

To prove the point, Thing disappeared. Suddenly, the creature was inside their impromptu circle. Logan reared back in surprise and had to be steadied by Emma, who chuckled softly to herself. Or to everyone, since her giggle sounded inside their minds.

Opal gave Thing an appraising look. Had the maddening little creature left its own world only a moment ago? Or had it been waiting? How did Thing know they'd be right here, now? What had it been doing since they last met face-to-face?

*I've been expecting you. What part of my message was unclear?*

Opal swore Thing's eyes twinkled with amusement. It looked the same—little green body, big black eyes—but also . . . different. Fuller? More . . . itself?

*There's been a lot going on*, Opal sent in a testy tone.

*More than you know.* Thing tilted its bulbous head. *What in the Void are you wearing?*

*Wetsuits.* Nico moved closer to Opal. *We're not taking any more chances with the Rift. We have our daggers too, in case there's trouble.*

There was an edge to Nico's voice. He wasn't messing around.

*No enemies are nearby at present*, Thing reassured them. *But we shouldn't dawdle.*

*Your message!* Emma zipped in next to Nico. *What did it mean?*

*And why all the secrecy?* Nico added irritably. *A cryptic note and a single chess piece? Why not just tell us what's going on straight out?*

Thing's tone grew icy. *We're not the only beings who travel this realm. Or have you forgotten the Takers? I didn't want to send anything that revealed too much. Plus, I knew you'd figure it out. And since you're here, I assume you did?*

Opal nodded. *I've been investigating the life of Yvette Dumont. She was a governess aboard a ship named the* Dauphin. *There was a ward in her charge. A girl named Aster. I . . . I think she's here with you.*

Thing's grin widened. *Excellent. I'm not entirely sure how the balance works—as I said before, it's not one-to-one—but I had no idea Aster was here until I returned. Yvette and I had assumed she drowned when the ship sank. Aster being alive on my world is a missing piece we never considered. Not in all the years that Torchbearers tended the Rift.*

Nico's voice growled in everyone's mind. *You're saying she's on your planet right now?*

*Yes, Nico. That's exactly what I'm saying.*

*How is that possible?* Emma asked in amazement. *Her ship went down hundreds of years ago!*

*Only in your timeline. On my world, it's been less than ten months.*

Everyone stared at the tiny alien in shock.

Opal was thunderstruck. A girl who'd been lost at sea over two hundred years ago was not only still alive, but in her life only a few seasons had passed. It was almost too overwhelming to consider.

Emma's spectral form began to shimmer. With excitement? *If Aster returns to Earth with us, everything will be back where it belongs! The balance will be fixed!*

*What about the Beast?* Tyler countered, frowning. *He's not from our world, but he's there now.*

Thing pursed its thin lips. *Interesting. Have you communed with the leviathan lately?*

Tyler shook his head glumly. *I can't seem to make contact.*

Thing shrugged. *The creature* can *communicate. Beastmasters had a method, I'm sure of it.*

*You don't know?* Tyler asked. *How* is *that* possible?

Thing shrugged. *I had little interest in events I could never see. I was trapped in a jar on the houseboat, you might recall.*

Before Tyler could say more, Logan's voice entered Opal's head. *Maybe we should leave Aster where she is until we know whether she and the Beast balance each other out.* He held up a hand as Opal whirled on him. *Think about it! We don't want another Dark Halloween situation. Plus, everything is a disaster on Earth right now. What if we make it worse?*

Opal glared at Logan so hard she thought he might blip out of existence. *We are not leaving someone behind. That's horrible, Logan! We have to bring Aster back and figure it out from there.* But then a strange thought struck her. *Does she want to return, Thing?*

*Of course.* Thing glanced at the glimmering Rift into its world. *She's healthy and eager—though she's certainly had some hair-raising experiences. Remember, Aster would be returning to your world little older than when she left. And we must hurry. We're running out of time.*

*Out of time how?* Nico demanded, but the tiny green alien was already arcing away. Thing slipped through its swirling gateway, then returned a beat later leading someone by the hand.

*Aster,* Opal breathed.

Thought or a sending, she didn't know.

The girl wore an old-fashioned blue dress and brown lace-up boots. Some kind of glowing purple substance stained her footwear, and her skirt was torn at the hem. Aster's sleeves were rolled up, her expression one of determination. She looked to be a year or two older than Opal. Her hair was bound in a single braid thrown over her shoulder.

Opal reached up to touch her own braid. It wasn't like looking in a mirror or anything—the girl was taller, and her hair was dark blond—but Opal felt an immediate connection. This was someone who knew the world wasn't always as it seemed.

Colors began to twist and spin around them. Opal thought she heard a low, faraway roar. Not animal in nature, but . . . *nature* in nature. As if a world was groaning. *But which one?*

*The Void has become unstable*, Thing sent in distress. *The balance has tilted once more.*

*We thought of that.* Opal unwrapped the parcel in her hands and held out the chess set. Aster's gaze locked onto it. The board had clearly belonged to her, and she seemed astonished to see it again.

Thing nodded swiftly. *Smart thinking. I'll take this back across and perhaps a tenuous stability will return.*

Aster turned her head sharply to regard Thing. A warning look smoldered in her eyes. Not fear, exactly. More like she knew something Thing wasn't saying. Thing seemed to be studiously ignoring her glare.

*Are we sure this is a good idea?* Tyler sent, eyeing the chaotic swirls around them. *What if we take her back and she, like, poofs into ash like the Avengers?*

175

Thing's tone was clipped. *Aster has done well for a human, but it's unsustainable. She cannot survive on my world forever.*

Opal met the girl's eye. Felt a challenge there.

*It's not up to us*, Opal sent. *She makes the call.*

The older girl nodded. Pointed to the Timbers Rift.

Opal gave a mental snort. *You see? There's nothing left to say.*

*Not that she's said anything.* Logan folded his arms to glare at Thing, accidentally listing to one side before righting himself. *My dad claims the end of the world is coming. He said that the Torchbearers knew it, and nothing can prevent it. Do you know what he's talking about?*

Thing's expression became guarded. *The end of the world is always coming. No matter which one you're on. The Order understood this.*

Nico threw up his hands. *What does that mean? And how many Torchbearers are there? How many Rifts into our world? What haven't you told us yet, Thing? We've been to Yellowstone, you know.*

Opal's gaze slid to Aster. She felt powerful emotions radiating from her, but couldn't decipher them. Why didn't Aster speak?

The Void bulged like a blown bubble, then seemed to squash down around them.

*There's no time for this right now*, Thing sent, avoiding Nico's questions.

*We gotta go!* Logan started flailing up toward the Timbers Rift, which was glowing white-hot. *Looks like now or never!*

Opal regarded the girl from another time. The one whose name was carved into Torchbearer lore. She'd lost her possessions. Her parents. Her world.

Aster glared at the group, unblinking. Then she reached out and gripped Opal's fingers.

*She's willing to take the risk*, Thing said.

The set of Aster's jaw confirmed it. And then, like a lightning bolt, words seared into Opal's mind.

Sharp and clear, a new voice rang in their heads, one tinged with having been other places, seen other things.

*I'm coming with you*, Aster said firmly. *I'm going home.*

# PART THREE
# THE HUNT

# 17
## NICO

Frigid gusts hammered the houseboat's front door.

A thin layer of ice now coated the pond outside—not yet sturdy enough to walk on, but getting there. Nico, Tyler, and Logan huddled in the foyer, peeling off their sodden wetsuits. Tyler's teeth were chattering nonstop. Nico's fingers burned from the cold. He tried to control his ragged breathing.

The journey home had been nothing short of terrifying. They'd never tried to reenter the Darkdeep on their way *back* through the Rift before. For a heart-stopping few moments Nico couldn't find its black current as he scrambled around underwater, spinning in frantic circles at the bottom of the ocean. His mind nearly blanking with panic, he'd thought they were going to have to surface in the storm-swept Pacific, miles from land, with no prospect of getting rescued from the ruins of the ancient oil rig that had concealed the Rift for decades.

But at the last instant, he'd sensed the Darkdeep's pull.

Linking hands, they'd kicked hard, running out of air as they surrendered to its gravity. Just as Nico was about to despair, the Darkdeep seized them. Sucked them into its nothing space. The inky flow swallowed them whole, shooting the Torchbearers down its length and spitting them out at the bottom of the island pond in Still Cove.

Nico had torpedoed upward and hit the newly formed ice, then punched through it with a roar of desperation, shattering the delicate patina into a thousand tiny shards as the group sloshed for shore, gasping and blowing. Then the bitter cold had set in. His legs had barely sustained him as they staggered across the stepping stones out to the houseboat.

*We could've died.*

Nico had never felt so frozen. His brain was numb as he dragged dry clothes on over his stinging, tingling limbs. The three girls were in the showroom, changing in privacy. Logan had slumped to the floor beside Tyler in rumpled jeans and a hoodie, rocking back and forth as he tried to rub feeling into his extremities. Tyler's lips were blue as he yanked a second sweatshirt down on top of his first.

"Let's n-never d-d-do that ag-gain, okay?" Tyler stuttered.

Logan cackled unexpectedly. "Wassa matter? You didn't like j-j-joining the p-polar bear c-club?"

Nico zipped a fleece jacket tight, his head and neck steaming like an ice cube. "I should've thought about reconnecting with the Darkdeep *before* we left the Void," he scolded himself. "We almost ended up deep-sea castaways during a freaking snowstorm."

"Don't beat yourself up." Logan wobbled upright and began stamping ice from his boots. "I first considered it while floundering twenty feet below the ocean waves." He shivered from more than low body temperature. "Not a pleasant experience."

Nico nodded, still disappointed he'd overlooked such a basic detail. That little mistake nearly landed them in deep, deep trouble. *Use your head next time! Aren't you supposed to be a leader?*

Tyler rubbed both hands over his face, then sneezed loudly. "Let's never do that again, okay?" he repeated, though at least he'd stopped sputtering from brain freeze.

"We're gonna have extra figments to deal with." Grimacing, Logan glanced at the front door. "Hopefully tamer than our missing attack wolf." Then his voice dropped to a mutter. "If that *was* a figment, anyway . . ."

"Not just the wolf," Tyler said. "Don't forget Mr. Reamer's boat-sinking cat."

"We don't know for sure if those things are Darkdeep-related." Nico tucked his hands inside his sleeves, wincing through the pins and needles of getting his fingers to thaw. "But we *do* know what happens when *we* dive through the well. There should be at least five new figments on the island, up to who-knows-what."

Logan waved a lazy arm at the door. "We should . . . you know . . . get them."

"Later," Tyler groaned. "If I step back outside right now, I'll be a Tyler popsicle."

"Same." Nico sighed. "We're in no shape to go hunting for trouble. And we need to talk to this Aster girl first anyway."

Logan walked to the showroom's entry curtain and reached out a hand, but then paused and stepped back, leaving the velvet undisturbed. "So, like . . . do you think they've finished changing clothes?"

"Give it a minute," Nico and Tyler both blurted in unison.

"Right." Logan spun and strode away, his face reddening. "Right right right."

A beat later Opal's voice carried into the foyer. "Okay, guys! You can come in!"

Logan glanced at Nico. "You first."

Nico rolled his eyes and moved past him. He still wasn't ready to accept Logan's olive branch—it's not like his father's transfer had been magically reversed.

In the showroom, Emma and Opal were flanking a seated Aster, who seemed shaken by the extreme voyage. Nico was jarred at how different she looked decked out in modern clothes. Aster wore athletic pants and Opal's form-fitting lavender zip jacket. Nico had to remind himself that he was facing a girl born in the mid-eighteenth century, before the invention of computers, cars, or even electricity. *How will she possibly adapt?*

Aster was staring fixedly at the floor with her arms wrapped around her midsection. Emma looked up, and Nico read the concern in her eyes.

"Aster," Opal said quietly, gripping the nonresponsive girl's hand in her own. "We're back on Earth now, in a tiny cove not far from where your ship went down."

"The place where we almost drowned a few minutes ago?" Logan added earnestly. "That's what sunk your boat. The Rift must've swallowed the ship whole and spit out its wreckage on the sea floor."

Nico shot Logan an exasperated look. "Dude!"

Logan blinked. He noticed everyone but Aster was glaring at him. "What? *I'd* want to know."

A rasped voice emerged from the hunched-over girl, carrying an accent Nico couldn't place. "The *Dauphin* was not consumed. It broke apart. I . . . I grabbed on to a trunk, but it fractured and I was left holding only my chessboard as I was dragged down into that . . . that . . . *hole* in the world." She shivered and fell silent.

No one spoke for long, awkward seconds. Nico had zero idea what to do next.

Aster looked up suddenly. "I was the only one in that other place. Did anyone else . . . are there survivors here?"

Opal gave her a pained look. "As best we can tell, only your governess escaped the disaster. Yvette Dumont lived in Timbers for a long time, in a house painted purple to remember you by."

Aster's eyes were hard. "Lived? What is the meaning of that? She is here now?"

Nico stiffened. "Thing didn't tell you?"

Aster turned her laser-like gaze on him. "The little green creature? Tell me what?"

Opal moved to crouch in front of Aster, catching and holding the girl's eye. "Aster, a *lot* of time has passed on Earth while you were in Thing's dimension. It's been over two-and-a-half centuries since the *Dauphin* sank. But from what we can tell, Yvette lived a long, full life. And she never forgot you."

Aster stared at Opal, eyes widening. A flush crept up her neck and into her cheeks. Then she shook her head rapidly, and glanced away. Another period of brutal silence followed.

"Um, guys?" Tyler was suddenly staring out the showroom's bay window. "We just left Earth like Aster. Did we, um . . . do you think time jumped for *us*, too?"

For a moment, Nico's eyes popped. But then he relaxed. "We never entered Thing's world, only the Void. We've been in that empty space before, and it didn't affect our timelines. I think you have to go all the way through to Thing's dimension."

Tyler nodded quickly in relief. Nico noticed deep exhales from the other Torchbearers, too.

Opal returned her focus to Aster. "I know this is hard, Aster. I'm sorry we have such bad news. From what we've been able to learn, Yvette Dumont spent most of her life trying to prevent another tragedy from happening like the one that struck your ship. She did a lot of important things."

Finally, Aster spoke again. "She was a hard woman, Madame Dumont. My father hired her, and we disagreed at times. But I am glad she . . . I am glad *someone* . . ." Tears formed in her eyes. Aster buried her head in her hands. No sobs followed, but her shoulders shook noiselessly.

Aster sniffed loudly, wiping her eyes where the others couldn't see. Emma put a hand on the girl's knee, but at the touch, Aster's head rocketed back up. She stood abruptly and began pacing the room in shaky steps.

"Easy now," Tyler said, raising both palms as if to calm a spooked horse. "No need to rush around. It's been a day."

"We can help you," Emma said earnestly. "I think it's part of our job, in fact."

Aster halted. She turned to the group, her gaze flicking from face to face. "Who are you?"

Nico was surprised by the question. "We're the Torchbearers. Thing didn't tell you about us?"

Aster made a dismissive gesture. "I barely know this Dax creature. The tiny green goblin only said it had contacts in my world, and that they would come and *rescue* me." Her eyes blazed at the word, but a beat later her stern expression softened. "Which, you did. So . . . thank you. For your assistance."

"Anytime," Logan deadpanned. "But maybe now you could answer some of *our* questions?"

Aster eyed him suspiciously. "What questions do you have of me?"

"Who are you?" Tyler asked. "Sorry if that's rude, but we don't really know, is all."

Aster drew up to her full height. "Fine. A short introduction is appropriate. My name is Aster Caraway. My father is"—she went rigid, then continued in a harder voice—"*was* a capitaine for the Dutch East India Company. I was born in Toulon, in the south of France. Upon my eighth birthday, I began boarding school in London. On my fifteenth birthday, I was allowed to accompany my father on a trading expedition to the Far East, under the rigorous stewardship of a governess, Madame Yvette Dumont. During the voyage we were blown off course by a terrible storm and pushed across nearly the entire Pacific Ocean, according to the navigator." She exhaled deeply. "At last we sighted land, and sailed for it, but our ship foundered in a sudden, vicious whirlpool. You know the rest."

Nico felt a sudden chill. "Your *father* was captain of the *Dauphin*?"

Aster swallowed. Nodded.

Tyler went rigid. He leaned over and elbowed Opal surreptitiously, whispering, "Lieutenant Commodore *Caraway*. From the old ship's manifest I found in my Beast book. That's her dad!"

Opal nodded, felt her heart breaking. Aster's father had gone down with the *Dauphin*, and to her it had been less than a year. The human loss of the shipwreck hit Opal for the first time. *History is just real people's struggles from another time.*

Another terrible quiet ballooned inside the showroom. Nico was staring at his hands.

Emma finally broke it. "What happened to you over there?" she asked gently. "You crossed the Void and visited another planet. How did you survive?"

Aster's expression became guarded. "I do not wish to talk about that. Not yet. It was . . . hard. But humans can survive in that place." Something flickered in her eyes, quickly masked. "If one is careful."

Tyler frowned. "What does *that* mean?"

She gave him an icy look. "Dax's world is not a safe place. Not a realm I should like my home connected to."

Nico felt a prickle walk down his spine. "Aster, is there something we need to know about?"

Logan stepped forward, eyeing the girl intently. "My father is *convinced* the world is going to end, but he won't say anything more. Do you know what he means by that?"

Aster met Logan glare-for-glare. Something worked behind

her eyes, like she was weighing possible responses. Then her gaze slid past him, finding Emma instead.

"You wish to know what happened to me? Here it is: I was pulled through the Rift, as you call it, and became stranded within the in-between space. I lost consciousness for what may have been days. Years. Who knows how long? When I awoke, I was alone. Scared. I did not know what to do. I felt *certain* I was going to die." Her voice deadened. "Then I saw a glimmering circle and decided to enter it. What else could I attempt? It led to another world and solid ground. There is food there, of a kind, and terrible, brackish water that will keep you alive. I . . . I avoided trouble and stayed as quiet as possible. A little mouse. For weeks. Then long months. Then this . . . this devilish green creature appeared. You seem to have figured out the rest. Dax put a note in a bottle, I carved a replica for my chessboard, and now I am here."

Nico was spellbound by Aster's story, but he had a weird feeling that she was intentionally leaving things out. What wasn't she saying?

"What trouble did you avoid?" Tyler asked. "Takers?"

Aster went very pale. "Dark Ones. Yes. I hid from them. And . . . others."

"What others?" Logan pressed.

Aster's eyes grew hooded. Her glance cut to Nico, then away.

What was *that* look?

Logan seemed about to push the issue when Aster swayed on her feet. Her eyes rolled up into her skull.

Opal and Emma leaped over as one, catching Aster before she crumpled to the floor. They gently eased her down onto the bench. Opal's red-hot glare swung back to encompass all three boys. "Enough. She needs rest. Can you imagine how traumatic this must be for her?"

Nico flinched. It's not like they'd been interrogating Aster. And there were important things not being said, he felt sure of it. But now wasn't the time. "Sure, Opal. No problem. Really."

Emma was already digging into their store of camping supplies. "We can set up a space for her to sleep." She glanced at the woozy girl. "You shouldn't leave the houseboat just yet, Aster. A *lot* has changed since your time, and it might be too much to handle all at once."

"Stay away from the Darkdeep," Tyler warned, though he seemed unsure whether he was being understood. "In fact, don't go downstairs at all. It's super dangerous."

If Aster heard either of them, she gave no sign. She'd curled into a ball with her head on Opal's thigh. A moment later her breathing softened and she appeared to be asleep. Emma laid out a sleeping bag, then helped Opal slowly ease the older girl down into its warm cocoon.

Opal glanced up. "You boys can go now."

It wasn't a request.

"Gee, thanks," Logan shot back. But he wilted at Opal's flared eyebrow. "Okay, okay!"

Feeling vaguely affronted, Nico gathered his things and led Tyler and Logan to the curtain. He paused and glanced back at the three girls, one snoring gently, the other two huddled over her like worried hens.

Nico sighed. "We need to learn more about . . . everything, guys. And soon. We're no closer to answers than when we dove into the Darkdeep."

Opal nodded. "Tomorrow."

Nico waved goodbye. Then he ducked through the curtain and headed for the door.

# 18

## OPAL

Opal swore under her breath.

*Crap! Not now.*

Looking out her bedroom window, she saw a grinning, googly-eyed dollar sign bouncing down Overlook Row. The figment—for that's obviously what it was—must've sprung from their trip through the Darkdeep yesterday, and she was pretty sure whose mind had created it.

"Nice job, Logan," Opal muttered, rushing to grab the Torchbearer dagger she kept hidden in her desk. *An impossible-to-explain creature, on the loose right here in town. Just what we need.* At least this one came from someone inside their group, meaning it should be easier for them to dispel. She hurried downstairs and outside, ready to jab the thing and send it packing.

Logan appeared on his porch a few houses down, gripping his hair as the goofy dollar sign boinged happily toward him, humming tunelessly. He was wearing full SpongeBob pajamas.

"That has to be yours!" Opal whispered-shouted, pointing repeatedly at the prancing figment. *"Get it get it get it."*

"I think about more than just money, you know!" But Logan vaulted down to the sidewalk and crouched in front of the capering cash symbol. "For example, I was just dreaming that the two of us got stuck on a Ferris wheel overnight, and we had to convince a talking caterpillar to help us down. So this doofus doesn't *have* to be my idea. Now gimme that knife!"

*Overnight?* Opal felt a weird twinge as she hurried to join him. "Just take care of it. Here!"

She tossed him the dagger. Logan caught it deftly and lunged at the sparkling dollar sign. It took a couple of tries—the glowing nightmare kept bobbing around like a deranged kangaroo—but Logan finally tapped the blade against its side and the figment blipped out of existence. Opal and Logan breathed twin sighs of relief.

Opal gave Logan a once-over, then covered her mouth. "Nice jammies."

Logan didn't flinch. "SpongeBob rocks. I'll wear these until they fall apart."

"There's gotta be more figments out there," Opal said, doing a quick scan of the block to make sure they hadn't been observed. Thankfully, it was early enough on a Saturday morning that the street was still empty. No other figments were in sight, either.

"Four at least." Logan frowned. "Five, if Aster made one on her way back from the Void—I'm not sure how that works. And that joker almost made it into Timbers."

"I take it you still need to change?" On their way home the night before, she and Logan had planned a trip to the public library to double-check Aster's story. It wasn't that Opal didn't trust their new friend, but it never hurt to be sure.

*Are we friends? Can I call her that?*

"I wonder what mine'll be," Opal muttered anxiously. "I wasn't thinking of anything specific when I jumped into the Darkdeep, just that we needed to get through the well and reach the Rift. It could be anything. At least yours is handled."

"We don't know stupid Dollar Guy was mine," Logan insisted stubbornly, before pivoting and stomping back into his house. Minutes later he reemerged in a BEAST PATROL sweatshirt he'd designed himself. Without another word, he started quickly up the street.

Opal had to jog-trot to catch up with him. "Okay, fine. *Sorry.* It's not a big deal."

They reached the end of the Row, where it met Main Street. Opal glanced both ways, and also up at the sky, making sure there weren't any other rogue figments close by.

"Your figment will probably be a giant notebook," Logan muttered, his jaw tight. "Or, like, a . . . a *nagging* monster."

Opal whirled to glare at him. Logan shrugged. He looked away with a small smirk.

"My figments are never that literal," Opal snapped, gripping her braid. "You just have a very *basic* mind."

Logan clamped both hands over his heart. "Ouch. Sick burn."

They turned the corner and headed uphill toward town square. Logan's foul mood didn't lessen. "Nico's figment is probably *super* basic. Like, a walking billboard that says, 'I blame Logan for everything.'"

"Maybe it'll be his house, asking him not to move away," Opal shot back. Now *she* was mad.

Logan went silent. Opal stole a glance at him, and saw that his face had completely fallen. In spite of herself, she felt bad. The morning was off to a terrible start.

Logan had lived through a rough few days himself, with his dad falling apart and raving about the end of the world. Her anger at the Nantes family felt like a cheap shot to use against him.

"I shouldn't have said that. I know you feel bad about the transfer."

"I didn't have anything to do with it," Logan mumbled. "I wish people would believe me."

"*I* do."

But did she? Opal knew Logan had taunted Nico about his dad possibly getting shipped out of town, in what felt like a lifetime ago, back before they were all Torchbearers. He'd cornered Nico in the school cafeteria and *really* been a jerk. But they'd gotten over it and become friends since then, or so she'd thought.

Nico clearly hadn't forgiven everything.

She and Logan continued toward the town center. Reaching the library, they found the place empty. Of course—it was the Saturday after Thanksgiving. Opal sighed in relief that the building was even open. Old Lady Johnson, the librarian, must have as little else to do as Mrs. Cartwright in the Nantes museum.

"Hello, Opal!" Emelda Johnson wore a red sweater with twinkling lights stitched across its front. The last time Opal had come by, the gray-haired librarian had worn an orange vest covered in sequined pilgrim hats. "Did you have a nice Thanksgiving?"

"You bet," Opal said with false cheer.

"Probably our last," Logan muttered.

"Did *you* have a good holiday?" Opal said quickly, stepping slightly in front of him.

"Oh my, yes," Emelda said. "I still have my sister in town, so I'm afraid the library will be closing early today. You're the only ones to come by anyway."

"We'll be quick," Opal promised.

Ms. Johnson sat back down in her chair. "Go on ahead. But please don't dawdle! I'm already hankering for a leftover turkey sandwich."

Opal led Logan toward a quiet corner of the building that

housed a local history section. The creaky stacks smelled like old paper and polished wood. She passed the bulky leather chair where she'd spent hours reading as a kid, patting its arm like an old friend.

"This is a waste of time," Logan griped. "I definitely want to fact-check Aster's story as much as you do, but what can we look at in here that we haven't already?"

"I'll show you."

Opal led him down a narrow, rarely used aisle. She pulled a dusty book from a shelf crammed with them, but replaced it after a cursory glance. Moving deeper into the gloom, Opal scanned the cracked spines and flaking titles, towing a reluctant Logan in her wake. Finally, she spotted what she was after: *Shipwrecks of the Pacific Northwest*. Within moments she'd located the correct chapter.

"We're not *fact-checking* the girl we rescued, Logan." Opal felt weird phrasing it that way. "We're merely seeking additional, corroborating information."

Logan sniffed. "You might be. I'm here to see if she's telling the truth. I don't trust her."

Opal shot him an icy glare. "Aster's dad went down with the *Dauphin*, Logan. Maybe some of her friends, too. Can you imagine being trapped alone on another world, then coming back to find out everyone you knew was gone?"

"Doesn't mean she's being honest." Logan tapped the book in her hands. "Impress me."

"There's only one page about the *Dauphin*." Opal began reading aloud. *"In 1741, a shipwreck occurred in Skagit Sound, near a stretch of coastline that would later be incorporated as the hamlet of Timbers, Washington. The only survivor, a governess named Yvette Dumont, became a founding settler in the area, but the vessel—a deep sea trader named the* Dauphin*—was a total loss. The only debris to ever wash ashore were empty trunks marked with the logo of the Dutch East India Company. How the* Dauphin *came to be in the region at all is an enduring mystery, as the company did not operate in the seas of the Pacific Northwest at that time. Throughout her long life, Ms. Dumont refused to speak publicly of her experience."*

"You see?" Opal said, slapping the book closed. "When I read that passage earlier, I thought it was random trivia and not super useful. But those facts matter now—they confirm Aster's story."

Logan looked skeptical. "That's pretty weak info, Opal. There's nothing about a whirlpool or anything."

Opal straightened her shoulders. "Most of the wreckage was probably sucked into the Rift along with Aster. That's why almost nothing was found, not even those poor people's bodies. What else could explain it?"

Logan made a face. "Sharks."

"Gross."

Logan snorted. "For all we know, Dumont sunk the

ship on purpose. *Her* story doesn't totally check out, either."

Opal rolled her eyes. Then they nearly popped from her skull as she remembered something. "I forgot!"

She dropped to a knee, ripped open her backpack, and removed the passenger manifest Tyler had discovered in his Beast book. The first name immediately caught her eye. "Tyler reminded me of this yesterday. Logan, *look*." She stuck the sheet in his face. "The captain of the *Dauphin* is listed as Lieutenant Commodore Henri Caraway. It's right here in black and white." Opal ran her finger down the page. "And there she is—Aster Caraway, student, age fifteen."

"That's what Tyler found?" Logan frowned at the list. "Okay. Fine. Unless she gave us a fake name."

Opal squeezed her fingers into balls, holding them up before her as she squinted at Logan in annoyance. "And what *possible* purpose would that serve?"

"I dunno. Maybe she's an outlaw. Or a pirate." He snapped his fingers. "An outlaw pirate *running from* outlawed pirates."

"Genius. You've cracked the case." Then Opal's expression grew pensive. "Aster must've had a really interesting life."

"Lonely, if you ask me."

Opal glanced at Logan in surprise. "Why do you say that?"

He shrugged. "If her story is true, it doesn't feel like a

happy one. Aster went to boarding school when she was just a little kid, and her dad captained for a global trading company. He was probably gone most of her life. I bet she begged onto that last voyage just to get to know him. Her mother definitely wouldn't have been invited—not on an active trading vessel. Just this governess Dumont, whom we know wasn't exactly Mary Poppins."

Opal quickly scanned the manifest. "No other Caraway is listed," she confirmed, then looked at Logan. "I guess I never thought of it that way."

Logan scratched his head. "Kids were often distanced from their parents back then. Aster has no siblings that we know of, and how do you make close friends when you're shipped around the globe all the time? It's not like they had cell phones to keep in touch. Like I said—lonely."

Opal placed the book back on the shelf. She'd think about what Logan said later. How did he understand Aster so well? The thought gave her pause. Did *Logan* feel lonely, like he assumed Aster did?

"We should get going," Logan said. "I don't want to stand between Old Lady Johnson and her leftovers."

Opal shook her head to clear it. "Okay. So. We have double confirmation of Aster's story—from a history book and the manifest. Her dad was captain of the *Dauphin*, a trading vessel for the Dutch East India Company that sank in Skagit Sound in 1741. Aster Caraway was also a passenger and thought to be lost at sea. Only she's here with us, now, in Timbers."

Logan leaned back against a shelf. "It's not like we have pictures proving it's really her or anything." At a glare from Opal he added, "But she does seem to be telling the truth. I'll give you that. I just wish I knew what was bugging me about the whole thing."

"Opal? Logan?" Emelda Johnson's round face appeared at the head of the aisle. "Time to go, please."

"Yes ma'am." Opal strode quickly out of the stacks. She didn't want anyone else thinking she was on a dating barrage with Logan Nantes.

"It's nice to see young people take an interest in this region's history," Mrs. Johnson said, smiling contentedly. "Maude mentioned that you two been by the timber museum."

Opal and Logan exchanged a glance. *Great*. The Timbers senior gossip network had noticed their interests. *And associations*. Opal's face reddened slightly.

"School project," she explained with a hasty smile. "Extra credit."

"Even better when the schools get involved." Reaching the entrance, the elderly librarian held open the door. "Button up those coats, dears. Wouldn't want you to get wet. I hear there's more nasty weather on the way."

Out on the steps, Opal turned to Logan. "So? Should we get the others?"

Logan was tapping on his phone. He pulled up a website about the old Dutch East India Company and its logo appeared—a large, dark *V* superimposed over an *O* on the left and *C* on the right.

"Let's see if the owners of the *Dauphin* ever filed an insurance claim after it sank," he said. "If a document like that exists somewhere, it'd list any lost cargo, and explain what the ship was supposed to be doing on its voyage. Then we could quiz Aster and see if her answers line up."

"How long do you plan on mistrusting her?" Opal shoved her hands into her pockets so she wouldn't punch Logan in the arm. Why was he being the worst?

"Until I'm 100 percent sure," Logan replied. "We need to be more confident than 'probably' where the Darkdeep is concerned."

Opal grunted in exasperation. Turning her back on him, she pulled out her phone and messaged Nico.

Aster's story seems to check out. What have you and Tyler found?

"Who are you texting?" Logan asked.

Opal didn't answer, popping her phone back into her pocket. "Let's go."

They descended to a small courtyard beside the library. The snow on the grass hadn't melted yet. In fact, it seemed *not* to be melting. Opal bent down to touch it. It wasn't the heavy, wet snow they usually got in late fall, if they got any at all. This was powdery and fine, the kind you saw people slaloming through at the Olympics.

"*Opal*," Logan rasped in a strangled voice. "You're not gonna believe this. She's here!"

"Who's here? Another figment?" But a second later, she saw.

Aster Caraway was strolling across town square, plain as day, hands tucked inside the jacket Opal had lent her, a wide-brimmed work hat covering her head. Where had she found that?

*I'm dreaming*, Opal thought. But there was no mistaking Aster's rigid bearing, or the old-fashioned boots on her feet.

"What's she doing here?!" Logan hissed. "We told her to stay on the houseboat!"

"No idea. Come on." Opal arrowed straight for the older girl. "Maybe she's lost? Or got scared?"

"You'd think everything about Timbers would freak her out." Logan waved at the vehicles and businesses lining the park. "Like, she doesn't even know about streetlights. How is she just cruising around, totally unfazed?"

Opal scoffed. "She managed to survive alone on an alien planet in another dimension. I'm sure she's seen worse."

"Well, let's get her the heck out of here. Cool cucumber or not, she's going to attract attention eventually."

"You're right. Let's hurry." Opal began walking faster.

A block ahead of them, Aster was casually peering around, glancing at store windows and a group of passing cyclists. Opal and Logan jogged past a gaggle of kids in parkas making snow angels, and a puffy, chubby dog wriggling joyfully in the drifts alongside them.

*Wait.*

Opal skidded to a stop. Swung around.

"Weird-looking dog," Logan said, also glancing back.

Opal felt her pulse thump at her temples. "That's no dog."

The wriggling creature had a wide, snuffly nose. Deep indigo fur. And very sharp teeth.

Logan coughed into his fist. "Is . . . is that a—"

"It's a freaking Dog Beast." Opal shook her head. "For crying out loud, Tyler."

Sensing their attention, the figment blinked ginormous black eyes at them. It was almost kind of cute, if you ignored the slathering jaws that could rip off an arm in one bite.

"Right in the center of town. We have to dispel it!" Logan angled slowly toward the monster, a hand sliding into his jacket. "Hey buddy. Good boy. Here Beastie, Beastie."

The creature tilted its head at Logan. Then the Dog Beast yapped manically and took off across the park, bombing in the direction of a giant toddler snowball fight taking place near the monkey bars.

Logan raced after it, calling over his shoulder. "Come on, Opal. Help me!"

Opal glanced back at where Aster had been, but the girl was lost from sight. There was no choice to make. The figment had to take priority.

But as Opal began sprinting after Logan, she could only think of one thing.

*What is Aster doing?*

# 19

## NICO

Nico scampered back from the frigid surf.

*I can't believe we're doing this again.*

Tyler stood at the high-tide line, wrapped in his ceremonial scarlet bathrobe. Emma was side-stepping in a slow circle around him, recording on her phone as he lifted an algae-soaked stick with the Torchbearer's Beast flag tied to its tip. Tyler had his eyes closed, as if in deep concentration, but he periodically shot annoyed glances at the unwelcome videographer.

"Filming me is a terrible idea," Tyler finally snapped at Emma. "What if your mom checks your phone?"

"If this somehow works, don't you want to know what you did right?" Emma pinched her fingers against the screen, then looked up with a calm smile. "Besides, I password protect. I'm not a noob."

"You can't keep anything secure online," Nico grumbled,

popping his jacket collar to deflect the frosty breeze. "Yesterday I searched for a story about LeBron, and now my Instagram feed is nothing but basketball-shoe ads. Everything gets data-mined."

"Don't forget the cloud!" Tyler added, hitching his dad's terry-cloth robe farther up on his shoulders. "*Everything* goes into the cloud, and nobody has a clue what it is."

"You guys are so paranoid." Emma began taking a panoramic shot of the motionless, fog-shrouded expanse of Still Cove. The beach was silent and cold. They rarely took the rowboat out to the island anymore—the tunnel was far more convenient than a back-breaking paddle across open water—but this was the second time Tyler had dragged Nico over the ridge that week. He was determined to contact the Beast.

The Beast, however, didn't seem as interested in a reunion.

Nico watched Emma's documentary efforts with growing irritation. "This better not wind up on your show, Emma."

Her head whipped to face him, blue eyes narrowing to slits. "Are you implying I would *lie* to you, Nico? Is that what you're saying?"

Nico felt his cheeks heat up. "No. But you haven't exactly been mistake free when it comes to keeping Torchbearer secrets."

"Nice of you to remind me," Emma replied coolly. She clicked her phone into rest mode and shoved it into her jeans. "When we miss a big moment, just remember it was *your* call."

Tyler resumed waving his totem overhead in a slow figure eight. "Beeeeast. Beeeeast," he murmured, almost like a mantra. "Come on, big guy. Sun's going down."

"It's eleven thirty in the morning," Nico muttered, confused.

"Shush," Tyler shot back. "I'm trying to connect on a metaphysical level."

"Kindred spirits."

"You don't need to be here, Nico."

"You specifically asked me to be here, Tyler."

Emma snorted. "Maybe it *is* better I'm not recording this."

Tyler tossed his flag-stick to the wet sand. "This is pointless. I can't do it. I'm no Beastmaster, and that's all there is to say."

Nico felt a rush of sympathy for his friend. "Hey, we're not even sure if the Beast is still around. He's been missing since the Rift fight. He could be circling Taiwan right now, for all we know."

Tyler shook his head. "We both saw that wake last time, right at the end. It must've been him." He slapped his hands together in frustration. "I bet Thing knows *exactly* how to do this. I wish we'd had more time inside the Void. I'd have wrung answers from that little booger's scrawny neck."

Emma sighed, kicking a loose pebble. "Well, I hope the Beast isn't gone. It'd be a huge loss to the town."

Tyler whirled, losing his temper. "The Beast is not a tourist attraction, Emma. Or a cool story, or a way to get clicks. It's a living, breathing being that saved our butts on that oil rig. Stop treating our most important ally as an *object*!"

Emma's face went beet-red, then very still, as if she were trying not to cry.

Nico stared at Tyler. He'd never seen his friend blow up at Emma like that. Those two were as close as siblings. Maybe closer. *But siblings fight. And when they do, it can be worse than anything.* Arguments with his brother, Rob, had devolved into wrestling matches more times than Nico could count.

Nico lifted his palms. "Okay, let's all calm down. Maybe we should take a break from—"

"I *never* treat the Beast like an object," Emma seethed, practically spitting the words. She turned and stormed toward the forest, and the path leading back over the ridge that encircled the pond. She'd nearly reached the dark trunks when she stopped dead. Went rigid.

Tyler reached a hand out toward her. "Emma, I'm sorry. I shouldn't ha—"

"Shhhhhh!" Emma waved him off without turning.

Nico chewed his bottom lip, at a loss. "Emma? Do you . . . are you okay?"

"Just be quiet!" Emma hissed. "For like one single second!"

Tyler seemed to bristle. "Look, I admit was rude, but it's not like . . ." He trailed off, eyes going wide.

Nico didn't know what was going on. Then he heard the sand shift as Emma hauled butt back to where he and Tyler were standing. "Tell me someone brought a dagger!" she shouted.

A heavy branch flew from the understory and landed in the water. Dark laughter followed.

Colors and shadows began to flicker among the trees.

*Figments.*

"Not good," Tyler whispered. "And no, we don't have our daggers."

Emma gasped as shadows in the tree began to blend. "Where did these guys come from?"

"The Darkdeep," Nico said. "We went in again, remember? Here's the result."

A noise was rising—a harsh symphony of shrieks and squawks. Nico felt his stomach lurch. Why hadn't they brought their only useful weapons? How many figments were massing in there? There was nowhere to run but into the icy cove. *We'd be snow cones in minutes.*

Tyler shielded his eyes, squinting at the snow-slicked boles. "I don't like this. What are they this time?"

"Depends on what we were thinking about, right?" Emma's foot was tapping spastically. She licked her lips. "We should draw them into the open, so we can at least see what we're up against."

"But what if they charge?" Tyler squeaked, shrinking into

his robe. "Because we don't want a group of angry figments to charge."

"We don't have a lot of options," Nico whispered. "We have to get around them somehow, then sprint back to the houseboat. We can arm ourselves or wait it out there."

Emma took a tentative step forward. "Hello? Come out, come out, whatever you are!"

All noise from the woods ceased. Nico felt his blood turn to ice. The sudden silence was even creepier than the yowling had been.

"Do you think they left?" Nico breathed.

"Nico." Emma was staring at something in the forest canopy. "What is *that*?"

A huge bird of prey was perched on the topmost branch of a massive oak. Twice the size of a bald eagle, the massive predator was glaring at them with glossy eyes. As Nico watched, its gaze flashed golden-yellow, pulsing with an internal light that sent shivers down his spine.

Nico opened his mouth to point out the figment, but then stopped. A harsh peppery odor was billowing down from the treetops.

Nico could swear the bird *smirked* at him. Then it dropped out of sight.

He went cold all over.

That smell. Those yellow eyes.

*Whatever these things are, I don't think they came from our minds.*

"Did you see it?" Nico whispered.

Emma nodded, face pale.

Tyler wiped sweat from his brow. "Maybe it's time we went for a jog down the bea—"

A deep, bone-shaking growl carried from the water at their backs.

Nico stiffened. Turned slowly.

*The Beast.*

It was right behind them.

Water drained from the sea monster's back as it crouched menacingly, razor-sharp claws gouging furrows in the sand. A snarl escaped the creature's mouth, so low its vibration rattled Nico's toenails.

Nico lost all capacity to think. *Not again. Trapped on the beach.*

A sharp rustling shook the trees. Whatever creature had been there was gone.

Tyler faced the Beast, arms shaking as he raised one hand. "H-hi there. Mr. Beast. I m-mean, hello. I'm T-Tyler. I've been . . . t-trying to g-g-get in touch."

The Beast's eyes locked onto the trembling boy as he stooped to retrieve his algae stick. Tyler raised it cautiously, and then wiggled the banner ever-so-gently until the flag unfurled.

The Beast blinked. Snorted.

Then, impossibly, the sea monster settled down in the surf like a cat.

A keening noise echoed from its throat. One massive paw lifted from the shallows, gripping a silvery-scaled fish.

The Beast dropped it onshore.

Emma was shaking from head to toe. "Tyler, whatever you did, um . . . keep doing it."

Tyler didn't respond. From the look in his eyes, he was somewhere else entirely. A slow smile spread across his face. Tyler abruptly strode forward, walking down to the water line. After the barest of hesitations, he placed a hand on the Beast's snout.

Nico stopped breathing. His blood stopped pumping. The cells in his body stopped dividing.

The Beast quivered under Tyler's touch. Then it seemed to calm.

"Hi," Tyler said simply.

The Beast growled, but ducked its head lower under Tyler's hand.

"This is it," Tyler whispered. "I really am a Beastmaster."

The Beast pulled back abruptly, tossing its head and thundering so loudly that the forest shook. Then the sea monster turned and swam back out into the cove, disappearing under a line of wake so soft that the ripples faded in moments.

Leaving three stunned kids on the beach, trying to get their hearts restarted.

# 20

## OPAL

Found her.

Opal hit send and put her phone away. She was lurking behind a van parked across the street from Pacific Pizza. She'd located Aster only a moment before—the girl from another time was glued to the restaurant's front window, and seemed to be breathing in the smells.

Opal's stomach growled. She clapped a hand over it. There'd been no time for lunch.

*Maybe that's why she left the houseboat.* Did Aster simply crave better food than the snacks they'd left her?

Opal didn't think so. Even as she watched, Aster turned from the storefront and looked around, a canvas tote bag draped over one shoulder. Opal was sure Aster hadn't been carrying it earlier that afternoon, before the figment appeared. Where had it come from? What was inside it?

Aster glanced up at the sky, as if she were trying to estimate the time of day. Opal got the distinct impression she was on the hunt for something else—something *specific*. But what?

Opal's phone vibrated. A response from Logan: Where?? Tie her to a lamppost!

Hoping to cover more ground, she and Logan had split up after running down and dispelling the Dog Beast. And it worked—Logan had caught sight of Aster first, outside the Custom House. He'd called Opal after spotting the older girl waltzing out the front doors, as calm as could be. Then she'd somehow given him the slip. They were determined not to lose her again.

Opal studied Aster. She was still wearing that ridiculous floppy hat, yet somehow pulled it off. No one was taking much notice of her. Aster's confidence helped her blend in with the crowd. *The girl has guts.*

Aster didn't seem fazed by the modern chaos surrounding her. Opal was amazed she'd managed to locate Timbers at all—the town was five miles north of Still Cove, and it wasn't like there were road signs pointing the way. Plus, how did Aster locate the secret tunnel off the island? Or had she used the rowboat? Opal wasn't sure whether they'd left it on the beach or not. *So many questions.*

That's why Opal elected to hang back a bit and observe her quarry. She hoped Aster would decide to return to the houseboat on her own, but the girl didn't seem in any hurry to leave town.

*And what's inside that stupid bag? Tell me she didn't go shoplifting!*

The door to the pizzeria opened and Aster stepped deftly away. Opal's heart skipped a beat. Evan Martinez exited and began attaching three large boxes to the back of his bicycle. Opal dove completely behind the van to avoid being seen. But she couldn't resist peeking once again.

*He's a delivery boy now? Maybe I should get a job there, too.*

Evan straddled his bike and pulled on his helmet, adjusting the strap. Quick as a wink, Aster's hands darted out. She grabbed the top pizza box and slipped it from the pile, then ducked into a narrow alley beside the store as Evan pedaled away.

Opal stifled a laugh. Wow. Poor Evan when he got to his delivery.

*But Aster can't just go around stealing.* Opal was about to cross the street and tell her so when Aster reappeared with the pilfered pizza and began strolling down the block, acting natural, like she'd done nothing wrong and had every right to be there. Smack dab in the middle of Timbers, almost three hundred years after she'd been born in France.

Opal texted Logan: Town Square. Bring handcuffs.

"What are you doing?" a voice demanded suddenly.

She wheeled to find Carson Brandt looming behind her. His sunburned face was shot through with pale splotches, and freckles stood out on his nose. Carson's sandy hair looked like it hadn't been combed in days.

Opal felt sorry for the guy. He'd seen the worst of Dark Halloween, and it was definitely haunting him.

"Just looking for a friend." Opal tried to smile politely and brush past him at the same time. She spotted Aster at one of the picnic tables near the square's small pavilion, eating her stolen meal with evident pleasure.

"You mean Holland?" Carson whispered a bit too loud. He and Parker used to torment Nico alongside Logan, but Carson's eyes were weirdly hopeful at the moment. "I need to find him, too."

Opal stopped short. "You do? Why?"

"He and Logan . . . they helped me that night on the beach." Carson's eyes were restless, as if he couldn't stop them from moving. "This crazy sphinx thing was attacking me, but Nico knew what to do. He knows about nature. It's even, like, his dad's *job*." Carson stepped closer to Opal and dropped his voice even lower. "Strange stuff is still happening, Opal. This morning, I swear I saw some kind of dog monster playing in the snow. I *have* to talk to Nico."

Opal stole a glance back into the park. Aster had nearly finished the whole pizza. She rose, leaving the crust-filled box on the table—first larceny, now littering!—and strode toward the woods at the north end of the park. Then Opal spotted

Logan over by the swings, panting and tugging on the knees of his jeans. Their eyes met as Aster vanished into the trees.

Logan pointed at Aster and gave a thumbs-up, trotting for the snow-covered woods.

Opal realized Carson was still standing right next to her, eyeing her with rekindled suspicion.

"Carson, I have to go, okay? Take it easy."

"Wait!" His hands balled into fists, desperation edging his voice. "Tell Nico I *really* need to speak with him! I was wrong to fight against you guys. We need to join forces and form a plan."

"Will do." Opal pointed in the opposite direction of where Aster and Logan had gone. "And hey, I think I just saw Emma heading down toward the docks. Maybe she knows where Nico is. Gotta go!"

When Carson looked away, Opal darted across the street and up the block, skirting town square plaza. Reaching the forest, she scurried over to the trail that Aster and Logan had taken. Winter-brittle branches dumped wet snow on Opal's head as she pushed through the foliage. She rounded a corner and emerged into a clearing, nearly running smack into Logan and Aster, who were standing there facing each other.

Arms crossed, Aster was casually leaning one shoulder against a tree. Logan yawned, hands in his pockets, attempting to mirror her blasé.

"Hello," Aster greeted Opal, without a hint of surprise.

"Logan and I were just discussing the importance of respecting personal space."

Logan chuckled dryly. "Our new friend here doesn't like being followed."

He sounded almost . . . charmed. *That stupid French accent.*

Opal suddenly felt guilty. "We weren't following you."

Aster raised an eyebrow. Opal's face heated up like a furnace.

"Not at first," Opal amended awkwardly. "But you were supposed to stay on the houseboat!"

"I already asked what she's doing in town." Logan was still playing it cool. "Apparently, she's having a look-see."

Aster nodded. "I am being a—how do you say? Sight-goer? Is that the right word?"

"Not quite." Logan coughed into his fist. "We usually say 'tourist' now, but 'sightseer' works too. So what's in the bag? Kind of hard to shop when you don't have any money."

"I found a few things that interest me." A smear of tomato sauce daubed Aster's chin, but she still sounded refined. "I like exploring my surroundings whenever possible. My father always urged me to experience a place as if one lived there. Go where they go. Eat the foods they enjoy." She wiped her mouth with the back of her wrist. "He taught me to see a place as it is, instead of how others might wish it to be."

Sadness infused Aster's voice as she spoke of her father. Opal felt a yank at her heartstrings, but also something else.

Distrust.

She didn't think Aster was telling the whole truth.

"We should return to the boat," Opal said diplomatically. "It's not safe for you out here."

Aster pouted slightly. "But I have not finished my tourist."

"Tour," Logan corrected with a grin. He was clearly warming to the girl.

Opal tried to be reasonable. No one liked feeling like a captive. "What else would you like to see? We can show you around ourselves." She pivoted on the trail. "Shall we visit the timber museum? The marina?"

"You've already visited the Custom House," Logan slid in. "Interesting choice."

Aster's expression sharpened, then smoothed to a pleasant blankness. "Perhaps another time. It *is* a long way back, and that exquisite meal—what is it called?—has made me tired."

*The meal you stole.* But Opal just smiled encouragingly.

"It's called pizza," Logan blurted. "Pepperoni pizza is the best."

"Pizza," Aster repeated, as if tasting the word. "Wonderful. Do they serve it every day?"

Logan nodded vigorously. The kid was all over the place.

"How'd you get here from the Cove?" Opal asked. The question had been driving her nuts.

"I have been reading to make my boredom less." Aster

221

removed a hand-drawn map from her pocket. *Not the shoulder bag*, Opal noted.

"This was on the house-ship," Aster continued. "I believe friend Tyler is the artist. It depicts your secret tunnel and a path toward the town. *Timbers.*"

"Pretty gutsy to follow it all by yourself." Opal pulled her jacket tighter against the chill. "But not smart. The town is in a frenzy these days, and strangers attract notice."

"I was careful," Aster replied indulgently. She locked eyes with Opal. "Unless I am a . . . prisoner?"

"Of course not!" Opal sputtered. She heard Logan's chuckle as he covered his mouth. "It's just . . . we don't want anything bad to happen. Staying on the houseboat is simply a precaution."

Aster tilted her head. "Staying near the bottomless black well that leads to a fissure between worlds is . . . the safest place for me?"

Logan bit his lip. "Um."

Before Opal could reply—and she wasn't sure how she was going to—Aster lifted her palms in a gesture of acquiescence. "I understand, of course. I will stay aboard the ship. Especially if you bring more *pizza*." She smiled, eyes twinkling.

"No problem!" Logan said. Opal imagined him paddling out to the island with a delivery box wedged in the rowboat and resisted an urge to roll her eyes.

"Should we all head back now?" Opal said hopefully.

"Do not trouble yourselves." Aster pulled the bag tighter, waving her other hand in a semi-bow. "I have a talent for navigation. I never get lost."

Opal's voice hardened. "It's no trouble. Really. We want to make *sure* you arrive there safe and sound."

And they did. Opal and Logan walked Aster every step of the way, over the hills, through the underground tunnel, and down to the stepping stones across the pond. At the houseboat's front door, Aster paused. "Would you like to come inside?"

Opal felt a stab of resentment. *She* was inviting *them* in?

"I have to go home," Opal said, trying to regain the upper ground. "We'll see you tomorrow."

Aster nodded, gently shutting the door. Not quite in their faces, but close enough.

"I wonder if she'd like a cheeseburger?" Logan mused, nearly losing his footing as they hopped back across the stepping stones. "I could bring one by tomorrow, so she could try it out."

Opal rubbed the bridge of her nose. "I can hardly wait."

Logan snorted. She ignored him, glancing back at the houseboat.

A lamp glimmered in the bay window, outlining a lone silhouette.

Aster was watching them leave.

# 21

## NICO

Nico stepped from the secret tunnel.

The island was cloaked in a swirling mist as chilly as the bottom of the ocean.

Opal and the others emerged behind him in a ragged line. The bike ride from Timbers had been done in silence, the rising sun still blocked by the eastern hills. Opal and Logan appeared to be in the middle of some argument they weren't discussing, while Tyler had caught Emma shooting footage of the Pacific as they rode, and it had turned his mood foul.

Everyone seemed on the verge of a tantrum, but checking on Aster came first. Nico was still shaken that the strange girl had been exploring Timbers without them. Assembling the group that early had been a huge challenge—Nico hadn't been allowed out of his house all afternoon the day before—but they were finally together.

Nico was hoping the full weight of the group might help

keep Aster in check. *But she doesn't seem interested in listening to us.*

Tyler glanced around as they stood at the foot of the ridge. "Why's it so quiet today?"

Logan waved a hand at the trees. "It's freezing out. The owls must be sleeping in."

"Owls are nocturnal," Nico snapped, but he nodded uncertainly at Tyler. They all knew figments were on the loose. *Three more at least. And maybe that bird. And the wolf. And a bobcat?* "We'd better get to the boat. Hopefully Emma's donuts will put Aster in a stationary mood."

Emma held up the box. "I brought three jelly-filled, just in case."

"We can't keep her here forever," Opal said with a frown. "We need a long-term plan."

Nico sighed. "One thing at a time. Aster comes first, then we need to discuss the cave at Yellowstone. If there really *is* another group of Torchbearers out there, evidence of them has to be hidden somewhere here in Timbers. Letters. A list of names. Logbooks. Logan's grandfather obviously knew a second Rift existed. We need to find his private papers, or *something.*"

"I *have* been looking," Logan answered in a frosty tone. "But anything my granddad might've written down about the Order will be buried where people aren't supposed to find it. Obviously."

Tyler tugged on his ear. "Guys, something is up. Can't you feel it?"

Nico paused. Now that Tyler mentioned it—*twice*—he did feel a creeping sensation on his skin. The air had a strange crackle to it. Like the atmosphere was stretched thin. Nico got a bad feeling in his stomach.

"Come on." He began climbing up the steep-sided gully.

Even with a map, Nico was surprised Aster had actually managed to locate the tunnel at the bottom of this slope. She was resourceful, and headstrong to boot. Not one to take orders she didn't agree with. Nico's anxiety grew.

They reached the top of the ridge, but fog as thick as soup covered the ground. Nico couldn't see ten feet in front of him. Descending the other side quickly, they reached the field beside the pond. With every step, Nico felt an eerie tension ramping up around him. He was getting thoroughly freaked out.

The mists abruptly parted halfway to the stepping stones, though the houseboat was still only a vague shadow out on the water.

But Nico wasn't looking at their clubhouse.

He was staring at a host of figments meandering the beaten grass.

Tyler's jaw dropped. "What in the *what*?"

"So many," Emma murmured, eyes wide. "There should be only five!"

"Three," Nico countered. "Logan and Opal already dealt with two figments in town. But this . . . this is . . ."

Opal swung her backpack around. "Daggers out!"

Logan glanced at Nico, then back at the mob of imaginary creatures. "Do these ones look . . . *different* to anyone else?"

Nico blinked. He focused on what he was seeing. Logan was right. These figments were all people.

"Oh no." Opal covered her mouth as she pointed to the water's edge.

Aster was perched on a small trunk, dripping wet and shivering under a sodden blanket. She was smiling.

Tyler slapped a hand to his scalp. "Good gravy, she did it. She went into the Darkdeep!"

Emma seemed to be counting in her head. "Quite a few times, by the looks of it. Incredible."

As they watched, Aster rose and opened the trunk, removing a tea kettle. She poured something into a chipped porcelain teacup and offered it to a nearby figment. To Nico's complete astoundment, the shimmering gentleman—he was wearing some sort of old-timey doublet and leg hose—took the cup from her and put it to his lips.

The man sipped. Steaming liquid poured through his ghostly body, forming a small puddle on the ground.

Nico was gobsmacked. *What was that?*

Aster began passing out tea to more figments, all of

whom nodded in thanks and took the proffered cups. Nico's stunned gaze shot to Opal, who stared back at him in astonishment. "They're *holding* the cups," she breathed. "Like it's no big deal!"

None of the figments noticed the Torchbearers as they huddled in a disbelieving mass, gaping at the impossible event taking place before them. Aster seemed as happy as a lark, though her lips were blue, and her teeth were chattering loud enough for Nico to hear them twenty yards away.

"Is she crazy?" Tyler squawked. "She used the Darkdeep to . . . to . . . *throw a tea party*!"

Aster finally glanced their way, and Nico saw her flinch. She rose unhurriedly and walked over to join them.

"Hello," she greeted coolly. "Good morning to you all."

"Good morning?!" Tyler exploded. "Is *that* all you have to say?"

Aster affected a puzzled look, but it didn't reach her eyes. Nico felt his temper slip a notch. *She knows what she's done. And she doesn't care what we think about it.*

Logan took a step forward, a stone Torchbearer dagger gripped tightly in his fist. "Let's deal with these figments first."

Aster raised a palm. "There is no need. We are finished."

She spun and rejoined the unearthly gathering, circulating among the figments and shaking hands with them. Each time she did, the figment bowed, curtsied, or doffed their hat. Then they disappeared.

Nico put a hand to his nose and squeezed. "Am I awake? Is this really happening?"

Aster finished dismissing her guests. She returned to the group, pulling the wet blanket tight around her shoulders. "If it is all right with you, I shall return to the house-ship. I am terribly cold. Besides, there are unfriendly beasties roaming the woods today." She giggled. "Apparently, *they* do not like tea."

With that, she turned and made her way toward the stepping stones.

"Okay," Emma said, shaking her head in disbelief. "Aster is kind of clutch."

"We'll see about that." Nico growled. "Logan. Emma. Can you keep a lookout for those other figments? Sounds like they're still on the island. I don't want to leave anything wandering freely if we can help it."

Nico thought Logan was about to protest, but he nodded sharply instead. "Fine. Come on, Emma."

"Keep an eye out for strange animals, too!" Tyler warned.

Emma nodded. "I've got an extra dagger up my sleeve with that wolf's name on it." She and Logan moved to the tree line and began scanning for threats.

Nico led Opal and Tyler in pursuit of Aster. He'd chosen the two of them specifically for this confrontation. They'd be just as appalled by Aster's foolishness as he was. *Right?*

Inside the showroom, Aster had changed into dry clothes

and was sitting on the floor, carefully cleaning the tea set. Nico wasn't sure where the porcelain cups had come from—there were still a few trunks he'd never looked inside, an oversight he promised to rectify as soon as possible.

Aster knew what was coming. "Before you say anything, please know that I was very careful."

"Careful?!" Tyler could barely contain his outrage. "You dove into a supernatural well we spent *weeks* getting under control, and we weren't even here! Remember us? The only people who've done it before, and know how the Darkdeep works."

"Kind of know," Opal muttered, though her glare didn't falter.

Aster's expression went blank. "I did not know I needed permission to investigate my own surroundings."

"Well, you do!" Tyler snapped. "You *very much do*."

"You're not a Torchbearer," Nico said quietly, but with steel in his voice. "Only members of the Order are allowed to enter the Darkdeep. It's simply too dangerous, and there's too much at stake."

"Very well," Aster replied, but with no hint of apology. "How do I become one of these Torchbearers?"

Nico stared. No one else spoke. Aster had literally struck them all dumb.

Aster crossed her slender arms. "You have asked me to stay on this ship, but did not tell me about the dangers I might face. There are strange, glowing animals roaming the island, but I have been given nothing to protect myself with. You have withheld information about the unnatural portal below our feet, yet expect me to twiddle my thumbs and wait until you deign to confide in me."

Nico swallowed. "Okay. Some of that is fair. But why'd you think it was smart to jump into an unstable space-time vortex?"

Aster shrugged, resumed cleaning the kettle. She nodded at the Torchbearer logbook resting on Thing's pedestal. "I read every word of your notes. Decided to see for myself. You see? I was not irresponsible. I was informed."

Tyler threw his hands up, but seemed at a loss for words. Opal strode over and gently removed the kettle from Aster's fingers. She let it go without comment, but her eyes blazed.

Nico tried to regain control of the confrontation. When explained calmly and efficiently, Aster's actions didn't seem as crazy as before. "How'd you make those figments so real?" was all he finally managed.

"Pardon?" Aster replied, her brow furrowing.

"The figments had *tea* with you," Tyler blurted, his whole frame thrumming like a bowstring. "They saw you, took a cup, and swigged. How'd you make them so . . . *interactive*?"

"I don't understand," Aster said slowly, glancing at the logbook. "I made a thought, held it hard in my mind, and went into the well. Just as you explained in the pages. My countrymen emerged as I swam out of the lake. That is what I did every time."

Opal glanced at Nico. Mouthed, *She doesn't know what she did is special.*

Nico shrugged, then cut off the exchange with a chop of his hand. Aster was watching them closely.

In spite of himself, Nico was impressed. In less than a day Aster had learned how to both conjure and dispel figments. Shaking hands to banish them had worked just like the daggers. Nico wondered if living on Thing's world for a time had somehow given Aster an important perspective. *She might see possibilities that we don't. Or be in tune with something we aren't?*

A commotion in the foyer pulled him back to the present. Logan and Emma had entered the showroom. At a glance from Nico, Logan shook his head. "Nothing in the woods nearby. But that doesn't mean they aren't still around."

Nico nodded unhappily. Returned his attention to Aster.

"If everyone had been here yesterday," Tyler grumbled, "we could've dealt with *our* figments already."

"Opal and I handled two of them just fine," Logan shot back, giving him an irritated look. "Plus, *we're* the ones who verified—" He darted a glance at Aster, who wore a deepening frown. "Er . . . learned more about Aster's story. Why didn't you three handle the others yourselves?"

"The Beast showed up!" Emma spat. "That's kind of distracting."

Tyler wheeled on her, scoffing. "Like you could be more distracted, Spielberg. You wanted to film it all!"

"The nerve!" Emma turned away. "I'm the only one thinking big picture here."

Nico felt his patience snap. "Is *that* what you call it?"

Logan grunted loudly. "Can we please focus on Furiosa over here? We have to figure out what to do about Aster."

"What to *do* about me?" Aster's voice was a block of ice. "You could stop treating me like a little child, for one."

"She has a point," Opal said, looking troubled. "We haven't told her enough."

"Hey everyone, Opal's taking the new girl's side!" Logan called out sarcastically, rolling his eyes. "Shocker."

Voices erupted in anger, with everyone shouting at once. Nico felt his pulse spike. This was going nowhere. Tensions were bubbling up from deep places and spilling out of control. He was about to add his own spice to the mix when a roar echoed across the pond. The argument died as everyone went still.

The deafening shriek sounded again.

Closer.

Right outside.

# 22

## OPAL

The houseboat groaned and shook.

Opal ran out onto the porch, nearly knocking Nico into the pond in her rush to see what was happening. She pushed up against the railing. "What's out there? Emma, tell me you didn't imagine a kraken or something."

"I was trying to think about bunnies when we dove in," Emma promised. She moved to stand beside Opal, squinting into the rolling mists. "But I *have* been watching a lot of monster movies lately."

"You're always watching monster movies!" Tyler scolded. "Whose figments are still unaccounted for?"

"Nico, Emma, and me," Opal said, ticking names off on her fingers. "Logan had to be Money Man, and the Dog Beast was you, right?"

Tyler shrugged. "Probably. Are we sure the leftover ones are especially bad?"

Logan gave him a look. "Do you *hear* that?"

Thunderous steps shook the island. Trees quaked.

Something silvery gray, like coalescing fog, was moving through the forest.

Nico nervously rubbed his temple. "I wasn't thinking about figments at all when I jumped in. Mine could be anything. Let's get to shore and take a look."

"Watch out for a yeti," Emma warned, as the group crossed the stepping stones. "I've been reading about yetis for my show. They're, um, big."

A voice sounded right in Opal's ear. "How can I assist?" Aster had joined her on the last rock. Opal leaped to dry land, then turned to the older girl. Aster's tone had been wary, but not fearful.

*At least she has* some *sense of self-preservation.*

"These figments resulted from our trip through the Darkdeep to rescue you," Opal said, hoping her point wasn't lost on Aster. "Unless you created more than just tea party friends?"

Aster shook her head. "Nonetheless, I will help."

Opal gave her a searching look, which Aster ignored. The group cautiously approached the woods, eyes roving for signs of danger.

A low, squat creature emerged from the trees—smallish in size, with mothlike wings folded against its back. The figment's mouth took up almost its entire head, and it didn't seem to have any eyes. Every step the monster took was heavy. It was the same dull color as the fog swirling the island. In each paw it gripped another figment, dragging them by the scruffs of their necks.

"Oh wait, *that's* me." Emma pointed to the monster's right fist, where a smiling, koala-faced figment dangled, its shiny pink fur streaked with grime and mud. A golden horn protruded from its forehead.

"I'm pretty sure the other captive's mine," Opal said, her face heating up. It was a giant turkey with pencils sticking out of its rump instead of tail feathers. She heard Logan stifle a laugh. "Still thinking about Thanksgiving, Opal? And, um, office supplies?"

"Shut it."

Opal lifted her Torchbearer dagger. The others did the same.

Aster pointed at Emma's weapon. "Where can I obtain such a poignard?"

"Sorry," Tyler snapped. "We didn't bring extras."

"You can just shake hands with them anyway, right?" Logan said sarcastically.

Opal noticed that Nico hadn't moved. He licked his lips, seemed to hesitate. Opal frowned. The gray creature holding the other two was likely his creation. She eyed the figment again, and felt a shiver travel her spine. It certainly was ugly— and looked more solid than earlier ones—but they'd dealt with similar things before.

Opal told herself that as she took a step forward. *No problem.*

The gray monster screeched suddenly, a sound so piercing that Opal nearly dropped her knife to cover her ears. Then it lifted the fluffy pink figment and stuffed it in its mouth.

"No!" Emma cried in horror. "Don't eat Koalicorn!"

Opal sucked in a breath. She heard Nico do the same. They'd never seen a figment harm another of its kind before.

The gray creature chomped down once, its neck moving in a huge swallow.

"*Gahhhhhh,*" Emma moaned, stamping a foot in distress. "That's not okay, dude!"

Tyler snorted. "If No-Eyes wants to ace the other nightmares for us, let it do whatever!"

"Can they really consume each other?" Opal wondered aloud.

Before anyone could answer, the figment howled a second time. The terrible mouth stretched wide again, expanding almost endlessly as the creature raised its other arm and dropped Opal's pencil-turkey between its gaping jaws.

Logan rubbed sweat from his forehead. "Let's get rid of this guy. He's giving me indigestion."

They moved in. The howler stood rock-still as the circle tightened. Then it bellowed another horrid scream, the teeth-rattling blast stopping them all in their tracks.

Except Nico. Pale and trembling, he shot forward, diving and rolling close to the monster's webbed feet. Then he popped up and swung his dagger in a tight arc under the creature's chin. The figment disappeared with a shriek, leaving the forest silent and empty again, as if the three conjurings had never existed at all.

"Good riddance." Logan wiped his dagger's blade on his pant leg, even though he hadn't used it. "That one was awful. What have you been dreaming about, Nico?"

"My business, not yours," Nico growled.

Logan persisted. "Tyler's was the Dog Beast. Emma made a stupid koalicorn. Opal imagined a fancy writing turkey. Which means that screeching, stomping, other-figment-swallower was *yours*, Holland. So what gives?"

"*You* brought us a humming, bouncing dollar sign," Opal slid in acidly.

Logan ignored her, eyes on Nico.

Nico shook his head in disgust. "Does anyone in your family ever *not* think about money? Or themselves?"

"Way to change the subject," Logan fired back.

"Keep running your mouth, and I'll change *it*, too."

Opal leaped in between them to diffuse the situation. "Done is done, okay? We've all created a wild figment or two, so no one should be mocking any of them."

Tyler snapped his fingers. Once. Twice. Having got their attention, he brought a finger close to his eyes and pointed it at the pond. "The ice just cracked," he whispered. "Big time."

Everyone turned to face the water. Then Opal heard what

Tyler had—a series of high-pitched pops and snaps. Sheets of ice began bobbing on the surface. As she watched, a long fissure in the ice grew closer to shore, shattering into thin shards not far from where they stood. Fog slid in to cover the break.

Logan was squinting into the gloom. "I think I see . . ."

Something long and dark slithered from the pond.

"Oh dear," Emma breathed.

"Watch out," Nico hissed. "Whatever this is, it can move on land."

A grunt-like cough echoed from the mists. Opal took a step back, accidentally bumping into Aster. The older girl steadied her without looking. Aster's whole focus was on the fog, and whatever it might conceal.

"This lake," she said quietly. "It is home to natural woodland predators?"

Opal shook her head. "None that we've ever seen."

"I see. So this is not likely a normal animal, then. Make ready with your dagger."

Opal's back stiffened. She swung her blade up. Aster was right. Whatever it was, they'd have to handle it.

A low, guttering rumble trickled from the broken reeds where the shadow lurked. Then two glowing yellow circles appeared.

Nico blanched. "Those eyes, again," Opal heard him mutter.

The silhouette crept along like a whisper, sliding into a shaft of moonlight that revealed a long green snout and protruding teeth. The ghost of a breeze swept over the pond, pushing back the fog. The creature's narrow head appeared, golden eyes pulsing like twin lighthouses. A fiery pepper scent filled Opal's nostrils.

Beside her, Opal felt Aster tense. She heard a sharp gasp escape the girl's lips.

"Get the heck out of here!" Tyler hissed. "That's a . . . a . . ."

"An alligator," Nico said in a disbelieving voice. "In our ice-covered pond. In November."

Logan barked a wobbly laugh. "Someone call the zoo. We found an escapee."

The alligator zipped forward a few steps, causing everyone to jump back. Logan's grin died. Shining reptilian eyes scanned the group before locking onto Aster. Its thin lips retracted in what seemed like a ghastly smirk.

"*Impossible*," Aster croaked, putting a hand to her chest. "Not here. Not in *this* place."

"Creepy," Emma said quietly. "I feel like it's . . . watching us."

"Must be a figment," Nico answered firmly. "We just have to take care of business."

"That is *not* a figment."

Opal twisted around in shock. Saw Nico do the same.

Aster was glaring at the alligator, naked hatred lasering

from her eyes. Quick as a thought she snagged the dagger from Opal's fingers. Aster strode past the Torchbearers, gripping the weapon tightly.

The animal glared at her, its yellow orbs strobing like camera flashes.

"Stalker," Aster hissed.

The gator rose up on its legs.

"*Fugitive*," a voice rasped.

Aster reared back and threw Opal's blade.

The beast vanished in a cloud of black vapor, which gathered into a thick contrail and began streaming toward the woods. The peppery smell redoubled, nearly causing Opal to gag as the sinister current slid between the trunks and disappeared. When the acrid fumes cleared, the space where the alligator had crouched was empty.

Logan staggered forward, then spun around in confusion. "What the heck just happened?"

Emma was staring into the woods. "You guys . . ."

A new set of glowing yellow eyes regarded them from beneath the snow-laden branches. As Opal watched, stunned, the wolf from the school attack strolled onto the frozen grass. It growled low, exposing long canine teeth.

"Oh man," Tyler said in a strangled voice. "Is this guy working with an alligator buddy?"

"No." Nico was wide-eyed in sudden comprehension. "These animals aren't working together. They're one being."

Opal started. "What?"

Nico's gaze shot to her, a terrible fear lurking there. "It's the *same* creature, Opal. The wolf. The bobcat. Even that bird from the beach. And now an alligator. The form varies, but the eyes never change. And that awful smell shows up every time!"

The wolf regarded Nico coldly, its lips pulling back in an impish smile. Another black cloud engulfed it, then faded as quickly. The odor of harsh spices flooded the field once more as a new form faced them: an elderly woman wearing a long raincoat.

"Oh my gosh," Tyler wheezed, grabbing Nico's arm. "That lady in the park! The last time we snuck to the Torch-bearer office."

Nico nodded. "I remember. She was watching us."

The creature scowled, its yellow eyes narrowing in contempt. *"Human scum."*

Despite everything, Opal felt her temper explode. "Whatever this monster is, we can take it. Spread out. Don't let it get away."

Nico nodded, some of the color returning to his face. "Tyler, Emma. Flank positions. Logan and Opal—you're with me. Aster, watch our backs." Nico curled his lips at the unfathomable life-form before them. "Let's take this punk down."

The group fanned out, but before they could do more, black smoke enveloped the creature yet again. When the haze dissipated, the huge bird from the beach was smirking at them. Fast as thought, the creature shot into the sky, flapped its giant wings—once, twice—and was gone.

"Whoa," Tyler said, still gripping his dagger with white knuckles. "That was *not* a figment."

Nico shook his head. "It could speak, though. Aster, you called it something?"

Logan looked around in confusion. "Where *is* Aster?"

They all turned as one.

The French girl was gone.

Opal did a quick scan of the field, but with the mists still swirling it was hard to see. "Did she bail?"

Emma nervously bit her lip. "Maybe she went back to the houseboat? That thing seemed to scare her pretty bad."

"We better check," Tyler huffed. "I don't want her swiping any more daggers. Y'all heard her angling for one."

"She called that creature a name," Nico insisted. "Like . . . like she knew it."

Opal felt a twinge of unease. "Come on. Quickly."

They hustled back across the field and over the pond. Opal kept darting glances at Nico. His expression was tight, his gaze unfocused. She sensed it was more than just the yellow-eyed shapeshifter—that howling gray figment had shaken him badly, even though he'd managed to dispel it himself. But Opal knew the scar was still fresh. Some dark corner of his soul had snuck out to say hello, and Nico clearly hadn't been prepared for it.

Opal shivered. Was this becoming more than they could handle?

*It always was*, she reminded herself. *We just have to keep trying.*

Opal reached the front door first and pushed it open. "Aster? Are you in here?"

Inside the showroom, Opal stopped in her tracks. A giant map of the world was spread out across the floor, with tea-cups positioned at marked locations.

Logan made a face, squeezing the back of his neck. "Weird."

Emma glanced around. "Is she here? Where'd she get a map?"

"This one came from the blue steamer trunk," Tyler said. "I remember it from our inventory. But it's nothing special—just a regular old world atlas, like you can buy in stores." He frowned. "Well, in stores thirty years ago, anyway. It's way out of date, so I never thought it had any use."

The chart was global, its edges crinkled and blurred. One of the cups had been placed over Still Cove. Another sat off the Pacific coast, where the Rift was located. Then Opal's eyes widened—over in Europe, smack-dab in the center of France, sat the tea kettle. More cups and saucers were positioned in different places around the world.

"Look." Logan pointed to a little plate. "She placed that one over Yellowstone. What's she doing? What does this mean?"

Worry lines dug across Nico's forehead. "Aster wasn't in town yesterday cruising around for pizza. She was investigating something. I wonder if she found her answers."

"We should've searched that bag," Logan said sourly, studiously avoiding a glance in Opal's direction. "Aster came out of the Custom House with it on her shoulder, and I'd bet my life that she wasn't carrying it before then."

"The Custom House?" Tyler flung his hands wide. "That's quite a place for her to visit, don't you think? What could she possibly have wanted to see in there?"

"She knows about the Torchbearer office," Nico concluded, clicking his tongue with finality. Then he bumped a fist against his chin. "Nothing else makes sense. But how? And did she get inside?"

"And if so, what'd she take out?" Opal finished. Then she sighed. "Looks like we need to have another chat."

"Anyone know what this is?" Tyler asked. He'd walked over to the wooden bench and picked up a single folded sheet of paper lying on it. "Seems like some kind of list. It's typed. Recife, Brazil. Vichy, France. Darwin, Australia. Wyoming is on here, too. There are fifteen places total."

"Places?" Nico was standing over the map on the floor, staring down. He jabbed a finger at it. "You said Brazil, right? I see a saucer in that country, near the coast. And . . . yep. A cup is planted in northern Australia, too." He rubbed his cheek anxiously. "Huh. Looks like she marked those specific cities on this map for some reason."

Then Nico leaped back. He shot an astonished glance at Opal.

Opal was staring back at him. "If she put Yellowstone and Timbers on there, along with these other locations . . ." She couldn't finish the sentence. Her heart was pumping like a shotgun.

"What are you saying?" Logan asked finally. "What's the point of it?"

Nico and Opal spoke at once. "It's a Rift map!"

Tyler flinched, eyes wide. He swung the list overhead, sputtering, "But . . . How . . . *where did she get this*?!"

Opal covered her eyes and groaned. "The Custom House. That sheet must've been what was in the bag."

Nico's face was green. "So she *did* go inside the Torchbearer office. But I can't understand how she even knew the room was there." His finger shot out. "And how did *we* miss that?! I've been in that room a dozen times and *never* saw that piece of paper."

Emma gasped suddenly, drawing every eye. She scrambled for her phone, scrolled furiously, then held it up for the others to see. "The teacups on the map—I recognize the pattern now. They match the wall holes in the Yellowstone cave. I've been staring at the pics I took in that chamber for days. Those niches have been bugging me ever since we snuck through there—they have to mean something, or why would the Order have drilled them? But look! Aster's recreated their positions on this map!"

Logan frowned. "You're saying the holes in the Torch-bearer cavern were some kind of . . . of"—he waved a hand as words failed him—"I don't know . . . old-school mapping system?"

Opal felt a jolt to her system. "*Of course*. A three-dimensional diagram of Rifts!"

"Hold on!" Nico demanded, waving for silence. "Are you sure, Emma? And how would Aster know what's inside that cavern? We never told her anything about it."

Emma paled. "I printed out my pics so Opal and Tyler could see them. I left the folder here on the houseboat for safekeeping. You know, with *all the rest* of our secret Torch-bearer stuff."

Tyler cleared his throat. "You mean these?" He lifted a stack of photos sitting farther down the bench.

"She put all the pieces together," Opal said with a gri-mace. "Right under our noses. But what is Aster looking for?"

Nico put a hand to his head. "Guys. If you're right about this, that would mean there were more than a *dozen* other Rifts." He looked like he was about to be sick.

Opal felt herself go lightheaded. *So many breaks in reality . . .* Then she had a sudden sense they were being watched. Opal glanced over at Thing's former pedestal, even though she knew the little alien was long gone. The spot was still empty, but movement caught her eye.

Opal noticed the wall panel behind the pedestal slowly inching closed.

There was a soft click.

Opal stared for a beat, then blurted, "Aster's in the stairwell."

Nico's face went sheet white. "Oh no. Why is she going downstairs?"

For a beat, no one moved. Then in a mad rush they all sped across the room, Opal in the lead. She shoved the hidden doorway open and clanged down the steps, hoping desperately that she was wrong.

*Too late.*

A pair of knee-high boots sat alone beside the Darkdeep.

Ripples expanded in shimmering rings from the well's black center.

Aster was gone.

# 23

## NICO

Nico stared into the black depths.

"We have to hurry!" Emma shouted, pulling her curly hair back into a ponytail. "Logan, go grab the wetsuit bag and bring it down here."

Nico sighed. "Hurry why, Emma? Aster will be splashing up through the pond in thirty seconds." A steely glower settled on his face. "And when she does, we're gonna have a serious talk. She's been holding out on us. How does she know core Torchbearer secrets that even *we* didn't?"

"She's not making more figments right now, you doof!" Emma shoved Nico with both hands, but only to get his full attention. "At least, that's not her goal—although we *do* need to remember that another one will be on the loose on the island when we get back. But Aster is headed for the Void!"

Opal grabbed Emma by the forearm. "Why do you think that?"

Emma gave her an exasperated look. "The map upstairs! Her shady recon trip through town. The fact that she snuck off again after confronting that . . . *shapeshifter* or whatever."

"What, is she going back to Thing's world?" Tyler's cheeks scrunched. "Why? Did she forget her favorite pet rock or something?"

Emma shook her head, her tone growing desperate. "I don't know Ty, but think about the map she made upstairs. Then she just left all her work out for us to see, after all that secrecy? I think she's done planning, and doesn't care what we know now. Because she's leaving! I swear I'm not wrong!"

Nico thought hard as the Darkdeep stilled below his feet. Then he nodded sharply. "Emma's right. I'm not sure why, but I think Aster *is* trying to pass through the Rift again, and we already showed her how to do it. It's the only conclusion that makes sense."

Logan twisted his hands at his sides. "What makes *sense* about it?"

But Opal was nodding, too. "Aster has gone through every scrap of Torchbearer information we collected on this boat. Who knows how long she spent in the office, too. By now she knows as much about the Rift as we do, maybe even more. And she's heading for it. Alone."

"Or she's outside by the lake, freezing her butt off with a new figment pal. Hold on." Logan ran upstairs. They heard the front door creak open, followed by silence for a full minute. Then Logan's sneakers clomping back down the steps as

250

he dragged the giant wetsuit duffel bag behind him. "Okay, she's not there. So either the dumb girl drowned or she made a break for the Void."

"Don't say that!" Opal scolded. "Did you see anything else?"

Logan shook his head. "Aster's figment is probably too stuck up to bother with us."

"Later," Nico grunted. "We'd better move fast if we want to catch her."

They suited up in silence, each lost in their own thoughts. Nico didn't want to risk another trip into the Darkdeep, but he couldn't imagine not following Aster now.

*Why didn't she tell us about the other Rifts? How did she recognize that yellow-eyed monster outside? What is she doing now?*

They had to know what Aster did. And there was only one way to do it.

The others were clearly of the same mind, even Tyler, though his friend was muttering under his breath as he dragged on his diving gear.

Soon they were ready. Nico called the equipment check. Everyone responded affirmatively.

It was time.

"See you on the other side," Logan said softly.

Surprisingly, he dropped in first.

Nico blinked at the well in astonishment. Logan had never led a dive before—that was Nico's role. Logan had always been the most freaked out by the Darkdeep's mysterious nature. *Maybe he just wants it over with.*

Nico went in next. He felt the vortex grab him and pull down, down, *down.* The Darkdeep sucked him toward its icy heart, blasting Nico into a vacuum blacker than the water surrounding it. He rode an invisible slipstream until it fired him through the blue-green blur that led into the Pacific Ocean.

The glow of the Rift bloomed below his feet. Nico watched something swim through it.

*Logan?*

No response. Nico arrowed for the same spot. Breath burning in his lungs, he kicked into the glimmering ball of light.

A blast of heat. Blinding radiance.

Cold that burned a hole through his brain.

Nico's mind caromed like a rubber band, then he was floating.

The Void.

Colors and shapes swirled around him like a Tilt-A-Whirl. Nico would never get used to it. He spotted Logan hovering a few yards away and zipped to his side. *See Aster anywhere?*

Logan nodded. *I spotted her when I first entered this funhouse, but she shot away like a cork.* He pointed toward a cartwheeling, color-bending area of the Void to their right.

Nico glanced down at the Rift into Thing's world gleaming just below their feet. *She didn't go through there? You're sure?*

Logan scowled. Pointed again. *That way, Holland. Not down there.*

*Okay, okay.*

Opal dropped in beside Nico, followed by Tyler and Emma. Logan again explained what he'd seen of Aster.

*Let's go then*, Opal sent. *We should be able to find her if we hurry.*

*How?* Tyler flailed both arms in frustration. *There are no true directions here. Everything looks exactly the same except for Rifts.* Then his jaw dropped open. *That's it! That's the answer! Aster is searching for another Rift!*

Opal's hands shot out to grip Tyler's shoulders. *Wasn't somewhere in France on that list?*

Tyler's nose crinkled in concentration. *Yeah. Vichy, I think the place was called.*

Nico nodded excitedly. *The tea kettle was positioned there on the map, almost like a centerpiece! I bet that's the one she's looking for!*

Emma spun in a slow circle, peering at the chaos surrounding them. *But how do we find it?*

Surprisingly, Tyler spoke up. *The same way we find anything in these spaces. Concentrate, and let your mind take you there. Right?*

Emma tackled him in a bear hug. *Yes! Let's try it.*

*Release me*, Tyler moaned.

*Clear your thoughts*, Opal instructed. *Think about a Rift, and . . . I don't know. French stuff.*

*French fries?* Logan joked. *French kissing?*

*Hilarious. I was thinking more like the Eiffel Tower. Baguettes. The beaches at Normandy.*

Nico closed his eyes and pictured a Rift—that shimmering slash through the fabric of reality. Then he added a French flavor to the image, cheesy stuff he'd seen in movies. An accordion began playing in his head. A juggling mime danced around the Rift as the Arc de Triomphe appeared behind it.

Nico almost laughed, but then, suddenly, he felt a . . . *calling* somewhere to his right. Faint, but there.

He didn't open his eyes. Nico surrendered to the magnetism, willing his body to move in that direction. Something about the sensation felt . . . *off*. Broken, in a way he didn't understand. But Nico didn't peek from behind his eyelids until he stopped careening through space.

He blinked. Nico was hovering before a gnarled crease in the substance of the Void. It looked like a wound sewn shut, or fragments of metal welded together. Nico knew instinctively that he was in the right place, but it clearly wasn't an active Rift.

With a start, he realized Aster was floating right beside him.

*Aster?*

The girl didn't respond. She had her head buried in her hands.

Nico ordered his mind. *Everyone! I found Aster, and maybe the France Rift. But something's wrong. Home in on me.*

A moment later, tiny specks on the horizon grew rapidly until Nico recognized Opal, Logan, Tyler, and Emma. They zoomed to his side, keeping a polite distance from Aster, who was clearly crying.

*Is she okay?* Logan sent. He pointed at the knobby space-scar in front of them. *What's this ugly mother?*

*The France Rift, I think.* Nico had been working it out while the others arrived. *But it's busted somehow. Or closed, which I didn't even think was possible.*

Opal glided to the weeping girl's side. *It's okay, Aster. It's easy to visit France in our world. Transportation improved dramatically while you were gone. You can fly to Paris in like twelve hours now.*

Aster's head flew up. *I don't want to visit France. Not here, in this time. I want to go home!*

Nico was astonished. He'd never seen Aster show weakness before. It was like watching a flower wilt.

Emma's eyes widened. *You were trying to go back.*

Aster glanced at her, then away. *Oui. And now I never will.*

*Can someone please explain what's happening?* Logan huffed in a loud sending. *Because I'm lost.*

Emma kicked at his shin. *She was trying to travel back in time! To when she first entered the Void. That's why she was searching for a Rift to France.* Emma regarded Aster with sad eyes. *It worked one way, so why not the other?*

Logan grimaced. *But this Rift is toast. Bummer.*

*"Bummer," you say?* Aster spat, twisting the word in her

French accent. Bitter tears streaking her cherry-red cheeks. *Bummer? My family is lost forever. I will never see my own time again. And soon there will be nothing left of your world. But you call this a* bummer?

Nico felt his heart stop. *What do you mean about our world?*

Aster turned hot eyes on him. *Follow me and see.* She shot away into the Void.

*After her!* Nico mind-shouted. He focused on Aster's face, and felt a tug toward wherever she was headed. He arrived there seconds after she did.

Nico knew where they were this time. He was staring at the Rift into Thing's world.

*Let me show you a real* bummer, *my friends*, Aster snarled acidly. Without another word, she leaped through the opening.

Nico stared at the glowing gateway. The others closed in around him. He pointed.

*Why follow her?* Tyler whined. *She's off the chain.*

*Aster wants to show us something.* Opal's gaze shot to Nico. *We should go and look.*

Nico nodded. He felt Logan and Emma silently agree. Finally, Tyler bobbed his head, too.

One by one, they stepped into the Rift.

# 24

# OPAL

A craggy, pitted landscape stretched out before Opal.

"*Nightmare*," she whispered.

"It's like Yellowstone got hit by an asteroid," Nico breathed.

They were standing atop a high plateau of rust-orange rock. Around them, Thing's world was a jumble of twisted, serrated stones in fantastical formations, rising up to form mountains and dipping down into ravines and canyons. Strangely animate brown plants grappled amid cracks and fissures. Heavy, roiling clouds hung low in a bruise-purple sky. Opal saw eerie green lightning streak across the plain below. Deep holes in the earth erupted with spurts of yellow and white-hot steam.

Whirling, Opal looked behind her to make sure the Rift back into the Void was still open. She exhaled in relief to see the ragged tear shimmering a few yards away.

"This is insane." Tyler swallowed, then pointed a shaky finger. "Look. Is that a lake?"

One plateau over, an expanse of midnight-blue liquid filled a depression in the center of the formation. The bubbling lagoon reminded Opal of the Darkdeep.

"I'm not going for a swim," Logan joked, with a nervous giggle. "See the fumes coming off it? That water could probably strip paint."

As they watched, an enormous head parted the lake's surface. Then another.

Emma clutched Tyler's shirt in her fist. "Are you seeing this?"

Tyler spoke in an awed tone. *"Beasts."*

Opal hugged her body close, rubbing goosebump-covered arms. This world thrummed with an overwhelming feeling of menace. *How did Aster manage to live here for a single day, let alone ten months?*

Aster.

She was standing near the edge of the cliff, her back to them as she gazed out over the broken horizon. Opal led the others over to join her. As if Opal had asked her question out loud, Aster spoke.

"I hid," she said softly, observing the torched landscape. "Watched. Waited. *I survived*. Always looking for a way home. Then Dax found me."

"Where does Thing live?" Emma said. "Are there more beings like it here?"

Aster shook her head. "I never saw any others. But this world is not as it once was."

Tyler's brow furrowed. "What do you mean? How could you know what this planet used to be like?"

Aster's lips formed a grim line. "This devastation is all I have ever seen. But Dax told me it was different before." She straightened to her full height, like an arrow in a bowstring, seeking a target. "It said to me, *This world was a paradise before it was eaten.*"

Opal shivered, though twin alien suns were beating down on them and she'd already begun to sweat. Her lungs felt heavy, like she was sucking air through a wet towel. Opal was surprised humans could breathe at all in such an alien environment.

*The Beast survives on our world. I guess we can handle his. At least temporarily.*

Logan was looking around. "Are there no, like, *human*-ish people on this rock? Or did they all get . . . eaten?"

"Intelligent species used to live there." Aster pointed to a nearby cliff.

At first Opal couldn't tell what she meant, but then she noticed low alcoves dug into the cliffside. Remnants of ladders stretched between the abandoned dwellings, hanging for-lornly, like driftwood littering a beach after the tide goes out.

Opal squinted, trying to get a sense of the scale. Would something like Dax have lived there? Climbing and moving along those byways?

"Let's find Thing," Logan suggested, then he snorted. "Unless you think it wants payback, and will put *us* in jars."

"Do we *need* jars?" Tyler asked nervously. He sniffed the air, nose curling in distress.

Opal suppressed a shudder. *We need to get out of here. Why are we on this world at all?*

"I don't know where Dax went after I left." The steel in Aster's voice had given way to exhaustion. Opal could only imagine how brokenhearted she must be. Aster had been searching for a way back to her family and friends. A path to recovering her old life. All that was gone now.

"Just how close are you and Thing really?" Logan asked suspiciously. "Because you acted like the two of you had barely talked when we first met."

Aster said nothing.

Opal stepped closer to the French girl's side. "What did Thing tell you, Aster? I've been thinking about your map in the showroom, and how you knew where the secret Torch-bearer office was hidden. Was Dax the one who said where to find the Rift list?"

Aster didn't answer for a long moment. Then her head dropped. "What does it matter now?"

"Lying to us definitely matters," Logan growled. "You've been playing a game this whole time, and making us look dumb in the process."

Aster shot him a glare, but stubbornly held her tongue.

Bolts of electricity rained down like fireworks on the broken plain below.

"So, this . . . *eating* you mentioned." Tyler was keeping a close watch on the Rift behind them, though he kept darting glances at Beast Lake. "What, exactly, is that all about?"

"Guys." Emma's tone caused everyone to turn. She was peering into a canyon. *"Look."*

A dark, glossy river was flowing through the narrow gorge. A gully beside it also began to fill with the viscous fluid.

"That liquid," Opal said. "It looks . . . unpleasant."

Nico licked his lips. "Not water," he agreed. "Good thing we're up here."

Entranced by the bizarre flood, the group snuck to the very edge of the plateau for a better look. More of the surrounding canyons were filling up with it. Several of the flows reached a confluence at a deep chasm in the earth.

One of the inky rivers ran alongside the base of their plateau. There, the stream separated into strands—like mercury under magnetism—breaking and reforming in countless tendrils. The warped lines of black looked almost like . . .

"Takers," Opal breathed. "That's a . . . a river of . . . *Takers.*"

Nico jerked back and turned to stare at Opal, his face sheet white.

"Nope nope nope!" Tyler made chopping motions with both hands. "Let's get the heck out of here!"

Emma pointed at the giant chasm, which was filling rapidly as dark torrents emptied into it. "I think they're gathering in that hole."

"Oui. They are."

Everyone turned to Aster, whose face was a mask of dreadful resignation. Down on the cracked moonscape, the flood-like surge separated, Takers assuming their individual forms. They marched up onto the plain directly below where the Torchbearers stood.

"What is happening, Aster?" Nico voice was tight, barely controlled. "Please explain."

She was silent a moment, then her shoulders dropped. "This world is all used up. The Takers are hungry, but there's nothing left for them to consume. And not just those creatures—their master thirsts for a richer realm to devour." She faced the group squarely. "A fresh planet, unsullied and ripe for the picking. Ours."

Opal blanched. "You're saying they want our world? That, all of a sudden, they're coming for it?"

"They were always coming, Opal." Aster's eyes were downcast. "Why do you think I wanted to return to *my* time?"

"Wait! Just *wait*." Logan's voice was wild, bordering on panicked. "Is *this* what my father is talking about? Is this the . . . the *doom*, or whatever?"

Aster shrugged. But she seemed to consider his words, and nodded slowly. "If your father told you the end of the world was imminent, he's right. He must know about the Eater."

"The what now?" Tyler whispered, through a hand covering his mouth.

"They're definitely headed somewhere." Emma was still gazing over the cliff. "I don't—"

Emma's whole body went rigid. Her hands clenched at her sides as she stared downward, with eyes like Frisbees.

"Did you see something?" Opal joined Emma and followed her gaze. Her stomach dropped into her shoes.

An enormous, broad-shouldered creature had stepped from the shadow of a monolith and was moving among the Takers, crushing unlucky ones beneath its clawed feet. The Takers surged around it, humming with what sounded like reverence. With a flick of its wrist, the giant ordered them forward. Ghastly, doglike animals streaked from the gloom to flank the gathering horde on the plain. As Opal watched, horrified, several Beasts emerged from the bubbling lake and began climbing down to join the throng.

"Holy crap," Tyler groaned. "It's an army."

"The big one," Emma squeaked. "It's a boss monster. Like in a video game!"

The lead creature was massive—as tall as a building—and covered in mangy brown fur. Its red eyes gleamed as the monster roared a command at the crowd of creeping nightmares. Opal spotted blackened rows of razor-sharp teeth in its mouth.

"Do not let his barbaric appearance fool you," Aster said solemnly. "The Eater is very cunning. And relentless."

"What'd you call that thing?" Logan croaked.

"The Eater. Consumer of worlds." Aster spoke dully, as if no fight remained inside her.

The Eater thundered again, stepping onto a roughhewn wooden platform with colossal wheels attached on both sides. A swarm of creatures began moving in concert, dozens of Takers pulling their warlord forward on the massive cart.

Opal tracked the line of their march. In the distance, ahead of the monstrous army, loomed an enormous mountain, with a dark cavity dug into its side. Sickly yellow-green light glimmered from inside the cave, visible even from where the Torchbearers stood.

Opal pointed at the distant cavern. "That's where they're going. I think it's another Rift."

Nico stiffened at her side. "Not just any Rift. Those are the colors we saw at Yellowstone."

"An *unguarded* portal," Emma and Logan said at the same time.

Opal felt her insides turn to ice.

"The Eater has gathered his strength, and will take his army through." Aster's voice had a hollow ache to it. "I had hoped not to witness this, but the Stalker's presence on our world leaves little room for doubt. They are coming."

Opal flinched. "The Stalker? That yellow-eyed shape-shifter we fought on the island?"

Aster nodded wearily. "The changeling. A creature of

264

many skins that serves the Eater. The Stalker was doubtless sent to scout our world's defenses, though the presence of such a creature plays havoc with the weather of any world it visits. The Eater will be pleased when it reports how weak they are."

Tyler pivoted ever-so-slowly to face Aster. "What, exactly, does the Eater . . . eat?"

A familiar voice sounded inside Opal's head.

*He's finished here. The Eater seeks another world to devour.*

By the others' wide-eyed stares, Opal knew everyone had heard those words.

"Thing! Where are you?" Opal demanded. "We need help!"

*There's no more time. I'm trapped and cannot help. Return through your Rift immediately. Each second you remain here is multiplied on Earth.*

Nico cringed. "Oh jeez. Forgot about that. We better book it!"

But Opal didn't move, clenching her fists in frustration. "Tell us what to do, Dax! How do we stop that monster?"

*You can't, Opal. I'm so sorry.*

*It's already too late.*

# PART FOUR
# THE VOID

# 25

## NICO

Nico yanked on a dry sweatshirt.

He nearly fainted in pleasure. His pruny fingers still shook, but at least he wasn't soaking wet anymore.

Beside him, Tyler sneezed, then stamped his feet. "Man, I'm getting *tired* of these freezer plunges."

They were back on the houseboat, changing out of their wetsuits in the foyer. Logan seemed shocked out of his wits—he'd slumped to the ground with his back against the front door, eyes wide and barely blinking.

"What time is it?" Logan asked suddenly. "We left in the morning, but it's full dark outside. If we've been gone for like a century or something, they better have flying cars by now."

Tyler scrambled to read his watch. "Oh jeez! We've been gone all day! My mom is going to end me."

Nico heard Opal's voice through the curtain. "Okay, guys. Come in!"

"We'll worry about the time later," Nico said, although he imagined his father sitting at home, staring at the clock, and couldn't repress a shiver.

The three boys dragged themselves up and trudged into the showroom. Nico worried that this was the best they could do—assemble every so often to discuss the latest calamities, but with no idea how to solve anything.

*Some Torchbearers we are.*

Opal, Emma, and Aster were sitting on the floor in a circle. Emma waved them over. Nico took the spot next to her and tried to gather his thoughts. But all he could think about was a three-story-tall monster with jagged teeth, surrounded by an army of Takers and other hideous creatures. How could they possibly fight against *that*?

"How long were we gone?" Emma asked immediately.

"All freaking day," Tyler answered glumly.

Emma tensed. "Same day?"

Tyler's eyes shot back to his wrist, then he exhaled a shaky breath. "Yes. Man, you scared me to death."

Nico rested his elbows on his knees. "Well, what now?"

"Tell them what you told us," Opal urged Aster, who was staring at her hands.

Aster sighed. "What is the point? We have no defense against this force of darkness."

"We're not giving up," Emma insisted. "We've beaten Takers before. They don't scare me." She swallowed before adding, "Much."

"You refuse to understand." Aster pressed her lips together. "The being you saw is called the *Eater*. He controls a force of demons that conquer and devour worlds."

Nico raised a palm. "Just explain it as best you can. Torchbearers have guarded the Rifts for a long time. Maybe we know some things that might help. We have to share information."

Aster seemed about to protest again, but closed her eyes instead. A moment later she sat up straighter. "The Eater feeds off life. The energy contained in living things. Dax told me its world was once a beautiful swamp, but our enemy came and ravaged it. There is nothing left."

"A beautiful swamp?" Logan snarked. "Now I've heard everything."

Nico gave him a cool look. "To a bullfrog, swampland is the most wonderful place in all creation. Everything is about perspective, Logan. Try to be less stupid."

Logan bristled, but at a sharp glance from Opal he kept his mouth shut.

"You were saying?" Opal prompted.

*Keep Aster talking*, Nico thought. *Maybe we'll finally get some real answers.*

Aster gripped her braid in both hands. "The Eater is a plague, like a swarm of locusts. He strips the environment bare and leaves only destruction in his wake. The Eater moves from world to world, never pausing, always feeding. His hunger is a bottomless pit that can never be filled. Those creatures that follow him? They have been enslaved to his will. Now they seek to feed always, too."

Aster went silent. No one else spoke, letting the older girl choose her own pace.

"And now the Eater has selected its next hunting ground," she whispered finally. "Through the Stalker he has discovered a way to come here, to our world. We cannot stop him. I wish it were another way."

"You're describing an apocalypse," Tyler said in a shaky voice, one hand worrying his cheek. "The end of the world." He glanced across the circle. "How did Sylvain Nantes know?"

Logan tensed, but didn't speak. He had no answer.

Aster shook her head. "I cannot say. I did not know any of these Torchbearers." Her eyes flashed. "But it seems they visited the world on which I was trapped, yet made no effort to find me. These are not good people."

Opal's cheeks flushed scarlet. "It's a complicated history. But remember—no one on this side of the Rift knew you'd survived the shipwreck, not even Yvette Dumont. For the entire time that Torchbearers have existed, you were thought to have gone down with the *Dauphin*. If anyone went to Thing's world through the Rift, they wouldn't have had a reason to look for you."

Aster seemed to mull this over in her head. "Very well. But I do not trust this Order, one that would imprison another being and keep it in a jar." She blushed suddenly. "Those members that are not *you* five, I mean."

"What else did Thing tell you?" Emma asked. "We figured out where you got that list of all the Rifts. The hidden office under the Custom House, right? We could've just shared information, you know. We're not your enemies."

Aster shot an abashed glance at Emma, then her gaze traveled the group, as if she weighed what to say next. At last, Aster sighed. "I suppose my distrust of everything Torchbearer was . . . misplaced. But I did not know if you would let me undertake my quest, and I was *not* prepared to be told no."

Logan barked a laugh. "That I can believe."

Nico surprised himself by chuckling, too. "For someone who hates the Order, you sure know an awful lot about it. More than *us*," he finished ruefully.

"Dax told me what to do," Aster explained. "The little alien understood what I was seeking—a way to return home—and it sympathized. Dax was equally concerned that you all might try to prevent my entering any Rift, should I find the right one. So we agreed that I would conduct the search on my own terms."

Logan *tsk*ed in annoyance. "So Thing told you where to find the list, and you matched those locations with Emma's photos of the Yellowstone cavern to locate a Rift in France." He frowned darkly. "I'm going to wring a certain scrawny green neck when I see it next."

"You shall do no such thing," Aster replied hotly. "Dax was a great help to me. It told me of a false-bottomed drawer in the desk of the Torchbearer office, which held a document detailing all known Rift locations. Even Dax was unaware of the full list, or so the tiny alien claimed. Dax never left the houseboat during its forced stay here on Earth. As an *unofficial* Torchbearer the Thing in a Jar was told much, and overheard more, but it was not trusted with the most sensitive information. More reason why *I* did not trust the Order in return."

"I hope that's no longer the case," Emma said. "We need to work together now more than ever."

Aster blinked several times, then rose and gave a small bow to the group. "Agreed."

Nico rose and began pacing. "We stopped a force of Takers at *our* Rift last month. A swarm came through, but we blocked the passage and the Beast drove them all back into the Void. If we did it once, we . . . we can do it again." He nodded curtly, as if to affirm his own statement.

"That was a small group," Aster said. "Perhaps sent to scout. And the Eater has apparently heeded the lessons you gave him. He sent his top lieutenant, the Stalker, on a direct mission to sniff out weaknesses. Now the Eater seeks a different Rift, one that is not so well guarded as the portal near Timbers. Tell me, Nico—who will stop his army at Yellowstone? You said that post has been abandoned."

Opal stood up and crossed her arms. "How long, Aster? When will the Eater come through?"

Aster seemed to consider. "Time moves much slower there, as you know. But we have no more than days."

Nico felt his anxiety level spike. "Some of us will have to go to Yellowstone again. We'll need to restore the balance somehow, and . . . and shut the Rifts down. Both of them. *All* of them. Forever."

Aster spoke in a quiet voice. "There are not enough of you, Nico. This will not be a small attack. *Invasion* is coming. The Eater will personally clear the way this time. Nothing can stand against him."

"We can't even defend our *own* Rift right now," Logan grumbled. "How are we supposed to handle double the work if both places are at half strength?"

"Like you care about keeping the group together," Nico shot back.

Logan's eyes smoldered. "I've had enough of you blaming me for your own problems, Holland."

"*My* problems?" Nico felt his temper sizzle. "Is that how you sleep at night?"

"Both of you, just stop it!" Opal stood up and crossed her arms. "You're acting like little kids. This has gone on long enough, and it's killing our teamwork. We've gotten slack at the worst time possible."

"Slack?" Tyler snapped. "I've been trying to get the Beast on our side for two weeks straight. Never saw *you* there, Opal. You've been wandering around with your head buried in a notebook."

Opal spun on him, seemingly taken aback, and not at all happy about it. "I was trying to solve a mystery, Tyler. Which, *by the way*, I did." She snapped a nod at Aster.

"Do not include me in your childish squabbling," Aster said primly. "Dax and I gave you unmistakable clues. Even the silly movie girl could have solved them."

"What's *that* supposed to mean?" Emma replied, indignant. "I have eight hundred thousand followers, I'll have you know. You think that just comes with signing up? No chance. You have to have *quality* content. Jeez, do you even know what YouTube *is*?"

Tyler rolled his eyes. "Can we please go one day without talking about your social media presence?"

Emma glared at her best friend. "Why? So we can wave algae sticks on the beach until the Beast feels sorry for you, and shows up to end your humiliation?"

Tyler popped up, jabbing his own chest. "I *communed* with the Beast, thank you very much. An ageless being from another dimension chose *me* to be its handler. Which might prove useful *when an army of darkness descends on Skagit Sound*!"

Suddenly, everyone was standing but Aster, who seemed indifferent to the group-wide meltdown. Nico struggled to control his emotions. Logan drove him crazy, but now really wasn't the time.

"We have to focus on the problem at hand!" Nico ground

a fist into his thigh, then took a deep, calming breath. "I want everyone to go home before our parents totally freak out. Summarize what you've learned in your area of expertise. Let's see if we can pull a strategy together." His finger shot out. "Tyler, look at how we can use the Beast to defend ourselves. Will he come when we need him?"

Still scowling, Tyler nodded curtly. It was the best Nico could hope for at the moment.

"Opal, you and Aster"—Nico eyed the older girl, who didn't even appear to be listening—"compile what we know about Thing's world and the Eater's invasion army. Is there anything we can do to keep them away?"

"I'll consult my *research*," Opal said acidly, firing a dark look at Tyler. Then she glanced at Aster. "And her."

"We must locate the Stalker." Aster spoke grudgingly. "That creature is too dangerous to be allowed free movement." She frowned for a moment before adding, "I have ideas."

"Great." Nico turned to Logan, and gritted his teeth. "Logan, find out what your father knows, and *how*. Don't let him put you off. Maybe some Nantes family history can help us decide what to do. And find out if your grandfather ever went to Thing's world. Someone in the Order learned about the Eater before Thing went home. The question is, how?"

Logan sneered. "Yes sir. Nico sir." But he didn't protest further, so Nico let it slide.

"What should I do?" Emma asked, chewing her bottom lip. Nico thought she was worried the group didn't think she had anything to contribute.

"Can you help me?" Nico asked gently. "We need to comb through the Torchbearer records, and see if there was ever a situation like this before. I want to check for any mention of the Eater, or if similar natural-disaster patterns were ever reported in the past. Perhaps a former invasion like this one was thwarted. If so, maybe *we* can do it again now."

Emma exhaled. Flashed an "okay" sign. Nico looked around the room, noted the hard stares and deep frowns.

They weren't a team right now, but everyone had their tasks. Hopefully it would be enough.

*Or maybe we're just spinning our wheels until the Eater shows up.*

Nico pushed the ugly thought aside.

"Come on, guys. We all have work to do. Let's give it everything we've got."

There was no cheer in response. Each Torchbearer seemed locked inside their own bubble of anger.

One by one, they filed out of the showroom.

# 26

## OPAL

I know you're lying."

Opal spun in the crowded hallway to find a fidgeting Carson Brandt behind her. Other students flowed around them on their way to the lunchroom, chattering about what they'd done over Thanksgiving break. More than one kid had been caught staring fearfully at the shiny new cafeteria doors.

Carson looked like he hadn't slept in days. His hair was more rumpled than the last time she'd seen him, but his eyes locked onto hers with a manic intensity.

*He's close to the edge.*

"We've been over this." Opal shifted her backpack farther up her shoulders. "*Freakshow* was responsible for the craziness on Dark Halloween."

She didn't feel guilty saying that, because it was pretty much true. If Colton Bridger hadn't gathered everyone on the beach that night, things would've gone—well, not *smoothly*, exactly—but better.

Carson shook his head. "That's not what I'm talking about. You're lying about *her*."

He jabbed a finger at Aster, standing with Emma a few lockers down. A knot of classmates eyed the new girl suspiciously, whispering about her accent and strange boots. Aster wore them paired with jeans, a wool sweater, and a long navy raincoat that belonged to Tyler's sister.

"She's not a foreign exchange student, or whatever." Carson spoke so low that Opal had to lean in to hear him. "Those kids come in January."

"Is that right? Then what is she, Carson?"

Carson fixed his jittery gaze on Aster. Opal noticed he wasn't the only boy staring.

The group had decided it was safer to bring Aster to school than leave her alone with the Darkdeep, but the jury was still out on whether it was the right call. They'd cobbled together a reasonably good cover story explaining why no parent had checked her in at the main office, but that wouldn't fool the school secretary forever.

*Oh well.* If the world lasted long enough for someone to expose their lie, Opal would happily face the music. Better that than the planet ending in an apocalyptic Eating.

"I think she's a spy," Carson said quietly, but with deadly conviction. "She looks like a spy."

Opal glanced at Aster, and her lips twitched. The combination of knee-high boots and dark slicker *was* kind of espionage-y.

"What would she be spying on at Timbers Middle School?"

"You know what," Carson said darkly.

Sighing, Opal took a step away from him. "Sorry, but I've got to go."

"*Conspiracy*." Carson said the word loud enough that a few heads turned.

Opal moved closer to him, attempting to put out a potential fire. *He'll draw everyone into his madness.* She widened her eyes in sincerity. "Carson. Buddy. I honestly don't know what you're talking about."

Carson tapped an index finger to his temple. "Foreign agents are attacking us by using *extra-foreign* agents. Aliens."

Opal's jaw dropped. Seriously?

*Although* . . . when she thought about it, he was kind of correct. The Eater was using the Stalker and other nightmare creatures to infiltrate Earth. Carson was closer to the truth than he knew.

He returned his frenzied gaze to Opal. "And *you're* trying to cover it up. You and your weirdo necklace friends. I think someone threatened your families or something, and you have to go along with whatever that girl wants . . . or *else*."

"Okay . . ." So Carson thought Aster was some sort of teenage assassin?

He shifted from foot to foot. "Now, I *think* you have good intentions. You're scared, and hope that if no one makes waves, everything will just sorta be okay. But spoiler alert: it *won't*."

Out of the corner of her eye, Opal spotted the French teacher, Mr. Pogba, approaching Aster and Emma. Farther down the hallway, Nico and Logan were in some kind of argument. *Again.* Logan looked up and frowned.

*This was a mistake. Why are we at school, pretending everything is normal?*

Opal's parents had hit the roof when she'd skulked into the house after dark last night, having been gone an entire day without checking in. She was on dinner dish duty for an entire month. Tyler got it worse—in addition to no TV, he had extra counseling sessions lined up to discuss his "sudden rebelliousness." And poor Emma was grounded from the Internet for a week, which was basically the most devastating thing you could do to her.

Nico had been spared, because his father had been out on his monthly owl-scouting rounds, and Logan's household was so out of whack that no one had even noticed him being gone. Still, the group's level of home surveillance was now at an all-time high, at the worst possible time. And here was Carson Brandt making everything more difficult.

Carson carried on like he'd decoded the Rosetta Stone. "The truth has to get out, Opal. That's the important thing. Before it's too late." Someone bumped into his shoulder and he rubbed it distractedly, but his eyes didn't blink.

As if sensing that Opal was cornered, Logan walked up

and gave Carson a guarded nod. He gestured at her phone. "You've got messages."

She glanced at the screen and read. Apparently Tyler was feeling the same way she was.

Guys, we should bail. Now. We're wasting time.

From Emma: Won't we get in trouble?

Nico: Doesn't matter. Everyone is staring at Aster. Her story won't hold up.

Logan: Let's do it. I'll rescue Opal.

Opal glanced up and saw Emma and Aster watching her. Tyler was farther down the hall, while Nico leaned against a nearby locker. They were all waiting. *Acting like a team again.* The group's bond was never clearer than at school, where no one else knew their secrets, or what was really going on.

Opal turned back to Logan and Carson's conversation.

". . . too cool to hang out with me and Parker anymore," Carson was saying, his face locked in a dreadful scowl. "Now that you've got *new* friends. We haven't taken the ATVs out in weeks!"

Logan rolled his eyes. "It's been storming nonstop for weeks, Carson. Not exactly outdoor sports weather, right?" He changed the subject quickly. "Opal, can I talk to you for a sec? *Alone.*" He avoided eye contact with his former friend.

But the skittish boy refused to let up. "Your family acts

like it runs Timbers, but if you won't help stop an alien invasion, what kind of people are you?"

Logan spun on Opal, eyes widening. "What have you been telling him?"

"Nothing! He thinks Aster is a secret agent working for extraterrestrials."

Logan stifled a laugh. "Oh." Then he grew pensive, muttering, "Well . . ."

"I'm standing right here!" Carson fumed.

Nico sidled up behind Logan, wearing an impatient frown. He pointed at his phone, mouthed: *Come on*. Opal shrugged in apology. There was no shaking Carson at the moment. He was busy letting Logan have it.

"I bet you've got a secret deal in place to sell the aliens precious lumber," Carson growled. "The Nantes family doesn't care about anyone but themselves."

Opal darted a look at Nico, worried he might pile on— he'd said similar things about Logan's family literally the day before. But Nico was staring at Carson in total befuddlement.

"Why would aliens want our . . . wood?" Nico mumbled.

"On *that* note . . ." Logan gave Carson's shoulder a hard squeeze, moving past him to stride down the hall. A moment later, Opal's phone flashed once again.

Logan had messaged the group:

Meet behind the school. By the batting cage.

Opal sensed Carson trying to read the text over her shoulder and blanked her screen. The other Torchbearers were already melting away down the corridor.

"That was my mom," she explained. "I have to go. But don't worry, I hear what you're saying. I'll investigate the French spy personally, from the inside. In the meantime, act natural and keep your head down."

Carson nodded seriously. "Understood. Thanks, Opal. I had a feeling I could count on you. Parker and I miss when you came four-wheeling, too." Exhaling in relief, he wandered off, his back a little straighter.

Opal caught up with the others at the rear doors. They slipped outside and ducked into a dugout by the baseball diamond. Logan was waiting there, practically buzzing with an idea. "I thought of a hotspot we could search for more Torchbearer stuff."

"Where?" Emma huffed. "We've already scoured the houseboat and the office."

"Your father probably burned all the contingency plans," Nico grumbled. "When he boxed up his Torchbearer responsibilities and dumped them under a floorboard."

Logan didn't rise to the bait, merely shaking his head. "I just asked myself, where would my dad hide something he didn't want found, but couldn't bring himself to throw away?"

"The houseboat," Emma said, still impatient. "We know that already."

"*Besides* the houseboat." Logan folded his arms. "He only put Nantes family stuff down there. I'm talking about *Order* things—Torchbearer items he might feel too guilty to risk damaging."

Tyler tilted his head forward, eyeing Logan in annoyance. "Maybe just *tell* us, bro."

"I'll give you a clue." The corners of his mouth quirked. "Our old buddy Roman Hale."

Opal thought of the skeleton they'd found in a ravine on the island. A shudder ran through her.

"Hold on." Tyler's voice dropped to a whisper. "Are you saying that your father *killed* Roman Hale?"

"No!" Logan barked, his brow forming an angry V. "Jeez, Ty. Real nice."

Tyler blushed. "Sorry! But you're being very confusing, okay?"

Logan glanced around, then continued. "Look, remember how we found Hale's private stuff stacked neatly in a storage bin? My dad *could've* thrown those things away after the guy went missing, but he didn't. He preserved them for some reason."

"*Ohhhh*," Emma said, raising an index finger. "In the company warehouse." They'd snuck into the huge building once before, locating Hale's personal effects and a critical piece of Torchbearer history. Could other secrets be hidden there, too?

Logan crossed his arms, his expression growing serious. "My dad may hate the Order, but he didn't sabotage it when he had the chance. Not with Hale, anyway. So maybe he's stashed *more* Torchbearer goodies away, just to be safe."

Aster glanced from face to face, as if watching a five-way tennis match. She spread her arms wide. "We need to visit this place, yes? This is clear?"

"It's a long shot," Logan admitted.

"Still a shot, though," Opal said firmly. "Let's take it."

# 27

# NICO

Slush was piling up on the warehouse roof.

The winter storm had struck out of nowhere—a sudden deluge of golfball-sized hail followed by a torrent of white, instantly covering the ground in a mantle of brittle, crackling ice. As Nico crouched behind the rear wheels of a parked tractor-trailer—its cargo bed stacked ten feet high with sawed planks headed for Seattle—he marveled again at the extreme weather.

*But Aster said the Stalker is causing it. How is that possible?*

Logan was ahead of the group, near the truck's front end. He peered around its fender, eyes locked on a garage door accessing the Nantes Timber Company's main storage facility. It was the biggest structure in the whole county, yet the building seemed strangely empty. Nico guessed everyone had gone home to avoid the blizzard.

Nico's pocket buzzed, nearly giving him a heart attack. He removed his phone and frowned at the message.

Warren Holland wanted to know why his son wasn't home.

"My mom texted me too," Opal whispered, reading over his shoulder. "I've got thirty minutes before I'm toast for not writing back."

"I've got ten," Tyler hissed from the rear bumper. "*Maybe.*"

"Then let's get moving already!" Emma scuttled up beside Logan and tapped his shoulder. He jerked around in annoyance, then pointed to something Nico couldn't see, whispering irritably.

Emma scurried back to join the others. "Logan says to wait one more sec. A truck is leaving now. His dad's inside the cab, so Logan thinks it's the last group. The driver just rolled down the loading dock door, but Logan doesn't think she secured it."

He was right. When they reached the rear of the warehouse—following Logan's hunched run across the icy parking lot like a line of stealthy ducks—the latch to the door wasn't padlocked. The workers obviously weren't worried about a break-in and hadn't wanted to dig around in the snow. Logan heaved the barrier up a couple feet and they all slipped inside.

The door dropped with a loud clang, engulfing the group in pitch black. For a nervy moment Nico was reminded of the

Darkdeep. Then halogen lights on the ceiling blazed to life. Logan was over by the wall, glancing around furtively, clearly hoping no one was left inside the building to notice.

"Big," Aster said in a small voice, looking around. "What could such an edifice be used for?"

"Lumber," Opal explained, wiping snow from her jeans. "Half the plywood in Washington comes from here."

"Okay, we're inside," Nico said, then grudgingly added, "Good work, Logan. Where to now?"

Logan rubbed his chin. "Hale's gear was in the Unclaimed Items room, but that time we had a locker number and knew where to look. For a blind search . . ." His expression soured. "This place is huge. If my dad hid something in the main stacks at random, we have almost no chance of finding it."

Tyler's brow dipped, but then he snapped his fingers. "Your dad wouldn't want Torchbearer stuff discovered by accident. Even in here, workers must root around in most areas eventually. He'd keep something ultra-private squirreled away where only he could stumble onto it. Know any places like that?"

"Just one," Logan answered thoughtfully. "His private office in the back of the warehouse. Obviously, no one goes in there without his permission."

"Until now," Emma quipped. "Let's burgle it."

Logan nodded. He led them down the center aisle, between massive stacks of shelving. The room stretched for almost a quarter mile, with every manner of lumber product filling the metal racks, alongside woodworking tools and oil-coated industrial equipment. Nico often forgot what a giant undertaking the Nantes Timber Company was. This was clearly a multimillion-dollar operation.

Finally, they reached the far end of the chamber, where a steel door was set into a movable wall. Logan tested the knob, then turned it, waving everyone inside. The lights were off. The place had a vacant feel.

Logan flipped another switch. "The executive section is in the very back. Come on."

They moved down a narrow walkway with a carpet runner extending over the concrete floor. The shelves here were smaller and more office-like. Nico glanced at the row marked "Unclaimed Items," where weeks ago they'd found Hale's cylinder.

*Remember when our problems were that simple?*

The aisle ended at another door. Logan reached up and ran his fingers along the top of the frame. There was a jangle as something small and metal hit the floor.

Emma scooped up a key and handed it to Logan. He unlocked the door and they all crammed through it. A short, wide hallway stretched before them, with a half-dozen rooms to each side and a wooden door at the opposite end. A name was painted on it: SYLVAIN NANTES, PRESIDENT & CEO.

It was also locked, but Logan dug into his jacket and

removed an old key ring. "This was my grandfather's set," he explained. "I snagged them from my house a few days ago, just in case. I doubt my dad ever actually got around to changing these deadbolts, but we'll—" He broke off as his hand turned smoothly and the door opened.

Inside, the office was disappointingly drab. The walls were bare except for a giant map of the greater Timbers area, with the acres being harvested outlined in blue. Red slashes covered large swathes of the region. Nico's spirits sank. Those sections were labeled "Protected" in angry block letters. Compliments of Warren Holland's work to protect spotted owls.

A desk sat at the back of the room. Two chairs faced it, flanking a small table. Beat-up metal filing cabinets lined the right wall. A row of bookshelves filled the opposite side. If something precious had been stashed in there, its first defense would be the complete lack of any indication that a valuable object would be left in such a dingy workspace.

Aster crossed her arms with a frown. "This is where the solution to everything resides?"

"It was just a guess," Logan snapped, rubbing his necklace. "This is one of the only spaces my father has complete control over. No one else uses it, and even he doesn't come here much. His main office is in the corporate building, down by the shore."

"Well, no point wasting time," Nico said, trying to hide his disappointment. "Let's spread out and look everywhere."

"I'll check the filing cabinets," Opal offered. Tyler moved to join her, and soon they were thumbing through reams of dog-eared files. None of it looked very interesting to Nico.

Emma and Aster began examining the bookshelves, leaving Sylvain Nantes' battered desk to Nico and Logan. They started on opposite sides of the swivel chair, each pretending the other didn't exist. The top drawers yielded nothing of interest. Nico moved to the lower compartment on his side while Logan began fiddling with the center console. But in minutes it was clear—the desk was a bust.

The rest of the group had finished their searches as well, and everyone grew quiet. Nico didn't know what they'd hoped to find, and they'd uncovered nothing worth the trip. Bleakness pressed down on his shoulders like a wet blanket.

"Welp," Tyler said awkwardly. "Do we search the lost items room?" His voice didn't carry much enthusiasm.

Nico was about to suggest they cut their losses when Aster pointed to the giant map. "This drawing, it is stuck to the wall? Perhaps with paste?"

"Tape, probably." Logan stepped closer. "Actually, it's pinned to a bulletin board behind it."

Aster cocked her head. "This board, it does not move?"

Nico blinked. "Why would it move?"

Aster gave him a patronizing look. "To hide something behind it, Nicolas. Like a safe. Or perhaps a secret window." She shrugged. "We do such things in France."

Logan smirked and rolled his eyes, but he ran a hand along the underside of the board. To his complete astonishment, something clicked and the map swung away from the wall. Nico gaped at the empty space behind it.

"You see?" Aster said smugly. "Not so different, I think."

Everyone crowded close to see. Nico expected to find a safe there, like Aster had said, but the hidden niche was too shallow for one. Instead, a stack of three rolled parchments filled the compartment.

"Bingo," Emma breathed.

Logan removed the documents and hurried to the desk, then carefully unrolled the first. He let out a low whistle.

"Another map!" Opal said excitingly.

"Maps behind maps," Tyler joked. "Why not?"

Delicate cartography depicted the entire world, but a much older version of it, littered with nations that no longer existed. Fifteen red circles were marked across its face, including one over the Washington coast.

"Rifts!" Emma crowed. "We've got them all now!"

"We can crosscheck this against the list and what we found in the Yellowstone cave," Nico said excitedly.

"You mean what *I* deciphered on the houseboat," Aster countered.

Logan moved to the next scroll. He wasn't speaking, and Nico noticed that his hands were shaking. How many secrets did Sylvain Nantes possess? Nico felt a sudden pang of sympathy for Logan, which surprised him.

The next parchment was less interesting—a drawing of the Darkdeep. Skillfully done, but ultimately just a piece of art. Everyone cooed over it for a moment before Logan set it aside. The last parchment seemed older and more brittle. Larger, too, at least double the width of the other two scrolls. Logan carefully unrolled it, weighing down its corners with objects on the desk. Seeing the ancient document held open by a Swingline stapler and a box of ballpoint pens gave Nico a weird dizzy sensation. *Worlds are colliding.*

The writing on the page was hard to decipher. Then Nico abruptly realized it was in French. He scanned to the bottom of the page, and recognized a signature. Yvette Dumont.

"Make room," Aster blurted, shoving past Nico to examine the crinkly document. "I know that handwriting. My governess wrote this." She read in silence for a moment, her lips moving slightly. Tears gathered in the corners of her eyes. Then Aster stepped back and hastily wiped them away.

"What does it say?" Emma pressed, barely containing her impatience.

"Nothing of use," Aster said dismissively. "Madame Dumont merely talks about the well."

Tyler frowned. "The Darkdeep? I'd say that's of use, fam."

Aster hissed in vexation, but began to read aloud. "'*The Deepness is a singularity on this planet. There is no feature like it at any of the other Rift locations. Dax is unaware of any such vortex on its world, either. Therefore, it is my belief that the Deepness is unique, and uniquely powerful.'* You see? Of no import."

"Translate it all, please." Nico was staring at the page. There were three more paragraphs, and he didn't think Aster had read them all the first time.

Aster's glare found the ceiling. "Fine. But my governess was never careless. She would not have trusted a great secret to pen and paper." She lowered her head and resumed. " '*The Deepness is of the local Rift, yet also not. It is a peculiar place outside the bounds of the emptiness beyond. I believe that a sentient being traveling the Deepness may be able to access thousands of worlds and in-between spaces from inside it. For that reason, it must never fall into unsafe hands.'* "

Aster glanced up, her annoyance gone. This *did* seem to mean something.

What, Nico wasn't sure. But he felt a creeping apprehension seize his insides. He swallowed. "Is that all?"

"There is one last section. '*The Deepness can create from mere thought, and therefore must be guarded. A being able to harness the power of the Deepness, and use it to travel the strands of space and time, would be unstoppable. For this reason, an Order must be established to protect against such a catastrophe. I shall be its first member.*' The page is then signed by Yvette Dumont."

Nico went cold all over. "She's saying the Darkdeep could be used as a weapon."

Opal's face had gone white. "One that must never fall into the wrong hands."

"You guys?" Tyler said slowly. "We've never really asked ourselves *why* the Eater is so determined to get here. He's been turned away at least once already. Maybe more times. You'd think he would try an easier world to conquer, right?"

Logan stiffened. "Unless we have something the monster desperately wants."

Emma made a squeak. "The Eater could use the Darkdeep to travel anywhere it pleases. Unlimited access to vulnerable worlds."

"Think of the *figments* such a monster might make," Aster whispered. "Minions called into being at will."

Nico's gaze shifted to the drawing, still lying unrolled on the desk.

The black depths of the Darkdeep stared back at him.

A weapon.

One unique to the universe?

And impossible to stop.

"The Eater wants the Darkdeep," Nico breathed. "He's coming to take it from us."

# 28
## OPAL

*T*his is it. No going back.

A sick gurgle roiled Opal's stomach. She ignored it, zipping her backpack closed while taking deep breaths. If anyone peeked into the bag, they'd probably think she was stowing away on an ocean-bound steamer ship. Blanket. Waterproof matches. Goggles. Flashlight. First-aid kit. Her leather notebook was sealed inside a series of overlapping plastic bags.

*I'm not running away from home. I'm protecting it.*

She'd never climbed out her bedroom window before. Never made a fake person in her bed the way teenagers did in cheesy movies. But an Opal-sized clump of pillows was now artfully propped underneath her heaviest quilt. And outside in the yard, a boy was waiting.

*Quit stalling.*

Opal slid the window open and climbed out onto the gently sloping roof. Stepping carefully across its ice-slick surface, she shimmied down an ivy-covered trestle bolted to the side of her house. Nico was right where he'd said he would be—in the bushes opposite the porch. He flashed a thumbs-up.

"The others?" Opal whispered.

"Already headed for the cove. We'll make our plans there." He led Opal down to Overlook Row, then arrowed across the street for a copse of fir trees in the park, where they'd stashed their bikes.

So far, so good.

"They left without us?" Opal hissed, glancing at her watch. She was five minutes late. It had taken longer than she'd expected for the lights to go off in her parents' room.

"Tyler got antsy," Nico said, as they began silently pedaling up the empty street. "Everyone just wants to get this over with." He paused, a hint of strain entering his voice. "Whatever *this* might be."

The night was frigid. A sandpaper wind bit at Opal's cheeks, kicking up snow that had fallen earlier. She shivered, glancing back at her house as it shrank behind them—dark now, the homey lights doused, its yellow exterior appearing blue-gray in the moonlight.

"Back soon," she whispered.

*I hope.*

———————

They arrived only minutes after the others. Topping the ridge, Opal spied several flashlight-wielding profiles crossing the stepping stones out to the houseboat. When she and Nico entered the showroom, an operation was in full swing.

Logan and Emma were going through the weapons chest, muttering over various daggers before setting them in piles. Aster was comparing her world map to the one Sylvain Nantes had kept hidden in his office. Opal heard water splashing somewhere down below.

"Good news," Logan said, without looking up. "We have six less figments to worry about, thanks to my intrepid leadership during the advance party."

Emma rolled her eyes. "He accidentally stepped on one. I don't know who was controlling the Darkdeep's creative processor when we went through yesterday, but this round was easy-peasy. After Logan screamed in terror and fell backward down the slope, Ty, Aster, and I mopped up a mini-version of King Kong, Squidward, a talking protractor, three dancing croissants, WALL-E, and a cartoon sloth."

Logan nodded. "An emphatic victory powered by my inspirational heroism."

Aster gave him a flat look. "You screamed, ran into a tree, and ripped your pants."

Logan's ears reddened. "I was taking the fight to the enemy. You're welcome."

To Opal's surprise, Aster giggled, shaking her head.

"What's going on?" Nico asked. "What's that gurgling sound?"

"The Darkdeep is acting wonky." Logan had moved to another trunk and was now counting torches. His expression grew anxious as he sat back on his heels. "I don't like it. I can't shake this feeling that the well *knows* we're planning to battle the Eater, and maybe doesn't approve."

Opal felt an unpleasant flutter in her chest. "What does *that* mean?"

Aster looked up from her maps. "Ignore the nervous boy. Tyler is keeping watch."

Nico stared. "You left Ty alone down there?"

Emma paused mid-lean, her rosy cheeks turning scarlet. "Uh . . . yeah. And, actually, it's been a minute."

"*Guys,*" Opal scolded. "Everyone agreed—we only go down in pairs now!"

Opal hurried for the trick wall panel. Descending the steps she stopped short, and choked down a gasp. Nico crashed into her from behind and they both grabbed the railing to keep from falling into a flood of black water that blanketed the floorboards.

The Darkdeep was overflowing.

Tyler was up to his knees in the dark liquid, staring at where the well's mouth would've been were its contents not spreading across the floor. The deluge had almost reached the bottom riser.

"Did you not hearing me yelling?!" Tyler squawked.

Nico's voice squeaked a full octave above normal. "What happened?!"

"The Beast!" Tyler seemed frozen in place. "It . . . it was here a second ago."

Opal blinked. "*Excuse* me?"

A wave of black ballooned outward from the center of the chamber, but then the water level dropped abruptly. As they watched in stunned silence, the overflow drained away like a plug had been pulled, gallons of inky liquid running back into the well. In seconds, the pool was gone.

Opal put a hand to her forehead. "Okay. What was that about?"

"I told you," Tyler said, trying to catch his breath. "Beast. Here. Just now. Big scary bad."

"You're saying . . . *The Beast* . . . attacked our houseboat?" Nico was incredulous. "Through the Darkdeep? How is it even in the pond?"

A roar sounded from beyond the wooden hull. Opal broke out in goosebumps.

"He didn't attack, Nico." Tyler was shivering head to toe, but Opal heard elation in his voice. "I called him, and he *came*."

A second roar shook the houseboat. Then, impossibly, it sounded to Opal like another bellow answered—similar to the first, but slightly different in tenor.

Nico flinched as if struck. "What . . . what was that?"

Logan and Aster clattered down the stairs in a tangle.

"What's going on?" Logan yelped. "Emma's on lookout—there are *huge* ripples moving in the pond. Is the Stalker attacking? Did you guys make another figment or something?" He tried to shove a dagger into Opal's hand, but she waved him away distractedly. Opal couldn't shake that second call. It had almost seemed like . . .

*No. Impossible. There's only one Beast on our world.*

Aster hefted a dagger as if testing its weight. "The giant water creatures are not friendly," she said, her voice grim. "Once they have your scent, they do not give up."

"Whoa, whoa, whoa!" Nico shouted, holding up both hands. "Everybody hold on a second!"

"That was *our* Beast," Tyler snapped. "I called him here."

Aster stared at him like he'd grown a third arm. "*Your* Beast? What insanity is this?"

"We've got one on the team," Logan explained with a nervous laugh. "It hates Takers. He's kind of our buddy."

Opal was still trying to get a grip on the situation. "How did you summon him, Ty?"

Tyler spoke rapidly, both hands darting for emphasis. "I was keeping an eye on the Darkdeep, because the well was acting funny. I was just staring at it. Not waving algae sticks, or old flags, or anything like that. I was only thinking, '*man,* if we have to go at this Eater dude, I wouldn't mind our giant sea monster pal helping out with the fight.' Like sixty seconds later, the Beast's head came up through the Darkdeep."

Opal stared, dumbfounded. "Its head. Was *inside* the houseboat."

Tyler nodded like a sock puppet. "Yup. It screamed at me once, then was gone. I nearly wet my wetsuit."

Worry lines dug across Logan's forehead. "But the last roar came from across the pond. Much farther away."

"There were two distinct calls," Opal said quietly.

Nico glanced at her, eyes pinched in alarm. *Did he notice it, too?*

Logan shook his head. "No. Same roar, different times. You're hearing things is all."

Opal's jaw firmed. "The second one sounded . . . strange."

Tyler rubbed his face nervously. "Like: *I'm mad at Tyler now*, strange?"

"No. Like: *I'm a different Beast*, strange."

Shocked silence.

Logan broke it. "No way. Come on. How could we have missed a second Beast all this time?"

Opal bit her lip, trying to make sense of the situation. She could've sworn the second roar was unique from the first, the way different people had different voices. But why wouldn't Thing have told them about another Beast? Had it not known?

"Wait!" Tyler snapped his fingers. "Not a second Beast. A Beast *figment*! Our Beast was just inside the Darkdeep, after all. He somehow made a figment copy of himself!" Then his eyes grew wide. Tyler actually started jumping up and down. "Guys! I've got it! That's what we have to do!"

Outside, two roars sounded in tandem. Everyone jumped.

Opal's blood turned to ice. Hearing them in concert was terrifying.

Emma came pounding down the steps. "Guys, there are *two* angry sea monsters circling the houseboat!"

"It all makes sense now," Tyler whispered. "The answer was staring us in the face this whole time."

Logan's voice cracked. "Do tell, Ty. What the heck is going on?!"

Tyler crouched, wiggling both hands out at his sides. "Earlier down here, I was *also* thinking about how we've got no chance against the Eater."

At an annoyed grunt from Nico, he shrugged. "Sorry, dude, it's true. He's got an army. We've got a few stone knives. But then Beastie Boy showed up in the Darkdeep, and now there are two of them doing laps out in the pond."

Opal gasped. "A figment Beast. And if it's as real as the conjurings Aster made—it could . . . could *help* us."

Nico grabbed his head with both hands. "Of course! This whole time we've been agonizing about how we could fend off an invasion. Meanwhile the solution is swirling below our feet!"

Energy sizzled through Opal. Could it be true? Was it that simple?

"We make our *own* army," Tyler growled, pointing at the Darkdeep. "We have the tool right here."

Aster placed her hands on her hips, a look of realization

dawning on her face. "'*The ultimate weapon*,' my governess said. '*Unique in the universe*.'"

"We just need to do what the Beast did!" Emma danced in a little circle, clapping delightedly.

Logan seemed almost in shock. But he began nodding as the idea took hold.

Opal looked down at the well.

*Make figments.*

*Create allies to battle the Eater and his army.*

*Can we really do it? Do we have enough control?*

Opal glanced at Nico. She could tell he was asking himself the same questions.

"Dangerous," he whispered.

"Playing with fire," Opal agreed.

Nico's eyes flashed. "But it's our only chance."

Opal took a deep breath. She turned to the group. Silence fell like a curtain.

"At first we didn't understand the Darkdeep," Opal said. "We made mistakes. But it made us face our fears."

The Darkdeep gleamed in the center of the chamber.

Opal's heart was pounding in her chest, but she grinned wickedly.

"Now, we'll use those fears to *fight*."

# 29

## NICO

Nico tugged on the sleeves of his wetsuit.

The well was churning again. Slowly, like on the day they first discovered this gloomy, freaky, nightmare of a hidden chamber.

*Into the Darkdeep, one last time.*

Nico winced at his own thought.

*Sheesh. Why did I think* last? *One* more *time, Nico.*

*One more.*

A tremor ran through him as he reached for his swim gloves. They'd decided to create figments to help battle the demon army. And, given the carnage such a clash would surely bring, the Torchbearers didn't want it taking place on this world. Not at Yellowstone, not at Timbers, not anywhere on Earth.

So they'd take the fight to the Eater. Stop him on Thing's world.

*You shall not pass.* Nico chuckled darkly to himself.

It was time to go.

"Everyone ready?" he asked.

The others nodded, bouncing on heels and shaking out arms and legs. Preparing to enter the Darkdeep's black embrace yet again. Where they'd make figments on purpose, and hope they could harness their power. *Use* them, for the very first time. Nico tried not to worry about *how* to actually do that. He tried not to panic at the thought of deliberately making monsters.

How would they control the creatures? Or keep them from running away?

This experiment ran the risk of loosing another horde of terrors on Timbers. Nico was afraid he'd think up something terrible, then never even *see* it, bobbing in the Darkdeep's nothing-space while whatever monster he'd conjured dragged itself over the cliffs of Still Cove.

He turned to Aster. "How'd you make them stay with you?"

Aster seemed lost in her own dark thoughts. She glanced at him, brow furrowed. "What do you mean?"

"The figments at your tea party." Nico suddenly felt this was vitally important. "How'd you make, uh, make them"—he spun his hand in a circle, searching for the right word—"I don't know . . . *attend*?"

Aster squinted at him in the semidarkness. "They had no

choice. I created them as guests of the festivity." Sadness filled her voice. "They were people I knew. Before."

*She imagined lost friends.* Nico felt a rush of sympathy for the girl from another time.

Opal straightened, eyes intent on Aster. "Explain that part. Inside the Darkdeep, we've only tried thinking of specific imaginings. We've never attempted to give our figments, like . . . I don't know . . ." She was also struggling to express her thoughts.

"Purpose?" Tyler chimed in.

"Yes!" Opal said. "Exactly, Ty." She turned to Aster again. "How did you make them want to show up?"

Aster looked from face to face, eyes suspicious, like she thought this might be some sort of trap. Then she shrugged. "When I enter the well, I think, *this is what I want.* Not, *this is what I wish to see,* or *this would be fun to play with.* I was particular, and the figments did as I wished."

Emma pressed a fist to her chin. "That's it! We forgot about the link!"

"The what?" Logan asked, eyebrows narrowing.

"The link to our minds!" Emma spun on Nico, talking excitedly. "Remember when we *first* read about the Darkdeep, in the old book from the Torchbearers' vault? The one that calls it the Deepness?"

Nico nodded, but didn't see where Emma was going.

"Well, it said that a part of the Deepness gets *inside* you, right?" Emma seemed to be working out her theory as she spoke. "The Darkdeep leaves a trace of itself in your mind, so it can feast on your hidden fears. That's what went so wrong originally. But maybe that link is more than just a nasty leach on our subconscious. Maybe we can *do* more if we concentrate harder!"

Aster was nodding. "Yes. I was focused. I thought, *Welcome, Uncle Pierre. I invite you to my tea party.*"

Nico felt like a door had been kicked open in his brain. Ideas were linking together like Lego bricks. "This whole time, we've been limiting ourselves. We've only thought about what we want figments to *be*. We never considered what we wanted them to *do*."

Tyler smacked his hands together. "*That's* how we build an army! We don't just make a bunch of figments and hope they help us—or don't kill us. We create allies whose *sole purpose* is to fight the Eater!"

Nico held up a hand for quiet, his mind racing. "Okay. So. When we go into the Darkdeep, only think about creatures who *want* to fight the Eater. Don't let their purpose get separated from their existence."

Logan shifted uncomfortably. "That sounds great, Nico. But how do we do it?"

Opal answered for him. "Think about monsters that could fight on Thing's world. In fact, think of them as *being there* already. Imagine that world for them—tell the figments it's where they belong. Then maybe they'll follow us. Through the Rift, into the Void, and over to the other dimension."

She seemed to falter as she laid out exactly what was needed. Could they really make all that happen?

Nico saw shoulders droop around the room. He couldn't let the group lose confidence.

"This *will* work," he said firmly, meeting eyes. "If we gather a strong enough force and block the Eater's army, we can stop this invasion from reaching Earth. We'll be in and out as quickly as possible, to avoid another time jump."

"We'd better," Tyler grumbled. "If I miss another whole day, I might as well chill there for a week, until I'm technically eighteen on Earth and can buy a plane ticket to Mars."

"We'll stay no longer than last time," Opal confirmed. "You've got the watch timer, Ty. When it goes off, we bail from Thing's world, no matter what. We can regroup in the Void if we have to."

"Right." Nico tapped the side of his head. "Smart and fast. We've got this, guys."

Emma and Logan both nodded, with only a trace of uncertainty, while Tyler gave a shaky thumbs up. Opal shook off her jitters, voicing agreement. For her part, Aster seemed confused as to why they were troubled at all.

*New girl thinks she's already a figment master.* But maybe she was?

In the hole below them, the Darkdeep coughed. Rotten-egg smell filled the chamber.

"No more debating," Nico said swiftly, preparing his things. "Let's get to work. Remember—don't just think of figments. Hold in your mind what you want them to do."

Emma lofted a hand. "Let's kick some alien butts."

High fives went around the circle. Everyone looked ready.

Nico approached the lip of the well. He looked down into its whirling, lightless depths.

*One last time.*

But this time, the thought didn't frighten him.

———————————

Splash.

Cold.

Blinding light, then a deep, dark pull.

Nico surrendered himself to the Darkdeep, found himself floating in its black emptiness.

He focused his thoughts on creatures that could fight. Some he knew from stories, others he made up on the spot. He let the menagerie race through his mind like a fever dream, hoping his friends were doing the same. The entire time, Nico imagined himself standing beside these figments, on the surface of Thing's planet, ready to fight the Eater.

Something electric ran through his body. Nico felt his mind skip the rails.

Pain lanced into his brain. Nico ground his teeth. Let out a mental scream.

As quickly as the spasm came, it was gone.

Nico found himself floating in the vacuum of the Darkdeep. Felt a pressure on his wrist.

Opal.

She was holding hands with Emma, who was linked to Logan. Tyler and Aster joined the chain on Nico's opposite side. The group floated in the Darkdeep's current, everyone seemingly exhausted by what they'd attempted.

But they were alone.

No figments.

No army.

Nico's head dropped in despair. Had they unleashed those terrible thoughts on their own town?

A hiss echoed in the darkness.

Nico looked up. He squinted into the ether.

A small glow appeared at the edge of his vision.

As he watched, the circle of light expanded, became a shimmering band of fire. Its blinding radiance arrowed toward them, picking up speed as it closed.

Nico felt the bottom of his gut fall out.

The fiery band separated into a dozen individual points. Then two dozen. Then a hundred.

The mass was barreling straight for where they hovered.

*Nico?* Opal sent.

He licked his lips. *Um, yeah?*

*Those lights are coming on fast. Can you make out the center one?*

Nico peered as hard as his sight would allow. Then he let out a soft whimper.

Similar groans sounded all along their human chain.

*You mean the dragon?!* Tyler sent, in more of a mental gasp than anything like words.

*That's the one!* Opal squealed.

Emma's voice crashed into Nico's head. *Sorry! She's mine!*

*A bit more dangerous than my rude uncle.* Aster's whole body was quivering.

Nico spun, searching for a way forward. For the nebulous path out of the Darkdeep's clutches and into the Rift.

The pinpricks of light took clearer form.

Figments.

Snarling and howling. Tearing across the emptiness.

Headed straight for them.

Tyler edged backward in space. *They know they're supposed to fight for us, right?*

*Let's not wait to find out.* Nico closed his eyes and imagined his destination. The Rift. Suddenly, he felt its awful gravity.

The figment pack streaked closer. Shrieks echoed in the nothing-space.

Nico blasted the Rift connection to his friends while reaching for it in his own thoughts. His consciousness stretched like a rubber band. He felt himself hurtling through darkness as a ball of screams echoed in his mind.

---

He awoke within the chaos of the Void.

Opal was shaking him. *Get up, Nico! We're not there yet!*

Nico snapped fully alert. A vague memory of swimming down into the Rift flickered through his brain. He glanced around at the glimmering in-between space of color and light. Aster and the other Torchbearers were already arrowing for the Rift to Thing's world.

Nico heard a rumble behind him. Turned. Found himself nose-to-nose with a snarling, reptilian snout. He rocketed backward, away from the dragon's gleaming teeth. The creature crashed through the Timbers Rift, eyeing Nico like a prize morsel. Beyond it a stream of deadly creatures were piling up in their rush to join the party.

The figment army had followed. It was coming after them.

But would they fight for the Torchbearers, or have them for dinner?

*Nico, hurry!* Opal sent.

He glanced at the Rift into Thing's world as Logan and Aster disappeared into its radiance. Emma and Tyler were right behind them, jumping through hand-in-hand.

Nico felt hot breath on his neck. Every nerve in his body fired at once.

Choking back a squeal of fear, he fired down to join Opal beside the gateway.

*Let's go!* he mind-shouted, but she stopped him.

*Wait!* Opal's body shook with adrenaline. *We have to make sure they follow us.*

Nico looked up. Monstrous figments were pouring into the Void behind the dragon. Nico saw a Yeti, giant fireflies, and a band of snarling ogres. The group spread out in a disorganized mob of growling mayhem.

But Opal was right. They weren't following.

Suddenly, she shot forward, closing on the swarm in a blink.

*Hey monster squad!* Opal sent, then she spun around and pointed at Nico. *That way to fight the Eater!*

The horde exploded in angry shrieks. All eyes glared at Nico as they raced toward him.

*They know I'm not the Eater, right?!* Nico squawked in panic.

Opal was only a few lengths ahead of the creature avalanche. *Go go go!*

She streaked by him, eyes wild as she bombed into the Rift without stopping.

Nico gave the muffled yelp of potential dragon food and dove through after her.

# 30

## OPAL

Opal tumbled flat on her face.

Spitting out grains of purple-red dirt, she rolled to her feet an instant before a neon-orange velociraptor crash-landed right where she'd been sprawled. Other figments tumbled out behind it in a growling, rumbling mass.

Nico scrambled to his feet on her left. Linking hands, they bolted to where the others were huddled about fifty yards farther up the plateau.

They had returned to Thing's world. The Torchbearers were temporarily less disoriented than the arriving figments, who'd only seen this place in their minds, but it wouldn't last long. Hissing and baring their teeth, the monster horde threatened to splinter and tear into itself. The gang needed to direct them, fast.

*Assuming they don't just maul us instead of the demons.*

"Where's the Eater?" Nico asked in a rush. He had an

ugly scrape down his left cheekbone. "We'd better point our figments at the alien army, quick!"

Emma was jittering beside him, streaked with dust. Aster had an arm around Tyler, steadying him, while Logan had assumed some kind of fighting stance, looking around wildly.

"There!" Opal pointed to the stark mountain in the distance on the plain. Yellow-green light still shimmered from the cavern at its base, where they believed a conduit to the Yellowstone Rift lurked. "That's where the Eater was headed."

"Have they gone through already?" Tyler balled his fists. "Please say we're not too late!"

Opal tried to calm her breathing. Figments were still storming out of the Rift behind them, and some members of the swelling mob were eyeing the Torchbearers hungrily. "Remember, time moves more slowly here. Even though we were back on Earth for a full day, only minutes would've passed in this dimension. They can't have gone far." She squinted into the murky half-light, trying to catch a glimpse of the deadly creatures.

Her stomach sank.

The Eater's army had ballooned on the plain, an undulating mass of nightmares streaming toward the mountain. Takers. Beasts. Other monsters she couldn't name. And in the center, on its chariot, rode the Eater.

Opal's pulse thundered in her veins. *Thing, are you here?* she sent. *Can you help us?*

No response. The Torchbearers shrank into a tight circle as howling figments began stalking toward them across the plateau.

"We have to hurry," Opal said in a strangled voice. "Like, *really* hurry."

Logan barked a high-pitched laugh. "We know, Emma. And not just to avoid being figment food. I'd prefer not to miss the next few decades on Earth. What's our time, Ty?"

"We've wasted two minutes already," Tyler whined. "That can't be good."

Nico cleared his throat. "We, um . . . we have someone's attention, at least."

The dragon was slithering ahead of the other figments, teeth gleaming like razors.

"It's okay," Emma said, nervously eyeing the giant reptile. "Dragons are good. Magical and wise. Right?" But her voice shook, and the dragon wasn't flashing a welcoming grin. Beside it, a pack of video-game robots fixed their laser-like gazes on Logan. His creations, Opal was willing to bet. But could he control them?

Even Aster seemed overwhelmed, ogling a group of iridescent, sparking peacocks that were closing in on her. Opal darted a glance at Nico, whose jaw was clenched. He was tracking a group of gray howling creatures like the one he'd dispelled on the island. They were smaller than most of the other figments, and eerily silent, advancing with eyeless faces.

*Really, Nico? That's the best you could do?* But the sickly pallor of his face changed her mind. *Whatever they are, he's absolutely terrified of them. Nico made the scariest creatures he could imagine.*

Opal caught his eye, and their gazes locked. Nico took a deep breath. They'd been through so much together—there were times Opal thought he was the only person who truly understood her. Saw what she saw. Felt what she felt.

Sightless monsters as a weapon? She had to trust him.

More figments stomped onto the plateau. Ten. A hundred. They followed the dragon across the broken landscape to where the Torchbearers cowered.

Opal swallowed hard. *We may have made a terrible mistake.*

Suddenly, Tyler's voice rang out. "Stop. Hold!" His tone carried an authority she'd never heard before. He stepped out in front of the others, one hand up like an angry crossing guard.

The dragon paused, eyeing the skinny boy. The other figments milled around it in confusion. Tyler had their attention, but the moment balanced on a knife's edge.

*Maybe he really is a Beastmaster.*

"We still command them," Tyler hissed over his shoulder. There were Beast-like creatures in the mix that were surely his imaginings, but these were slender and winged rather than hulking sea monsters. "We made these figments with a purpose. We just have to, like . . . *show* it to them. Remind our fighters why they came here!"

"How?" Emma asked in a hushed voice. "They don't even see the Eater's army."

Logan sucked in a breath. Then covered his eyes. "Right. Opal, can I borrow your flashlight?"

She blinked at him. The plateau was lined with shadows, but it wasn't hard to see.

Logan thrust out a palm and snapped his fingers, eyeing the dragon, which was rocking side to side on its talons, as if working up to charge. Other figments growled and scored the dirt.

"Hurry, please."

Opal swung her bag around, dug into the pouch, and tossed Logan a light. "What do y—"

Logan flicked it on and bolted away from the group, waving the beam over his head. "Hey monsters! You should all look at me now, but don't bite!" He whirled and ran across the rocky mesa.

The effect was electric. The dragon's head snapped to Logan. Steam poured from its nostrils as it abruptly gave chase, like a cat pouncing after the dot of a laser pointer. The other figments roiled in confusion, then set off after their champion. In moments, Opal and the others were left alone, watching the pack of figments sprint away.

After Logan.

Who was running like a jackrabbit.

"Logan, *no*," Opal gasped.

"Fool," Aster swore. "Brave stupid fool!"

A hissing rumble sounded at their backs. Opal froze. She and others turned back toward the Rift.

A black cloud was exiting the Void. In a blink, it stretched into a slipstream and rolled closer to the Torchbearers.

Caustic pepper smell swamped the plateau. Opal felt a sickly tingle on her skin.

"He's here," Aster said quietly, but her voice quavered. "The Stalker has come home."

The cloud reformed a short distance from where they stood. Sparks ignited within its depths, then the vapor slowly faded.

The yellow-eyed wolf emerged, staring at the Torchbearers with a smirking tilt to its jaws.

But it was bigger. *Much* bigger, its broad shoulders towering higher than Opal's head. Teeth like warped swords crowded its salivating mouth.

A voice like sandpaper rattled from its throat. *"The end is nigh. You will be mine. It has been promised."*

The wolf stalked forward a step, but then froze as a thunderous roar erupted from somewhere out on the plain. The Stalker cocked its enormous head, grimacing. The shapeshifter spat on the dirt in disgust before turning to glare at them once more. *"Soon."*

Black smoke exploded around it, swirling into a tornado as the wolf disappeared and the bird of prey arrowed up into the sky, zooming out over the plateau, toward the Eater's army.

Opal took her first breath since the creature arrived. She noticed everyone was gripping their Torchbearer daggers tightly. "Why did it flee?"

"It did not," Aster said miserably. "The Stalker was called to heel by its master. The Eater is ready to invade. And we are not prepared to stop him."

Nico whirled. "Logan! He's alone. Come on!" He took off after the figment pack.

Emma and Aster were right behind him. Opal glanced at Tyler, who made an inarticulate groaning sound. "I hate hero stuff," he wailed. But they both raced after their friends.

A cloud of dust had billowed up ahead. Logan was surrounded by the throng, standing at the very edge of the cliff with his hands up, shouting, "Wait wait wait!" As the Torchbearers drew close, the figment circle tightened around him, hissing and spitting. Claws and paws darted out to jostle and prod.

"Look!" Logan spun, putting his back to the mob as he aimed his flashlight down at the plain. "Just *look*, okay?!"

The dragon glanced where Logan was pointing. It stiffened, exposing glistening incisors. The champion growled deep in her throat. She'd spotted the Eater. And was not pleased.

Other figments mirrored their leader's attention. Logan seemed momentarily forgotten as they began shrieking their disapproval down at the demons on the plain below. Logan cautiously slunk along the rim of the plateau until he was outside their sphere. Then he sank to one knee and threw up.

Everyone ran to his side. Tyler and Nico helped Logan off the ground and began anxiously dusting him off. Aster shook her head in disbelief. "More bravery than sense," she snorted, but something else flickered in her eyes.

"All right," Nico said. "Nice work, Logan. You're insane. But did they take the hint?"

The dragon let out a deafening roar. Fire arced from its jaws as it glared down at the Eater.

"I believe so," Emma whispered. "Yes."

Opal's fingers dug into the side of her wetsuit. "But they're stuck up here, with no way down to the plain."

"Whatever we do, we'd better move quickly." Logan pointed at the mountain. "Time is flying by, and the Eater is on the move."

Beside them, the figment horde was getting worked up. A bus-sized tiger swatted a paw over the edge, looking for a way to descend. But the monsters were stuck on a plateau well behind the Eater's army, which was arriving at the foot of the mountain.

*They're so close to the Yellowstone Rift.*

"How can we get in front of them?" Tyler said. "We're going to be too late!"

Emma's face brightened. "I have an idea!"

Before the others could react, she darted into the jostling pack of figments, sliding unnoticed among them until she reached the dragon's clawed feet. She waved a hand and yelled up at the enormous predator.

Opal nearly passed out.

"Emma," Tyler croaked, both hands pressed to his face.

The dragon went rigid for several anguished heartbeats, eying the little blond girl. Then the figment lowered its head.

Emma climbed up onto the dragon's back.

The other creatures stared at Emma. Opal felt the oxygen evaporate in her lungs. "I. Can. Not. Even."

"I told you dragons are wise!" Emma shouted back at the Torchbearers. "We can use flying figments to carry the others. We can still get in front of the Eater. Come on!"

Logan giggled in terrified surprise. "Okay, guys. You heard her! Let's attack from the sky! *Holy moly.*"

Aster aimed a shaky finger at her sparking peacocks. "Like the birds on royal grounds. I saw them once, on a tour with my father." She paused as two of the peacocks flapped glimmering wings, grabbing the massive tiger between them and hauling it into the air. "I made them larger. With better flying. And that excellent new invention, electricity."

The dragon rose off the ground, snaring the velociraptor in one set of talons and a slavering, red-eyed panda bear in the other. It lifted them skyward, Emma still perched on its back.

"Okay," Nico choked. "Emma is riding a dragon carrying a dinosaur and an evil panda . . . Sure. Why not?"

"Oh dear," Opal breathed, as a handful of griffins fluttered into the sky, arcing over to where they stood. Each dropped like a stone and seized a Torchbearer by the shoulders. Then they took flight.

Sharp claws pressed into her flesh, but Opal was too scared to notice.

---

*Don't pass out don't pass out don't pass out.*

Flying in the grip of a mythical creature wasn't like cruising on an airplane. Noxious clouds streamed around Opal, putrid up-currents choking her with the foul stench of sulfur. She felt weightless and powerless. A captive in every sense of the word.

And then, suddenly, they were diving.

The figment air force plunged downward, unencumbered flying creatures strafing the Takers and Beasts while their comrades deposited the land-based fighters in front of the massive demon army. The Eater's minions reared back in surprise. Opal felt her griffin flap its wings hard, once, twice to slow down. She was unceremoniously dumped on the ground.

The Order's defenders had arrived, gathering between the Eater's force and the cavern where the Rift hid. Opal heard terrible screams—Takers shrieking in anger, furious at the enemies now blocking their way.

Opal wanted to shut her eyes against the sight of so many of them, but she picked herself up and stood with the other Torchbearers, gasping as she tried to get her bearings. They nodded to each other, faces grim.

The Eater bellowed from his perch in the center of its army. He pointed forward.

Emma slid off the dragon and put her hands on her hips, like some kind of warrior princess. "Children of the Dark-deep! *Attack!* Stop the Eater!"

Opal wasn't sure whether the figments heard her or not—or what they thought of Emma's grandiose words—but the dragon charged a knot of Takers anyway, jaws snapping, tossing their ghoulish black forms into the air like toy soldiers.

Tyler's Beastwings lashed into the flanks of the Eater's army, zooming low over their larger sea-Beast kin to harass them from above. Logan climbed aboard one of his robots, shouting orders from its shoulder as they grappled with a pod of deadly snake beings. Aster jumped astride one of her sparking peacocks and signaled a charge.

The dragon rose and spread its wings, scorching the enemy with a stream of deadly fire.

Nico was kneeling on the ground, solemnly regarding the strange eyeless figments he'd created. They alone seemed to be doing nothing. Nico's head dropped into his hands. Opal noticed that nothing was attacking the squatty gray creatures.

*What is he doing?*

A scream behind Opal caused her to wheel. In a tight formation, her griffins plunged into a riot of Takers.

But the huge mass of alien creatures began pushing the figments back. Opal watched her griffins pull away, reeling in a disorganized flock. The peacocks were being battered aside, and other figments—smaller lizards, dinosaurs, ogres and warlocks—began blipping out of existence.

*The Eater has too many. We can't stop them all.*

Despair crept in. Opal heard another terrible shriek.

"We have to fall back!" Logan shouted, trying to organize his robots into a retreat.

The Eater's army pressed forward, hungry eyes fixed on the mountain cave behind Opal. She saw a trio of Beasts rear up and sink their claws into the fire dragon, pulling it down in an explosion of dust.

"*No!*" Emma yelled. "We have to help her!"

Tyler's Beastwings rose and banked as one, attacking the group of sea monsters swarming the figment champion. But the deadly army surged ever closer to the Rift. They were almost there. Opal heard the Eater's laughter echo over the battlefield.

*We need to regroup,* Opal thought. Where was Thing? Was it even still alive?

A voice sounded faintly in her mind.

*Help Nico.*

"Thing?!" Opal frantically looked around, trying to find Dax. "Where are you?"

There was nothing more.

Help Nico?

Opal ran toward her friend, and the strange gray creatures surrounding him.

"Nico!" she yelled. *"NICO!"*

He looked up, and something like relief splashed across his face at the sight of her. Their eyes locked and held. Then he turned to his figments and mouthed the word NOW.

They lifted to the sky on gossamer wings of silver.

Opened their wide, bottomless mouths.

And *HOWLED.*

Both armies froze in their tracks.

The line of howlers landed with a thud directly in front of the Eater's front ranks.

The demons quailed, wearing expressions of horror. They began to slink backward.

The howlers advanced a step in unison. The ground shook like an earthquake. They released a second earsplitting howl. Even the Torchbearers cowered from the awful sound.

Parts of the Eater's army turned and fled, racing back across the open plain.

"They're retreating!" Logan shouted, incredulous. "Keep doing whatever you're doing!"

Elation sizzled through Opal. They were winning! Saving their world from destruction. *It's working!*

Then she heard it.

Footsteps, like the breaking of stone.

A shadow, skyscraper high, parted the remaining mass of Takers and Beasts.

The Eater had come.

The destroyer of worlds towered over his broken army like a lightning rod of pure terror.

He stomped toward the cavern, tossing aside anything in his way—Takers, figments, pillars of stone—and halted before the line of eyeless creatures. Nico's figments opened their mouths to scream again, but the Eater struck first, unleashing a roar that shook the planet's surface.

The howlers vaporized into dust.

The Eater tossed its head back and thundered, a sound so terrible it froze Opal's blood. The fur-covered monstrosity leaped high into the air, red eyes glinting as its massive bulk sailed over the remaining figments, landing directly in front of the glowing cave entrance.

"No!" Nico shouted, his face draining of color.

The Eater looked back at the Torchbearers as they trembled in a ragged row. He laughed cruelly. Opal saw infinite coldness in those burning eyes, felt unfathomable power radiating from a being that had consumed and consumed for centuries. For millennia.

And.

In that moment.

A shriek sounded inside her own head.

*OPAL!*

"Thing?!"

The Eater lifted one fist with a smile. Dax was imprisoned within his meaty claws.

*It's too late!* Thing sent, fear coating its words like a weighted blanket. *Flee! The Eater can't be stopped!*

"We can't let him through!" Opal shouted.

Then she charged.

No plan. No chance.

*No choice.*

The others raced alongside her, desperation etching their features.

But Thing was right.

As Opal watched in terror, the Eater stepped into the tear between worlds.

# 31
## NICO

Nico couldn't catch his breath.

The Eater had gone through the Rift. There was nothing standing between it and Earth.

Behind Nico, the figment mob roiled, on the point of breaking. Takers and Beasts were closing a noose around the cave mouth again, ready to finish the Torchbearers and push through the Rift after their fearsome leader. Opal and Emma were huddled to his left, trying to rally the remaining defenders. Aster was helping a battered Logan to his feet, while Tyler was screaming instructions at his Beastwings.

Everything felt on the brink of collapse.

"We can't stop the army!" Logan shouted, eyes wild. "We should follow the Eater into the Void!"

Nico froze, unable to think straight. They couldn't let the big monster get away, but what about all the nightmares here on Thing's world? Wouldn't they just follow on their heels? How had things gone so wrong?

Takers screeched, slinking closer. Snake demons hissed. Beasts growled and stamped.

*It's over. We lost. We couldn't protect our home.*

Nico was about to call for a full retreat when a roar rattled his eardrums.

Out of the mass of terrible enemies, the dragon exploded upward like a phoenix, spewing flames from its mouth. On her back rode two of Nico's eyeless gray creatures. The dragon landed with a boom directly before the cavern, nearly squashing Nico and his friends as they dove out of its way.

"She's back," Emma cried, clapping her hands in delight. "Get 'em, dragon!"

The dragon spun slowly, regarding the demons opposing her. The remaining figments rallied around her, facing their attackers with new purpose. The two howlers dropped to the dirt.

The dragon bellowed in defiance at the Eater's army, shooting a stream of liquid fire into the purple sky.

Nico's creations stepped forward.

*My greatest fear. Fighting for me.*

The squat gray figments thrummed with sudden energy, expanding ten times in size to tower over the army facing them. Their mouths stretched to nearly swallow their own eyeless faces.

Takers shrank back. Beasts ducked and whinnied, tucking their tails between their legs.

Nico's howlers advanced another step. The Eater's army scampered in reverse.

Then the howlers . . . unleashed.

The pair of screams that tore from their throats seemed to stop time. Hundreds of Takers melted back into liquid form, streaming away from the mountain. The dragon launched skyward, bathing the remaining monsters in sizzling blue fire. Aster's electric peacocks charged. Logan's robots surged forward. A squadron of griffins and Beastwings buzzed low overhead.

The enormous howlers shrieked again, clattering Nico's bones.

The Eater's army backpedaled, broke, and ran, as a wave of enraged figments chased them back across the empty plain. Within moments, only the Torchbearers remained at the entrance to the cavern.

"We did it!" Logan cried, thrusting a shaky fist at Tyler, who ignored it completely, elbows on his knees as he rubbed his eyes in relief. Out on the plain, enraged figments harried the Eater's army into smaller and smaller groups that fled into the shadows of the broken landscape.

"*Human scum.*"

Nico went cold. He turned back to the cave.

A giant, snarling bobcat stood before the Rift, golden eyes pulsing with hatred.

Before anyone else could react, Aster charged forward.

"Monster!" she screamed, waving Torchbearer daggers in both hands.

"Where'd she get those?" Tyler blurted despite himself. "I *knew* she was going to steal one!"

The Stalker reared back, startled by Aster's rapid approach. Black smoke began to wreath its feline body as the horrible spice scent flooded the cavern.

Nico darted after Aster, cautiously leading the other Torchbearers inside the cave.

Aster halted a dozen paces from the Stalker. With a cry of defiance, she threw both daggers at the same time.

The Stalker flicked its paws contemptuously, deflecting the blades with a snarl.

Nico froze in place, unable to react. How could they defeat such a creature?

"Devil! You have hounded me for the *last* time!" Aster shouted. Nico noticed she had slipped one hand in and out of her pocket. Something small and round appeared in Aster's palm.

"*Foolish mortal,*" the Stalker rasped. "*You came back for nothing. Now you are mine.*"

The smoke around it increased, enveloping the huge bobcat.

In a flash, Nico realized what was happening. "It's about to change form!"

Aster seemed to have been waiting for just that moment.

As the toxic cloud thickened, she hurled the object nestled in her hand. It sailed into the cloak of vapors without a sound.

White light exploded within the dark cloud. The Stalker shrieked in agony.

The vapors turned a dull gray and drifted apart, revealing a small, ratlike being at their core.

"No!" the shapeshifter wailed. "Impossible!"

Aster leaped forward and kicked the tiny rodent squarely with her boot. The Stalker sailed into the Rift and was gone.

"What?!" Logan panted, eyes as round as dinner plates. "How did . . . huh? I can't . . ."

Opal, Tyler, and Emma were staring at Aster in shocked disbelief.

"Later," Aster snapped, tossing her dark blond braid over a shoulder. "The danger has not passed. The Eater alone can devastate our planet!"

Behind them, the dragon returned, landing at the cave mouth with a boom and eyeing Nico and his friends sternly. The plain was now completely clear of demons. Few figments remained, either. Those that did were fading slowly until they popped out of existence. Many wore satisfied smiles as they vanished.

Nico watched the figment champion warily. "I think she has some unfinished business."

Opal grabbed his sleeve. "We have to go!" She pointed at the yellow-green light. "The Eater is still ahead of us!"

"We *cannot* let him get to Earth," Aster insisted in a shaky voice. "Or else this battle will have meant nothing."

The dragon grunted loudly, steam pouring from its nostrils once more.

"Wait!" Emma waved both hands at once. "I think I know what she wants!"

Emma stepped outside the cavern and bowed to the dragon. Then she spun and pointed at the mouth of the cave. The figment snorted haughtily, but bobbed its head.

Emma ran back inside and grabbed Nico's forearm. "We have to go *right now*."

Nico blinked at her in confusion. So much chaos at once. Beyond the jagged opening, the dragon had drawn up to its full height, thick azure smoke streaming from her nose.

Suddenly, Nico understood *exactly* what was about to happen.

"Through the Rift!" he shouted, his voice cracking. "Like, immediately!"

Emma didn't hesitate, shooting forward and plunging into the yellow-green slash. Opal was helping Aster with Logan, who still seemed out of sorts. Tyler reached the gateway and turned, squirming impatiently as Nico and the others converged at his side.

"Another crack in reality," Nico whispered, then he laughed anxiously. "Let's hope we're right about where it goes, huh?"

337

"Doesn't matter." Opal's face was determined. "The Eater went through here, so we have to follow."

"Emma already went through!" Tyler was rigid with tension. "And FYI, my watch alarm went off a while ago. We've been here way longer than last time. You know what that means."

Nico grimaced. "Nothing we can do about it now."

Outside, the dragon stretched its wings and leaned toward the cavern mouth. Nico noticed the powerful figment was beginning to fade. Soon it would vanish, and the chance would be lost.

"Go go go!" Nico shouted, cajoling the others through one at a time, until only he remained.

The dragon roared. Opened its jaws wide. Nico dove into the shimmering gap just as brilliant blue fire flooded the cave and collapsed its walls, sealing the Rift under a mountain of broken, burning stone.

———————

The Void was in chaos.

Nico tumbled through nothingness, cartwheeling head-over-heels as the in-between space spasmed and quaked.

Opal grabbed his arm to steady him. Mouths dropping open, they watched as the Rift behind them blazed a brilliant mix of rainbow colors, thcn went dark, sealing with a hiss to form the same scabbed-over look they'd seen the day before.

*Just like the Rift to France,* Tyler sent in wonder. *The one Aster found.*

Logan was blinking in wide-eyed disbelief. *The dragon fried it! Rifts aren't indestructible!*

*Nico, come on!* Opal began towing him away from the wreckage. *The Eater isn't here, and we don't know where he's gone. We can't let him get away. That nightmare has Thing!*

Nico righted himself. Tyler and Logan were above him, supporting Emma by her shoulders. She was trying to catch her breath as words spilled out of her. Aster had arms crossed as she scanned the glittering Void. But they were alone.

Nico shook his head to clear it. *The Eater's going to Yellowstone, so a companion Rift to Earth should be close by. We need to concentrate and let our minds take us there.*

Tyler zipped down to join him and Opal. *That's the problem, man! Emma already did that, and she's back. The Eater isn't at the Yellowstone Rift! She even went through it to make sure.*

Logan floated close, one arm locked around Emma, who seemed shaken. Aster whizzed to her opposite side.

*The Eater wasn't in the underground chamber we found,* Emma confirmed in a wavery voice. *And a monster that size would've had to bash a way out through all those passages to reach the surface. But there was no sign of anything. We've lost him!*

Tyler seemed on the verge of tears. Nico briefly wondered

how Emma could've scouted Yellowstone so quickly—she'd only been a few seconds ahead of them. Then he remembered how time moved more slowly on Thing's world. A ball of ice formed inside his chest. How long had they been gone from Timbers? What was his father thinking right now?

Nico pushed the worry from his mind, trying to concentrate. *Opal, are you able to contact Thing?*

Opal shook her head miserably. *No response at all.*

*But we were so sure the Eater was headed to Earth.* Nico felt his cheeks blaze in frustration. *If he's not going to Yellowstone . . .*

Beside him, Opal gasped. *Oh no.*

Nico's eyes darted to her. *You don't think—*

*We're all here.* Opal could barely articulate her fears. *Not at the Timbers Rift. Not watching the Darkdeep.*

*Which is what the Eater wants in the first place!* Logan smacked his forehead. *How could we be so dumb?!*

*Hurry!* Nico mind-shouted. *Back to Timbers! Let's hope we're not too late!*

Nico closed his eyes and imagined the Rift leading home. He felt his body speed across the Void. When he opened them again, he saw the Timbers Rift dead ahead, growing in size as he rocketed through space. The rest of the group was right behind him.

Nico didn't slow. Didn't hesitate.

He leaned forward like a cliff diver and shot directly into it.

Frigid seawater enveloped Nico. He coughed out his air,

trying not to panic. He was in the Pacific, under the ruins of the oil platform the Torchbearers had used to hide the Rift for decades.

*But we don't want the ocean. We know where the Eater is going.*

A flash of movement caught his eye. Something huge was swimming away, into a jet-black current that seemed to both thrum and hold perfectly still at the same time.

The Eater.

The giant demon slipped into the Darkdeep's inky flow and disappeared.

The others were flailing underwater around him. Nico swung his arms frantically, then pointed.

Opal nodded, gripping Emma and Tyler by the shoulders. Logan spun around and grabbed Aster's hand as she struggled to keep from sinking. As one, the group swam down into the Darkdeep. Nico had never seen it look so distinct before. Almost like it *wanted* them to enter.

With a silent prayer, he swam for the inky flow and was pulled like a magnet into darkness.

———

Black.

Everywhere, black.

Nico steadied himself in the nothing space of the Darkdeep.

Silence blanketed the empty realm.

Opal appeared beside him, followed by the others in a ragged line. They were dripping wet, then suddenly not—in the Darkdeep, your mind controlled the environment. Soon they were facing each other, patting shoulders and bumping fists. They'd made it back in one piece.

*This is where figments are born. Where it all started. But where is the Eater?*

As if summoned, the monster appeared in front of them. As if he'd always been there.

The destroyer of worlds smiled wickedly, its belly rumbling as a humorless cackle sounded in their minds. Thing was still clutched in the Eater's massive paw.

*Foolish. You should not have followed me here.*

Nico reeled. The Eater had spoken! Threatened them!

He glanced at his friends, saw his horror mirrored on their faces.

A strangled voice cut through the ether. *Torchbearers, get away! This foe is beyond you!*

Nico's gaze flew to Thing, who was struggling to break free from the Eater without success.

Opal expression hardened. *We won't leave you, Dax. We can fight.*

Thing wagged its tiny head frantically. *The Eater is too powerful. The Darkdeep is open to him now!*

The Eater shook his paw, rattling Thing like a child's toy. Nico heard a wail from the little voice inside his head.

*This goblin is correct,* the Eater boomed. *Here, I am . . . limitless.*

The monster roared.

Behind it, a dozen figment versions of itself appeared in a row. Then a hundred more. Each smacked a meaty fist into its other paw, snarling with menace.

Nico sensed Opal falter beside him. She covered her mouth, as if to hold in a scream. The others quailed from the army of Eaters. Their hopes teetered on the verge of disaster.

*This is our mission,* Nico thought. *We're the guardians of the Darkdeep.*

He steeled his nerve. Nico straightened, squaring his shoulders against the monsters before them.

*We're the Torchbearers. This is* our *place.*

Nico felt his own lips snarl. He sensed his friends growing stronger beside him. Lines of connection began forming between the Torchbearers like a network of spiderwebs.

Against all odds, Nico smiled.

*You're not the only one who can be limitless.*

He closed his eyes. Focused on a single point of light in the darkness. Nico let that spark burn in his consciousness, splitting and replicating, its branches streaking across the Darkdeep like lightning bolts.

Faster than he could think, Nico sent a wave of instructions to the other Torchbearers. He felt their minds blaze in response.

Reality shifted around him.

Nico felt the Torchbearers meld. Join in purpose. Become one.

Opal. Tyler. Emma. Logan. Aster.

Their minds linked to his, and the bonds separating them fell away like cast-off chains. Everything twisted in service to the one vision in the center of Nico's thoughts.

A knight.

In armor.

Towering above the Eaters.

Gripping a broadsword in one steel fist.

The figment's armor was as red as Tyler's robes. One of Logan's torch necklaces hung from its neck. The outline of a flower was etched into its breastplate—an aster, surrounded by glimmering opal stones. In place of regular eyes, movie cameras whirred, gleaming beneath an owl-winged helm.

*Something from all of us. Here. Together.*

In the vacuum of the Darkdeep, Nico and his friends formed a super-figment.

With a roar, the Eaters attacked.

The knight that contained them all swung its sword, slicing through the first wave of Eater figments, which vanished into the ether. But more poured forward, springing into existence so fast Nico couldn't keep track. The real Eater held back, frowning its hatred at them. The knight swung and blocked, obliterating the monster's creations.

But more and more came.

*Too many*, Tyler wailed inside the knight.

*Keep fighting!* Aster and Emma spoke at once. As one.

Logan burned with fury. Nico felt Opal squirm inside his mind. *Maybe this will help.*

In the knight's other hand appeared a heavy stone dagger. The super-figment swung the knife in tandem with its sword, destroying more Eaters. But enemies came on and on. One Eater slipped through the knight's guard and slammed into its chest. The knight faltered, tumbling to a knee. Eaters rushed forward like rats, intent on finishing the fight.

Then, suddenly, they vanished.

A shriek of pain filled the Darkdeep's vacuum.

Nico peered through the knight's face guard and saw the real Eater on its knees. Fighting with something on its back.

*The Beast!* Tyler sent, in a cry of triumph. *The Beast is here!*

The sea monster had sunk its teeth into the Eater's backside and was shaking the demon back and forth. The Eater yowled and swung its fists, but couldn't reach the Beast. Thing dropped from his clawed fingers.

The little green man zipped away, skidded to a stop, then rocketed back into the Eater's midsection like a speeding bullet. The monster let out a surprised *oof.*

Abruptly, Opal was beside Nico in the mind of the knight. *Now's our chance!*

Nico bared his teeth. *Let's do it!*

The super-figment dropped the dagger and raised its broadsword with both hands.

Torchbearer runes blazed to life along the blade.

The Beast glanced up, then released the enraged Eater and scampered back into the darkness. Thing punched the monster under its chin and also shot away.

Screaming in rage, the Eater turned back to the knight, acid dripping from its fangs.

Too late.

Nico and Opal brought the sword down, slicing the Eater in two.

The monster blinked—once, twice—then dropped away below their feet. It fell into nothingness and was gone.

The knight shimmered.

Broke apart.

Five kids floated in the inky blackness.

# 32

## OPAL

Opal finished hanging the sign across the houseboat's showroom.

*WE'LL MISS YOU!*

She climbed down and stood alongside the others, staring up at the letters. *Goodbyes are the worst.*

Tyler had both hands buried in his pockets. "Man."

"I know." Emma's voice was quiet.

The banner had been Tyler's idea, as had the stockings hanging from Thing's old pedestal. A small fir tree stood next to the entry curtain, decorated with Torchbearer tokens they'd scrounged from the display cases. Charles Dixon's medal was affixed to its apex. The holiday season was coming soon. No reason not to make the boat festive.

"It looks good, Logan," Opal said. He'd designed the banner and had his local T-shirt supplier print it up. The words were in a script-like font with matching torch symbols at both ends—gold against a deep blue background.

"Thanks," Logan mumbled.

Emma's tone became a little *too* bright. "Hey, what about the food? Can I get a compliment, too?"

Opal blinked away tears, tried to rally. "It all looks amazing, Em."

Emma had covered a display case with a tablecloth and set out every conceivable packaged dessert. Ding Dongs. Twinkies. Cupcakes. Zingers. Ho Hos. Sno Balls. Three kinds of pizza sat inside their boxes, in the hopes they'd stay warm.

"This is Nico's favorite," Tyler said, setting out a two-liter bottle of root beer.

Opal steadied a four-level pyramid of her own contribution—pudding cups. *Like the ones we ate in kindergarten.*

The others were quiet. They'd worked hard to make this farewell party the best ever, but there was no escaping what it was. The end of something.

"You see Carson today?" Tyler asked Opal.

Opal cringed. "Yes. I even got a hug. He still buys that we turned Aster over to the FBI and she admitted to being a film student trying to make a name for herself. I told him he's a hero. That he saved Timbers from the greatest hoax since Colton Bridger."

Emma chuckled. "At least he's sleeping again. I saw him and Parker out on their ATVs yesterday. They didn't say 'hi' or anything, but they didn't try to spray me with mud this time. I call that progress."

Tyler shrugged. "Mayor Hayt lifting the youth curfew definitely helped. And we probably *do* need to thank Sylvain Nantes for holding that town meeting. Ever since he blamed all the weirdness on thrill-seekers from out of town, people finally seem to be getting over monster shock. The ones that *can*, anyway. Some folks will never accept that real nightmares didn't invade."

Opal breathed deep. "It's the best we could've hoped for. People don't even trust their *own* memories after a while, if they seem too irrational. I can't wait until the only thing that interests the outside world about Timbers are new eps of *Emma-mazing!*"

Emma beamed. "A new try-not-to-laugh post is dropping this week! It's called 'Get Wrecked' and is hosted by a giant animated talking dog named Flip."

Tyler covered his face. "Please make it stop!" he groaned, but Opal saw the smile behind his hand.

Voices carried across the pond. Opal peeked out the bay window, into a perfect, blue-skied mid-December day. The kind where the sun shone and your breath puffed in tiny clouds, and you felt glad to be alive.

Nico and Aster were hopping across the stepping stones, wearing fleeces and ski hats against the cold. Nico had Thing's jar in his hands and was moving extra-carefully.

"Get into position!" Opal hissed. "They're almost here!"

The others ducked behind trunks and bookshelves. Someone knocked an old metal platter over and it went clattering to the floor.

"*Shhh!*" Opal warned.

Emma giggled. "Not me!"

"It jumped into my way!" Tyler insisted.

"Quiet!" Opal found her own hiding spot and crouched out of sight.

Feet on the stairs. The front door swung open. A moment later, the green curtain parted.

"I've been researching," Nico was saying to Thing, as the trio entered the room. "Living somewhere like Yellowstone might give you the most freedom, because certain areas in the park resemble your own . . ." He trailed off, looking around with wide, blinking eyes. "Hey, where is everyone?"

"I do not know." Aster sounded confused. "They told us to meet here, yes?" Her precise, French-accented English had improved dramatically in the weeks she'd spent in Timbers. Opal spied her glancing at a new digital watch, the source of much pride. "We are certainly not late."

Nico shot a glance up at the banner. "I don't know *what's* going on," he announced, laying it on thick.

"SURPRISE!" Opal shouted.

The others jumped up from their hiding spots. Nico spun and gave Aster two hand-shooters, smiling wide as he juggled Thing's jar.

Dax grumbled in its liquid container. *Thanks for not dropping me.*

"What is all of this?" Aster asked. She sniffed. A grin split her face. "There is pizza here!"

"It's for you!" Opal pointed to the sign overhead. "We wanted to send you off in style."

Aster's eyes grew misty. "This is very kind." She placed her hand on a pizza box wistfully. "They may not have such delicacies in France."

"Don't worry, they do," Tyler said, slapping Nico five. "Good job, decoy. She had no idea."

Nico grinned. "I'm just glad this party isn't for me."

Opal beamed at him. "Well, consider it, like, your *un*-goodbye party."

Nico chuckled. "That's definitely worth celebrating."

Everyone attacked the refreshments. Aster lifted pizza slices in both hands, while Tyler scooped ice into plastic cups and poured soda. Logan gave Nico a friendly nod. Nico nodded back.

"I still can't believe our dads will be working together," Logan said, his mouth half-stuffed with pepperoni.

Opal couldn't help but jump in "Pretty crazy for you two. But also pretty cool."

Nico couldn't mask a nervous frown. "It might be a total disaster though. I mean, seriously. This could go *so* wrong."

"Maybe it'll be great," Opal countered. "It says a lot that they're both up for trying it out."

351

Desperately relieved that the world was *not* about to end, Sylvain Nantes had recently hired Warren Holland as an environmental consultant for the Nantes Timber Company, to help reshape the business into a more sustainable and eco-friendly operation. It meant Nico's dad was leaving the Park Service he loved, but it also meant the Hollands could stay in Timbers.

Opal thought it was cool to see Logan's father take a renewed interest in the health of his hometown. He still wouldn't touch his family's Torchbearer legacy, but at least he wasn't giving up anymore. Or standing in Logan's way—Sylvain spent days talking Logan through everything he knew about the Order, then officially turned the responsibility over to his son. He was out, but he wouldn't interfere.

*Or tattle, which is basically the same thing.*

"My dad's willing to give the job a year," Nico said, between bites of cupcake. "We'll just have to wait and see how it goes." Spying the tower of pudding cups, he snagged the topmost one and spun it in his hand. "Opal, did you bring these?"

"Of course. Is chocolate-vanilla swirl still your favorite?"

"You know it." Nico peeled away the foil and tipped the cup in a *cheers* gesture. "To the Torchbearers."

"Wait, wait!" Emma held up her drink. "We all need to get in on this."

The others followed suit, though Aster looked slightly confused. Inside its jar, Thing lifted a hand as well.

"*We watch the Darkdeep, and watch out for each other,*" Tyler intoned, quoting the Torchbearer oath they'd invented on this very houseboat. The others repeated it, Aster solemnly speaking the words for the first time.

"May I say something as well?" she asked.

"Of course," Emma said.

Aster carefully put down her cup. "I want to say that, as I embark on this new adventure, I will never forget you. I will return to visit as often as possible. And to tell you what I find, in France and with the other Rifts." She cleared her throat. "I am grateful. I have lost my family, but found true friends."

Emma threw her arms around Aster, accidentally splashing Sprite on the older girl's braid. "We're gonna miss you so much!"

"I made you one of these," Logan said awkwardly, stepping forward to hand Aster a carved Torch necklace. "We all have them. It's kinda, like, our own personal thing. For *this* group of Torchbearers."

"Thank you." Aster tied on the necklace and smiled. Logan turned a deep shade of crimson.

Tyler elbowed Emma in the ribs, spoke under his breath. "What's his deal?"

Emma shrugged. "No idea. Are there any Twinkies left?"

Logan cleared his throat, tearing his eyes away from Aster. "And one for you," he said, stepping over to Thing's new heavy-duty plastic jar, which was resting on the tiny alien's old pedestal. "Do I . . . what? Drop it inside?"

*Wood will boil into particles in my liquid environment.*

"Um, right." Logan placed the necklace around the neck of the jar. "This works fine."

*I am honored.*

Thing had instructed Opal on how to mix a new liquid habitat formula for him after they'd resurfaced through the pond. She hated that Dax was back in a jar, but Nico was investigating potential natural habitats for the little green hero. Until then, Thing intended to see as much of Earth as possible, now that its home world was all but destroyed.

"Okay, enough with the jewelry," Tyler snarked. "Let's get down!" He turned on a portable speaker sitting next to Thing. "This is gonna be more lit than a radish-festival remix."

Opal made a face. "Don't remind me."

But she joined the others, everyone laughing and bouncing up and down until Thing's jar wobbled to the beat.

---

*It's time.*

Thing was right, but Opal could tell the others felt the same way she did—a mixture of bitter and sweet. The group followed Aster down the winding staircase to the Darkdeep.

Logan grunted, scuffing a shoe. "Take care, Sure Shot. We're, um, gonna miss that cannon around here."

"Enough with the silly name, please!" Aster protested, but Opal could tell his joke pleased her. After their return to

Earth, the group had demanded to know how Aster had vanquished the Stalker.

*The onyx queen,* she'd said in a pleased voice. *A fitting tribute to my father and governess.*

Aster had guessed the same thing as Nico—that the harsh peppery smell blossomed when the Stalker was about to shape-shift, and the black cloud was meant to camouflage the creature during its transformation. By hurling the chess piece into the noxious vapors at exactly that moment, Aster had struck the demon during the only time it was vulnerable. Then she'd booted it right out of Thing's dimension.

They still didn't know what happened to the slippery, yellow-eyed monster—they'd seen no sign of it inside the Void—but that was a worry for another day. At least the weather was back to normal, which meant the Stalker wasn't likely on Earth. Aster had the other chess pieces in her backpack just in case, including her wooden queen to replace the one she'd sacrificed.

Opal watched her approach the slowly swirling well. After consulting their world map, Aster believed she could travel through the Void to reach a Rift in Germany. From there, she'd journey by train to her hometown of Toulon, then begin a survey of the marked locations, starting in Vichy. They still didn't know if other active chapters of Torchbearers were out there—or, if not, what had happened to them. Sylvain Nantes had rejected the Order early in his training and never learned that information. But this was the way they'd get answers. Opal felt a pang of jealousy that she wasn't going along.

"Still active," Tyler said, nervously eyeing the Darkdeep's motion. "I really hope we got all the figments from our last jump. I feel like we might've lost track."

"We counted a dozen times," Nico pointed out. "Aster will make another one *now*, though. The grind never ends."

"Thank you for taking care of that for me." Aster's voice trembled slightly. She cleared her throat. "My father always said to say *adieu* with enthusiasm. Because, if we do not see each other at the end of *one* grand adventure, we may meet yet again at a greater one."

Tears burned under Opal's eyelids. "Goodbye, Aster. Take good care of Dax."

Emma bowed regally, filming on her phone. "Bon voyage!"

"Ciao!" Logan added.

Tyler gave him a withering look. "That's Italian, you dork. They're going to Germany."

Logan scoffed. "I was being continental."

*Aster and I will report back what we discover.* Thing's smile was infectious. *I'm finally the explorer I always wished to be. I will put truth to the Traveler name the Order gave me.*

"We will examine the Rifts and search for more Torchbearers," Aster confirmed. "And you will let us know what you learn here."

She carefully placed Thing's jar inside a backpack Emma

had liberated from her parents' supply store. Aster strode to the edge of the Darkdeep, hesitated a moment, and then stepped off into the well.

In a blink, they were gone.

"Good luck," Nico said softly.

Tyler surreptitiously wiped his eyes. "Okay. So. That happened." He exhaled a deep, melancholy sigh. "At least we still have the Beast."

Days after their return, they'd spotted the sea creature cavorting in the foggy inlet. The Beast had appeared most days ever since, often regarding Tyler and the others with unfathomable eyes. It appeared that they were now acknowledged neighbors in Still Cove.

Logan clapped a hand on Tyler's shoulder. "Let's eat a ton of HoHos. I haven't eaten dessert in so long, I've forgotten was happiness tastes like."

"I've had it worst," Tyler clapped back, shaking his head in sorrow. "Your three weeks in solitary confinement are Easy Street compared to my new house rules."

Upon their return, the Torchbearers were horrified to discover that almost two full days had passed since they'd entered the well. The fallout from that time jump had taken a bite out of their lives ever since.

Opal's parents had gone to the police, even forming a search party. Nico's father had led it, canvassing the western hills while the Watsons and Fairingtons posted missing persons signs all around town. When the six of them had rolled back into town with a story about a storm-wrecked, wayward camping trip, a turned ankle by the French girl, and text messages they'd been *so sure* had gone through, the Torchbearers had been simultaneously swarmed with bear-hugs and scolded within an inch of their lives.

Groundings. Punishments. Loss of freedom. No one escaped unscathed.

Another schoolyard legend added to their reputation, but this one bought them a weird kind of respect. Things were just finally getting back to normal, though getting out to Still Cove remained tougher than ever. The party had been a care-fully orchestrated exception.

"It feels good to be home again." Emma linked arms with Logan and Tyler. "Let's go dance battle. Or do figment cha-rades. Or read old books. Whatever."

"Sounds good," Tyler said. They headed for the steps. Logan glanced back at Opal and Nico. "You guys coming?"

"In a sec," Opal answered, at the same time Nico said, "One minute."

Emma poked Tyler in the side. "Why are *they* being weird?"

"Who knows," he muttered. The trio tromped upstairs. Seconds later, music started blaring again. Opal felt a smile tug the corners of her lips. Nico chuckled softy.

At their feet, the black well churned. Slowly. Implacably.

Opal thought back to the beginning, when Nico's worst fear had appeared from the Darkdeep. A version of his father who didn't care about him at all.

"Remember your scariest figment?" Opal asked.

"Yeah."

"And now your dad is taking a new job for you."

"Well, don't forget the owls. He really loves owls."

"Right," Opal giggled. "But, I mean . . ."

"I know." Nico sucked in a deep breath. "He wouldn't have accepted the offer if it didn't interest him, but he still did it for me. For our family. For *now*," he couldn't help adding.

Opal wanted to hug him. Instead, she asked something else.

"I've been wondering. Those gray creatures—the howlers. What were they, really?"

Nico stiffened. Hesitating, he shuffled his feet awkwardly, wiping at his brow.

"You don't have to tell me," Opal said in a rush. "Not if you really don't want to."

Somehow, her hand found his. They stood there, fingers entwined. The way they'd held on to each other during their first battle inside the Darkdeep.

"Loneliness," Nico said finally. "Those creatures were loneliness in physical form. My *new* worst fear. Or maybe one I've had all along."

Opal exhaled in surprise. "And you summoned it voluntarily. To help us on Thing's world."

Nico nodded. "Because I know now that everything will be okay. Even if I have to move one day after all. As long as you guys are my friends, wherever I might be, I won't be alone." He cleared his throat.

"You're right."

Opal squeezed his hand. Nico squeezed back.

They stood together, watching the Darkdeep spin in quiet circles.

In her mind, Opal wished Aster and Thing safe journeys. Whole new lives were waiting for them.

*"Go and see,"* Opal whispered. *"Go and see what the world has for you."*